The
Central Intelligence Agency

DATE DUE			

The
Central
Intelligence
Agency

HISTORY AND
DOCUMENTS

EDITED BY

William M. Leary

The University of Alabama Press

Introduction, Bibliographical Essay,
and Index Copyright © 1984 by
The University of Alabama Press
University, Alabama 35486
Manufactured in the United States of America

Library of Congress Cataloging in Publication Data

Main entry under title:
The Central Intelligence Agency, history and documents.

   Bibliography: p.
   Includes index.
   1. United States. Central Intelligence Agency—
History—Sources. I. Leary, William M. (William Matthew), 1934–
JK468.I6C46 1984   327.1′2′06073   83-17896
ISBN 0-8173-0207-7
ISBN 0-8173-0219-0 (pbk)

Contents

Editor's Introduction
to
History of the
Central Intelligence Agency

Introduction

The Central Intelligence Agency (CIA) likes to trace its roots to the revolutionary struggle that gave birth to the nation. Precedents for contemporary espionage activities certainly abound in the eighteenth-century conflict. The Continental Congress used secret committees to conduct sensitive intelligence operations, employed spies, and authorized paramilitary missions against the British. George Washington—whom the CIA cites with evident pride in a bicentennial publication as "a skilled manager of intelligence"[1] —organized a secret intelligence bureau under Major Benjamin Tallmadge, sent secret agents behind enemy lines to assess the strength of opposing military forces, and was involved in counterespionage schemes. In fact, Washington spent $17,000 on secret intelligence during the war—if his accounting is to be trusted.

However, neither Washington nor his successors saw any need for a peacetime intelligence organization. American intelligence languished throughout most of the nineteenth century, with operations taking place on a sporadic, ad hoc basis, in response to immediate problems. Even the Civil War failed to produce significant change. It was not until the 1880s that permanent intelligence units appeared. In response to increased American involvement in world affairs and to a general societal trend toward organization and rationalization, the Navy created the Office of Naval Intelligence (ONI) in 1882, while the Army established the Military Information Division (later, Military Intelligence Division—MID) three years later. Congress funded the first full-time military attachés in 1889.

Military intelligence units, together with the U.S. Secret Service, played a noteworthy role in the Spanish-American War, but an extensive espionage system did not emerge until World War I. Army intelligence, under the initial direction of Ralph H. Van Deman, assumed extensive duties during the Great War. MID collected information, conducted counterespionage operations at home and abroad, and made significant progress in cryptography. ONI also flourished. With the enthusiastic approval of Assistant Secretary Franklin D. Roosevelt, Naval intelligence employed secret agents abroad and developed an extensive domestic surveillance network. In addition, President Woodrow Wilson gave the State Department wide authority in intelligence matters, including primary responsibility for the evaluation and dissemination of information. Frank L. Polk, counselor at State, took charge of coordinating the government's flourishing espionage bureaucracy.

American intelligence declined sharply in the postwar years. MID's budget fell from $2.5 million in 1918 to $225,000 in 1922, ONI's headquarters staff shrank from 300 intelligence officers to 24, and Congress slashed funds for the attaché program. In 1929, Secretary of State Henry L. Stimson dealt cryptographic work a severe blow when he withdrew the department's support from the government's code-breaking unit. But complete demobilization of intelligence did not take place. Military units continued to function on a reduced basis; attachés, if few in number, continued to report; and cryptographic work survived in the Signal Corps. The nucleus for later expansion remained in place.

War in Europe brought renewed emphasis on intelligence. As the government's espionage apparatus expanded, President Franklin Roosevelt recognized the need for a centralized structure. Five months before Pearl Harbor, he sought to remedy organizational problems by appointing William J. Donovan to coordinate intelligence activities. Charged with collecting and analyzing information bearing upon vital security interests, the energetic Donovan quickly put together the framework for a new and unprecedented national intelligence organization.

Donovan's intelligence unit—designated the Office of Strategic Services (OSS) after June 1942—attained legendary status during the war. Academics found employment and adventure in the research and analysis division, producing intelligence estimates for policymakers. Actors, lawyers, socialites, and soldiers undertook espionage and counterespionage missions, supplied guerrillas, conducted paramilitary operations behind enemy lines, and engaged in all manner of derring-do. The methods, procedures, and techniques of OSS, many personnel, and the unit's ésprit de corps, would carry over into the CIA.

In November 1944, General Donovan outlined for President Roosevelt the structure of a postwar centralized intelligence organization, reporting directly to the president [Document 1]. This proposal found little favor with other government agencies charged with producing intelligence. When FBI Director J. Edgar Hoover leaked Donovan's memorandum to the press, Congressional opponents of a peacetime executive intelligence unit forced Roosevelt to defer action on the controversial scheme.

Harry S. Truman became president upon Roosevelt's death in April 1945. The new chief executive recognized the need for an improved national intelligence system, but he sympathized with those who recoiled at the idea of a peacetime central intelligence service. Distrusting the power that might be wielded by such a large and secret organization, Truman disbanded OSS at war's end, parceling out its components to the departments of State and War. The president let it be known that he would not support the creation of "a Gestapo."

But the grim realities of confrontation with the Soviet Union and the difficulties in obtaining useful information from the various agencies charged with intelligence collection and analysis soon caused President Truman to overcome his distaste for a peacetime intelligence organization. In January 1946, the president issued an Executive Order (largely the work of administrative analysts in the Bureau of the Budget) creating the Central Intelligence Group (CIG) [Document 2]. Operating under the National Intelligence Authority (the secretaries of State, War, and Navy, and a personal representative of the president), the CIG was intended to coordinate the work of existing intelligence units and to provide intelligence analysis to senior policymakers. However, the new organization quickly became an intelligence producer, with authority to conduct independent research and analysis, together with clandestine collection capability. It was only a short step from the CIG to the CIA.

The National Security Act of 1947 gave birth to the CIA [Document 3]. As part of a general restructuring of the national defense establishment, the CIG became an independent department under the designation of Central Intelligence Agency. The law placed the new organization under a National Security Council (NSC) and made it responsible for coordinating, evaluating, and disseminating intelligence affecting national security. One provision of the act, authorizing the CIA "to perform such other functions" as the NSC "will from time to time direct," would provide the legal foundation for later expansion of the CIA's mission, especially in the area of covert action.

Indeed, it was not long before American policymakers saw the CIA as an offensive weapon in an expanding Cold War. In December 1947, the NSC gave the CIA authority to conduct covert psychological operations. Six months later, the NSC established a covert action unit within the CIA [Document 4]. And this was only the beginning. By 1952, clandestine operations claimed 60 percent of the agency's personnel and 74 percent of its budget.

The CIA, in common with many newly created agencies, suffered from organizational growing pains. Less than a year after the CIA came into existence, the NSC recognized that all was not well. In January 1948, it recommended to President Truman that a group of individuals not in government service be selected to undertake a "comprehensive, impartial, and objective survey of the organization, activities, and personnel of the Central Intelligence Agency." Truman appointed Allen W. Dulles, William H. Jackson, and Mathias F. Correa to undertake the task. Their report [Document 5] identified areas of organizational weakness and recommended changes to enhance the CIA's efficiency.

Although not implemented immediately, the Dulles-Jackson-Correa study became the basis for a major reorganization of the agency that took place in 1952. CIA Director W. Bedell Smith merged the units responsible for clandestine activities into the Directorate for Plans, grouped intelligence functions under the Directorate for Intelligence, and created the Directorate for

Administration. These changes fixed the basic organizational structure of the CIA for the next twenty years.

The CIA flourished during the heyday of Cold War confrontation between Communism and Freedom. Mysterious, omniscient, and deemed vital to national survival, it enjoyed unprecedented prestige and status. The agency's triumphs in Iran and Guatemala were given discreet publicity; its failures remained shrouded in secrecy. Led by Allen Dulles, the CIA turned aside witch-hunting attacks of Senator Joseph McCarthy and foiled attempts by Congress to exert legislative oversight.

The temper of the times can be seen in the Doolittle Report [Document 6] and the NSC 5412 series of directives that governed covert operations [Document 7]. Requested by President Dwight D. Eisenhower to forestall a possible inquiry by Congress, the Doolittle committee's examination found little fault with the CIA. The report spoke of "an implacable enemy," and the need to "subvert, sabotage and destroy our enemies by more clever, more sophisticated and more effective methods than those used against us." As revealed in NSC 5412/2, the Eisenhower administration saw the CIA in the forefront of the great struggle against international communism.

The Bay of Pigs fiasco of 1961 caused a disenchanted executive to institute tighter control over what Secretary of State Dean Rusk called "those spooky boys,"[2] but the CIA's role in the Cold War did not change. Clandestine activities continued to dominate the agency's budget, with major paramilitary operations launched in South America, Africa, and Southeast Asia. The late 1960s, however, marked a turning point in public attitudes toward the CIA. The trauma of Vietnam and the emergence of a credibility gap brought the agency under intense—and hostile—public scrutiny for the first time since its founding. In an atmosphere of suspicion and distrust, CIA Director William Colby recalled, the CIA came to be regarded "as an exemplar of the repugnant clandestine methods and secret manipulations that were seen characteristic of the Johnson and Nixon administrations."[3]

The road to Congressional investigation, in the most immediate sense, began with Watergate. In June 1972, the American people learned that former CIA officers E. Howard Hunt and James McCord had taken part in a bungled attempt to plant listening devices at the Democratic party's National Committee headquarters. Although there had been earlier contact with Hunt, the CIA had not been involved in the Watergate break-in. Nevertheless, the intelligence agency became caught up in the tide of events that would lead to President Richard M. Nixon's resignation.

A new era began at the CIA in February 1973 when James Schlesinger took over as director from Richard Helms, who had been fired for refusing to cooperate with the sorely troubled administration in a cover-up. Schlesinger placed new emphasis on collection and analysis of intelligence, conducted—heavy-handedly, some have argued—a needed purge of personnel in the agency's covert action component, and had drawn up a list of past activities that might have violated the CIA's charter ("the family jewels").

While Schlesinger struggled to put the CIA's house in order, the ills of Vietnam and Watergate continued to plague the body politic. The war's end and Richard Nixon's ignominious departure from the nation's highest office signaled the beginning of national recovery, but not before the CIA underwent a wrenching catharsis.

Congress had remained protective of the CIA during the troubles of 1972–74. Despite increasing restlessness on Capitol Hill, senior members of the Senate and House Appropriations and Armed Services Intelligence Subcommittees steadfastly maintained the loose and sympathetic oversight that had characterized relationships between Congress and the CIA since the agency's inception. This era of good feeling ended shortly before Christmas 1974 when Seymour Hersh reported in the *New York Times* that the CIA had conducted probes of the anti-war movement in clear violation of prohibitions against domestic spying.

President Gerald Ford sought to calm a mounting public furor—and preempt a more serious and less controllable legislative inquiry into CIA activities—by creating the Rockefeller Commission, a blue-ribbon panel charged with investigating Hersh's charges. But this action failed to mollify an aroused Congress. On January 21, 1975, the Senate established a Select Committee under Frank Church of Idaho to investigate the CIA. Unlike the Rockefeller Commission, the Church Committee had a broad mandate "to conduct an investigation and study of governmental operations with respect to intelligence activities and of the extent, if any, to which illegal, improper, or unethical activities were engaged in by any agency of the Federal Government."[4] Thus began the Year of Intelligence.

The Select Committee's staff, led by Director William G. Miller and Chief Counsel Frederick A. O. Schwarz, Jr. (considered by many to be the driving force behind the staff inquiry), promptly set to work collecting data and documents. Over the next eight months, the energetic researchers amassed a wealth of material and put together numerous studies that laid a solid foundation for hearings that began in September. Meanwhile, the House of Representatives overcame some initial confusion and launched a separate investigation of intelligence activities.

The dangers of sacrificing substance for political advantage remained constant throughout both inquiries. Indeed, the House Committee (chaired by Otis Pike of New York) soon became mired in leaks and controversy.[5] But the Senate's Select Committee maintained a sense of high purpose, producing what CIA Director Colby has termed "a comprehensive and serious review of the history and present status of American intelligence."[6]

The Church Committee concluded that the realities of world politics demanded an effective American intelligence system [Document 8]. However, the CIA's original mandate to collect, analyze, and disseminate intelligence to policymakers had been overshadowed by covert action. The Committee recommended that covert action—which for the most part had been unproductive—be undertaken only in extraordinary circumstances, that abusive practices be curbed, and that the CIA once again stress research, analysis, and coordination. Finally, Congress should provide the necessary guidelines and oversight to assure compliance with the rule of law.

President Jimmy Carter incorporated many of the Select Committee's recommendations in Executive Order No. 12063 of January 1978 [Document 9]. Designed to clarify the boundaries of legitimate intelligence activities, establish effective oversight, and specify the authority and responsibilities of the CIA's director, the Order should have been the basis for more permanent statutory foundations. Congress, however, became caught up in an acrimonious debate on provisions of a new law and failed to act on the administration's proposal.

Efforts to return the agency to its original mission of intelligence collection and analysis, in fact, had only limited success even before Ronald Reagan took office in January 1981. Determined to revitalize America's intelligence system, the new president issued a revised Executive Order to govern the intelligence community [Document 10]. Although continuing some of the restrictions of the earlier Order and retaining provisions for Congressional oversight, the new mandate expanded the CIA's authority in several areas, including the first permission to conduct domestic covert operations. At the same time, President Reagan placed renewed emphasis on clandestine action abroad. Although by the early 1980s remarkable progress had been made in restoring public confidence in the integrity of the CIA, the agency's proper role in government remained uncertain.

Fortunately, in the continuing debate on the propriety, utility, effectiveness, and accountability of the CIA, an authoritative historical perspective is available. The *History of the Central Intelligence Agency,* written for the Church Committee by Anne Karalekas, a talented young staff member who did graduate work at Harvard University, largely escaped public attention at a time when the nation's newspapers were filled with disclosures of assassination plots and drug experiments. Based on studies compiled by the CIA's historical staff, extensive interviews, and a variety of classified and public sources, it traces the agency's origins and development, clarifies the organization's changing functions over time, and discusses the relationship between the CIA and other branches of government. The *History* was used by the Select Committee to recommend changes in the CIA's organization and mission; it continues to provide the parameters for discussion of the correct place of a central intelligence organization in a democratic society. Given the Reagan administration's emphasis on secrecy (as indicated by the draconian provisions of the National Security Decision Directive of March 11, 1983), the

History is likely to remain the primary source of reliable historical information on the CIA for many years to come.

Notes to Introduction

1. U.S. Central Intelligence Agency, *Intelligence in the War of Independence* (Washington, D.C., 1976), p. 34.

2. Interview with Dean Rusk, February 11, 1981.

3. William Colby and Peter Forbath, *Honorable Men: My Life in the CIA* (New York, 1978), p. 309.

4. Senate Resolution 21.

5. See J. Leiper Freeman, "Investigating the Executive Intelligence: The Fate of the Pike Committee," *Capitol Studies* 6 (1977), 103–17.

6. Colby and Forbath, *Honorable Men*, p. 442.

History of The
Central Intelligence Agency

HISTORY OF THE CENTRAL INTELLIGENCE AGENCY

INTRODUCTION [1]

During the past two years the Central Intelligence Agency has been the object of continuing public scrutiny, much of which has focused on the Agency's abuses. The current political climate and the mystique of secrecy surrounding the intelligence profession have made it difficult to view the CIA in the context of U.S. foreign policy and the Agency's development as an institution. This history will examine the CIA's organizational evolution, evaluating the influences that have shaped the Agency and determined its activities. An historical study of this nature serves two important purposes. First, it provides a means of understanding the Agency's structure. Second, and more importantly, by analyzing the causal elements in the CIA's pattern of activity, the study should illuminate the possibilities for and the obstacles to future reform in the United States foreign intelligence system.

An institutionalized intelligence function is not unique to the United States Government. The tradition of formalized reporting organizations dates back to the 16th century in Britain, to the 19th century in France, and to the 18th century in Czarist Russia. In establishing a peacetime central intelligence body after World War II, the United States as one of the great powers came late to defining the need for an intelligence institution as an arm of foreign policy. Secretary of State Henry Stimson's alleged statement, "Gentlemen do not read each other's mail" reflected the United States' rejection of ongoing espionage activities. Over the course of history American presidents and the military services employed agents to engage in clandestine missions, particularly in times of war. However, the distinction between these sporadic activities and an institutionalized structure for generating information for senior officials was a significant one. The decision to create a separate agency implied recognition of the intelligence function as an integral part of the foreign and military policy process. Today the United States military and civilian intelligence establishment employs thousands of people and expends billions of dollars

---

[1] This history of the CIA is based on four principal groups of sources. Since classification restrictions prevent citing individual sources directly, the categories are identified as follows: (1) Approximately seventy-five volumes from the series of internal CIA histories, a rich if uneven collection of studies, which deal with individual Agency components, the administrations of the Directors of Central Intelligence, and specialized areas of intelligence analysis. The histories have been compiled since the late 1940's and constitute a unique institutional memory. (2) Approximately sixty interviews with present and retired Agency employees. These interviews were invaluable in providing depth of insight and understanding to the organization. (3) Special studies and reports conducted both within and outside the Agency. They comprise reviews of functional areas and the overall administration of the CIA. (4) Documents and statistics supplied to the Committee by the CIA in response to specific requests. They include internal communications, budgetary allocations, and information on grade levels and personnel strengths. This history of the CIA was prepared for the Select Committee by Anne Karalekas, staff member.

annually. The Central Intelligence Agency is one organization in that establishment.

In contemplating the role of a central intelligence organization and its relationship to foreign policy, one can define the objectives that the agency might achieve. It should gather information that is otherwise unobtainable; it should have the institutional independence that allows it to interpret information objectively and in a way that assists policymakers to make decisions; it should have the access that insures maximum use of its analysis; with appropriate direction from the Executive branch and oversight from the Legislative branch it might undertake clandestine operations in support of United States foreign policy.

The CIA has functioned in each of these capacities, but not with equal concentration of resources and attention to each area. During the past twenty-nine years, the Agency's overall effort and the relative emphasis among its functions have been affected by four factors: the international environment as perceived by senior policymakers; the institutional milieu created by other agencies serving similar functions; the Agency's internal structure, particularly the incentives which rewarded certain kinds of activities more than others; and the individual serving as the Director of Central Intelligence, his preferences and his relative stature. This study will examine the CIA's history, determining which influences were most important at which periods and evaluating their impact on the Agency's development.

Today the CIA is identified primarily in terms of its espionage and covert action capabilities, i.e. spying operations and political action, propaganda, economic, and paramilitary activities designed to influence foreign governments. However, the motivating purpose in the creation of the Agency was very different. Before the end of World War II American policymakers conceived the idea of a peacetime central intelligence organization to provide senior government officials with high-quality, objective intelligence analysis. At the time of the new agency's creation the military services and the State Department had their own independent collection and analysis capabilities. However, the value of their analysis was limited, since their respective policy objectives often skewed their judgments. A centralized body was intended to produce "national intelligence estimates" independent of policy biases and to provide direction over the other intelligence organizations to minimize duplication of efforts.[2]

Within two years of its creation the CIA assumed functions very different from its principal mission, becoming a competing producer of current intelligence and a covert operational instrument in the American cold war offensive. In size, function, and scale of activities the CIA has expanded consistently.

In addition, the problem of duplication among intelligence agencies remained. Since 1947 growth in the scale and number of United States intelligence agencies has paralleled the CIA's own growth. In fact, much of the history of the CIA's role in intelligence analysis has been

---

[2] "National" intelligence meant integrated interdepartmental intelligence that exceeded the perspective and competence of individual departments and that covered the broad aspects of national policy. "Estimates" meant predictive judgments on the policies and motives of foreign governments rather than descriptive summaries of daily events or "current intelligence."

a history of its efforts to emerge as an independent agency among numerous intelligence organizations within the government. Today these organizations and the CIA itself are referred to as the intelligence "community," although they have been and continue to be competitors in intelligence collection and analysis.[3]

This study is not intended to catalogue the CIA's covert operations, but to present an analytical framework within which the Agency's development and practices may be understood. The CIA's twenty-nine year history is divided into four segments: 1946 to 1952, 1953 to 1961, 1962 to 1970, and 1971 to 1975. Because the CIA's basic internal organization and procedures evolved during the first period, these years are treated in somewhat greater detail than the others.

---

[3] At the time of the CIA's creation in 1947 only the State Department and the military services engaged in intelligence collection and analysis. Today the organizations responsible for U.S. intelligence activities include:

—The National Security Agency (NSA) which was established in 1952 and is under the direction of the Defense Department. NSA monitors and decodes foreign communications and electronic signals. It is the largest U.S. intelligence agency and is a collector of data rather than a producer of intelligence analysis.

—The Defense Intelligence Agency (DIA), established in 1961, is responsible to the Joint Chiefs of Staff and the Secretary of Defense. DIA was intended to limit duplication among the service intelligence agencies. Its primary task is production rather than collection.

—The Bureau of Intelligence and Research, the State Department's intelligence component, has no independent collection capability of its own but employs Foreign Service reports in the production of analyses for the Department's senior officials.

—The service intelligence agencies, Army, Navy and Air Force, collect and analyze information related to "tactical intelligence," essentially regional intelligence on foreign military capabilities.

—The FBI, the Treasury Department and the Energy Research and Development Administration have intelligence capabilities that support their respective missions.

Part One

THE CENTRAL INTELLIGENCE GROUP AND THE CENTRAL INTELLIGENCE
AGENCY, 1946–1952

INTRODUCTION

The years 1946 to 1952 were the most crucial in determining the
functions of the central intelligence organization. The period marked
a dramatic transformation in the mission, size, and structure of the
new agency. In 1946 the Central Intelligence Group (CIG), the CIA's
predecessor, was conceived and established as a coordinating body to
minimize the duplicative efforts of the departmental intelligence components and to provide objective intelligence analysis to senior policymakers. By 1952 the Central Intelligence Agency was engaged in
clandestine collection, independent intelligence production, and covert
operations. The CIG was an extension of the Departments; its personnel and budget were allocated from State, War and Navy. By 1952
the CIA had developed into an independent government agency com-
manding manpower and budget far exceeding anything originally
imagined.

I. The OSS Precedent

The concept of a peacetime central intelligence agency had its origins in World War II with the Office of Strategic Services (OSS).
Through the driving initiative and single-minded determination of
William J. Donovan, sponsor and first director of OSS, the organization became the United States' first independent intelligence body
and provided the organizational precedent for the Central Intelligence Agency. In large part, CIA's functions, structure, and expertise
were drawn from OSS.

A prominent attorney and World War I hero, "Wild Bill" Donovan
had traveled extensively in Europe and had participated in numerous
diplomatic missions for the government after the war. A tour of
Europe for President Roosevelt in 1940 convinced him of the necessity for a centralized intelligence organization. Donovan's ideas about
the purposes an intelligence agency should serve had been shaped by
his knowledge of and contact with the British intelligence services,
which encompassed espionage, intelligence analysis, and subversive
operations—albeit in separately administered units. The plan which
Donovan advocated in 1940 envisioned intelligence collection and
analysis, espionage, sabotage, and propaganda in a single organization. Essentially, this remained the basic formulation for the central
intelligence organization for the next thirty years.

The immediacy of the war in Europe gave force to Donovan's proposal for a central agency, the principal purpose of which was to
provide the President with integrated national intelligence. Acting on
Donovan's advice, Franklin Roosevelt established the Office of Coor-

dinator of Informtion (COI) in the summer of 1941. COI with Donovan as Coordinator, reported directly to the President. Its specific duties were to collect and analyze information for senior officials, drawing on information from the Army, Navy, and State Departments when appropriate. A year after its creation, when the United States was embroiled in war with Germany and Japan, the Office was renamed the Office of Strategic Services (OSS) and placed under the direction of the Joint Chiefs of Staff.

The British provided invaluable assistance to OSS. British experts served as instructors to their American counterparts in communications, counterespionage, subversive propaganda, and special operations. In real terms the British provided American intelligence with the essence of its "tradecraft"—the techniques required to carry out intelligence activities.

OSS was divided into several branches. The Research and Analysis (R&A) branch provided economic, social, and political analyses, sifting information from foreign newspapers and international business and labor publications. The Secret Intelligence (SI) branch engaged in clandestine collection from within enemy and neutral territory. The Special Operations (SO) branch conducted sabotage and worked with resistance forces. The Counterespionage (X–2) branch engaged in protecting U.S. and Allied intelligence operations from enemy penetrations. The Morale Operations (MO) branch was responsible for covert or "black" propaganda. Operational Groups (OG) conducted guerrilla operations in enemy territory. Finally, the Maritime Unit (MU) carried out maritime sabotage.

Although by the end of the war OSS had expanded dramatically, the organization encountered considerable resistance to the execution of its mission. From the outset the military were reluctant to provide OSS with information for its research and analysis role and restricted its operations. General Douglas MacArthur excluded OSS from China and the Pacific theater (although OSS did operate in Southeast Asia). In addition to demanding that OSS be specifically prohibited from conducting domestic espionage, FBI Director J. Edgar Hoover and Nelson Rockefeller, then Coordinator of Inter-American Affairs, insisted on maintaining their jurisdiction over Latin America, thereby excluding OSS from that area.

These operational limitations were indicative of the obstacles which OSS encountered as a new organization in the entrenched Washington bureaucracy. On the intelligence side, OSS failed to establish a consistent channel of input. Roosevelt relied on informal conversations and a retinue of personal aides in his decisions. The orderly procedure of reviewing, evaluating, and acting on the basis of intelligence was simply not part of his routine. Roosevelt's erratic process of decision-making and the Departments' continued reliance on their own sources of information frustrated Donovan's hope that OSS would become the major resource for other agencies.

Nonetheless, General Donovan was firm in his conviction that a centralized intelligence organization was an essential element for senior policymakers. Anticipating the end of the war, Donovan recommended the continuance of all OSS functions in a peacetime agency directly responsible to the President. Having endured the difficulties surrounding the establishment of OSS, Donovan had by 1944 accepted the fact that a separate, independent intelligence agency would have to coexist with the intelligence services of the other Departments. In a November 1944 memorandum to Roosevelt in which he recommended the maintenance of a peacetime intelligence organization Donovan stated:

> You will note that coordination and centralization are placed at the policy level but operational intelligence (that pertaining primarily to Department action) remains within the existing agencies concerned. The creation of a central authority thus would not conflict with or limit necessary intelligence functions within the Army, Navy, Department of State, and other agencies.

Donovan's hope that OSS would continue uninterrupted did not materialize. President Harry S Truman ordered the disbandment of OSS as of October 1, 1945, at the same time maintaining and transferring several OSS branches to other departments. The Research and Analysis Branch was relocated in the State Department, and the Secret Intelligence and Counterespionage Branches were transferred to the War Department, where they formed the Strategic Services Unit (SSU). Although it is impossible to determine conclusively, there is no evidence that OSS subversion and sabotage operations continued after the war. SSU and the former R&A Branch did continue their activities under the direction of their respective departments.

The OSS wartime experience foreshadowed many of CIA's problems. Both OSS and CIA encountered resistance to the execution of their mission from other government departments; both experienced the difficulty of having their intelligence "heard"; and both were characterized by the dominance of their clandestine operational components.

II. The Origins of the Central Intelligence Group

As the war ended, new patterns of decisionmaking emerged within the United States Government. In the transition from war to peace, policymakers were redefining their organizational and informational needs. A new President influenced the manner and substance of the decisions. Unlike Franklin Roosevelt, whose conduct of foreign policy was informal and personalized, Harry Truman preferred regular meetings of his full cabinet. Senior officials in the State, War, and Navy Departments were more consistent participants in presidential decisions than they had been under Roosevelt. In part this was a result of Truman's recognition of his lack of experience in foreign policy and his reliance on others for advice. Nonetheless, Truman's forthright decisiveness made him a strong leader and gained him the immediate respect of those who worked with him.

Secretary of State James F. Byrnes had little diplomatic experience, although he had an extensive background in domestic politics, having served in the House and Senate and on the Supreme Court. Secretary of War Robert P. Patterson, a lawyer by training, had been immersed in the problems of war supply and production. In 1945 he faced the issue of demobilization and its implications for the U.S. postwar position. Secretary of the Navy James V. Forrestal was probably the individual with the most fully developed ideas on foreign policy in the cabinet. As early as May 1945 he had expressed concern over the potential threat of the Soviet Union and for the next two years he continued to be in the vanguard of U.S. officials who perceived the U.S.S.R. as the antagonist to the United States.

Among the Secretaries, Forrestal was also a vocal proponent of more effective coordination within the Government. He favored something similar to the British war cabinet system, and along with it a central organization to provide intelligence estimates. In the fall of 1945, Forrestal took several initiatives to sound out departmental preferences for the creation of a central agency. These initiatives were crucial in developing a consensus about the need for centralized intelligence production, if not about the structure of the organization serving the need.

Truman himself shared Forrestal's conviction and supported the Secretary's efforts to review the problem of centralization and reorganization. From October through December 1945, U.S. Government agencies, spurred on by Forrestal, engaged in a series of policy debates about the necessity for and the nature of the future U.S. intelligence capability. Three major factors dominated the discussion. First was the issue of postwar defense reorganization. The debate focused around the question of an independent Air Force and the unification of the services under a Department of Defense—whether there should be separate services (the Air Force becoming independent) with a Joint Chiefs of Staff organization and a civilian Secretary of Defense coordinating them, or a single Department of National Defense with one civilian secretary and, more importantly, one chief of staff and one unified general staff. Discussion of a separate central intelligence agency and its structure, authority, and accountability was closely linked to the reorganization issue.

Second, it was clear from the outset that neither separate service departments nor a single Department of National Defense would willingly resign its intelligence function and accompanying personnel and budgetary allotments to a new central agency. If such an agency came into being, it would exist in parallel with military intelligence organizations and with a State Department political intelligence organization. At most, its head would have a coordinating function comparable to that envisioned for a relatively weak Secretary of Defense.

Third, the functions under discussion were intelligence analysis and the dissemination of intelligence. The shadow of the Pearl Harbor disaster dominated policymakers' thinking about the purpose of a central intelligence agency. They saw themselves rectifying the conditions that allowed Pearl Harbor to happen—a fragmented military-based intelligence apparatus, which in current terminology could not distinguish "signals" from "noise," let alone make its assessments available to senior officials.

Within the government in the fall of 1945 numerous studies explored the options for the future defense and intelligence organizations. None advocated giving a central independent group sole responsibility for either collection or analysis. All favored making the central intelligence body responsible to the Departments themselves rather than to the President. Each Department lobbied for an arrangement that would give itself an advantage in intelligence coordination. In particular, Alfred McCormack, Special Assistant to Secretary of State Byrnes, was an aggressive, indeed, belligerent, advocate of State Department dominance in the production of national intelligence. President Truman had encouraged the State Department to take the lead in organizing an intelligence coordination mechanism. However, as McCormack continued to press for the primacy of the State Department, he encountered outright opposition from the military and from Foreign Service stalwarts who objected to the establishment of a separate office for intelligence and research within State.

Among the studies that were underway, the most influential was the Eberstadt Report, directed by Ferdinand Eberstadt, an investment banker and friend of Forrestal. Eberstadt's recommendations were the most comprehensive in advancing an integrated plan for defense reorganization and centralized decisionmaking. In June 1945, Forrestal commissioned Eberstadt to study the proposed merger of the War and Navy Departments. In doing so, Eberstadt examined the entire structure of policymaking at the senior level—undoubtedly with Forrestal's preference for centralization well in mind. Eberstadt concluded that the War and Navy Departments could not be merged. Instead, he proposed a consultative arrangement for the State Department, the Army and the Navy, and an independent Air Force through a National Security Council (NSC).

Eberstadt stated that an essential element in the NSC mechanism was a central intelligence agency to supply "authoritative information on conditions and developments in the outside world." Without such an agency, Eberstadt maintained, the NSC "could not fulfill its role" nor could the military services "perform their duty to the nation." Despite the fact that the Eberstadt Report represented the most affirmative formal statement of the need for intelligence analysis, it did not make the giant leap and recommend centralization of the departmental intelligence functions. In a section drafted by Rear Admiral Sidney Souers, Deputy Chief of Naval Intelligence, and soon to become the first director of the central intelligence body, the report stated that each Department had its independent needs which required the maintenance of independent capabilities. The report recommended only a coordination role for the agency in the synthesis of departmental intelligence.[1]

The Presidential Directive establishing the Central Intelligence Group reflected these preferences. The Departments retained autonomy over their intelligence services, and the CIG's budget and staff were to be drawn from the separate agencies. Issued on January 22, 1946, the Directive provided the CIG with a Director of Central Intelligence (DCI), chosen by the President. The CIG was responsible for coordination, planning, evaluation, and dissemination

---

[1] Amid this major effort to define the role of a central intelligence agency, only one individual advocated the creation of an independent agency which would centralize the intelligence functions in the Government. General John Magruder, Chief of SSU, openly questioned the willingness of the separate agencies to cooperate in intelligence production. On that basis he argued for a separate agency wholly responsible for the collection and analysis of foreign intelligence.

of intelligence. It also was granted overt collection responsibility.[1a] The National Intelligence Authority (NIA), a group comprised of the Secretary of State, the Secretary of War, the Secretary of the Navy, and the personal representative of the President, served as the Director's supervisory body. The Intelligence Advisory Board (IAB), which included the heads of the military and civilian intelligence agencies, was an advisory group for the Director.

Through budget, personnel, and oversight, the Departments had assured themselves control over the Central Intelligence Group. CIG was a creature of departments that were determined to maintain independent capabilities as well as their direct advisory relationship to the President. In January 1946, they succeeded in doing both; by retaining autonomy over their intelligence operations, they established the strong institutional claims that would persist for the lifetime of the Central Intelligence Agency.

III. The Directors of Central Intelligence, 1946–1952

At a time when the new agency was developing its mission, the role of its senior official was crucial. The Director of Central Intelligence was largely responsible for representing the agency's interests to the Department and for pressing its jurisdictional claims. From 1946 to 1952, the strength of the agency relative to the Departments was dependent on the stature that the DCI commanded as an individual. The four DCIs during this period ranged from providing only weak leadership to firmly solidifying the new organization in the Washington bureaucracy. Three of the four men were career military officers. Their appointments were indicative of the degree of control the military services managed to retain over the agency and the acceptance of the services' primary role in the intelligence process.

Sidney W. Souers (January 1946–June 1946)

In January 1946, Sidney W. Souers—the only one of these DCIs who was not a career military officer—was appointed Director of Central Intelligence. Having participated in the drafting of the CIG directive, Souers had a fixed concept of the central intelligence function, one that did not challenge the position of the departmental intelligence services.

Born and educated in the Midwest, Souers was a talented business executive. Before the war he amassed considerable wealth revitalizing ailing corporations and developing new ones, particularly in the aviation industry. A naval reserve officer, Souers spent his wartime service in naval intellience, rising to the rank of Rear Admiral. His achievements in developing countermeasures against enemy submarine action brought him to the attention of then Secretary of the Navy Forrestal, who appointed him Assistant Director of the Office of Naval Intelligence in July 1944. Later that year, Souers assumed the post of Deputy Chief of Naval Intelligence.

[1a] Participants in the drafting of the January 1946 Directive have stated that clandestine collection was an intended function of the CIG at that time, although it was not formally assigned to CIG until June 1946. See p. 14. It is unclear how widely shared this understanding was. Commenting on the maintenance of SSU, Secretary Patterson wrote to the President in October 1945, saying that "the functions of OSS, chiefly clandestine activities, had been kept separate in the Strategic Services Unit of the War Department as the nucleus of a possible central intelligence service. . . ."

The combination of his administrative skills and his intelligence background made him Forrestal's choice to head the newly created Central Intelligence Group. Souers accepted the job with the understanding that he would remain only long enough to build the basic organization. Holding to that condition, Souers left CIG in June 1946 and returned to manage his business interests in Missouri.

The close relationship between Souers and President Truman resulted in Souers' return to Washington a year later to assume eventually the position of Executive Secretary of the National Security Council, a job he held from September 1947 until 1950. It was probably in this position rather than as DCI that Souers exerted the most influence over the central intelligence function. His stature as a former DCI and his friendship with Truman lent considerable weight to his participation in the early NSC deliberations over the CIA.

Lieutenant General Hoyt S. Vandenberg (June 1946–May 1947)

The appointment of Lieutenant General Hoyt Vandenberg as DCI on June 10, 1946 marked the beginning of CIG's gradual development as an independent intelligence producer. Vandenberg was an aggressive, assertive personality. As a three-star general, he may have viewed the DCI's position as a means of advancing his Air Force career. His actions during his one-year term were directed toward enhancing CIG's stature. Soon after leaving CIG he became Air Force Chief of Staff, acquiring his fourth star at the same time. Vandenberg's background, personal connections, and strong opinions contributed in a significant way to changes which occurred over the next year.

A graduate of West Point, Vandenberg had served as head of the Army's intelligence division, G–2, and immediately prior to his appointment as DCI had represented G–2 on the Intelligence Advisory Board. This experience gave him the opportunity to observe the problems of directing an agency totally dependent on other departments.

One of Vandenberg's important assets in the never-ending battles with the military was the fact that he was a high-ranking military careerist. As such, he could deal with the military intelligence chiefs on more than equal terms. Vandenberg was also well-connected on Capitol Hill. The nephew of Arthur Vanderberg, ranking Republican on the Senate Foreign Relations Committee, Vandenberg gained wide access to members of the House and Senate.

Vandenberg's achievements touched on two areas: administrative authority and the scope of CIG's intelligence mission. He first addressed himself to the problem of the budget. The existing arrangement required the DCI to request funds from the Departments for operating expenses as they developed. There were no funds earmarked in the departmental budgets for CIG's use; therefore, the DCI was dependent on the disposition of the Department secretaries to release the money he needed.

Since CIG was not an independent agency, it could not be directly granted appropriations from the Congress. Vandenberg pressed the Departments to provide CIG with a specific allotment over which the DCI would have dispersal authority. Although both Secretary of War Patterson and Secretary of State Byrnes objected, arguing that CIG's budget had to be kept confidential, Admiral Leahy, President Truman's Chief of Staff, provided Vandenberg with the support he needed. Through the certification of vouchers, the DCI could pay personnel and purchase supplies.

Under Vandenberg, CIG moved beyond a strict coordination role to acquire a clandestine collection capability, as well as authority to conduct independent research and analysis.[2] During this period, CIG also replaced the FBI in Latin America.[3] When Vandenberg left the CIG, he left an organization whose mission had considerably altered.

Admiral Roscoe H. Hillenkoetter (May 1947–October 1950)

Rear Admiral Roscoe Hillenkoetter assumed the position of DCI at a time when the Central Intelligence Group was about to be reconstituted as the Central Intelligence Agency and when international pressures placed widely disparate demands on the fledgling agency. Under Hillenkoetter, the Agency experienced undirected evolution in the area of intelligence, never fulfilling its coordination function, but developing as an intelligence producer. In this period the Agency also acquired its covert operational capability. Hillenkoetter's part in these changes was more passive than active. Having only recently been promoted to Rear Admiral, he lacked the leverage of rank to deal effectively with the military.

Hillenkoetter had spent most of his almost thirty-year naval career at sea, and he remained a sea captain in mind and heart. A graduate of Annapolis in 1919, he served in Central America, Europe, and the Pacific. His assignments as naval attaché had given him some exposure to the intelligence process. However, the position of the DCI required bureaucratic expertise; Hillenkoetter did not have the instincts or the dynamism for dealing with senior policymakers in State and Defense.

In fairness to Hillenkoetter, he labored under the difficulty of serving during a period of continuing disagreements between Secretary of State Dean G. Acheson and Secretary of Defense Louis A. Johnson. With the Agency having to execute covert operations which were to serve the policy needs of the two Departments, the antagonism between the two Secretaries left the DCI in a difficult position. Hillenkoetter left the Agency in 1950 to resume sea command.

General Walter Bedell Smith (October 1950–February 1953)

It was precisely because of Hillenkoetter's weakness that General Walter Bedell Smith was selected to succeed him in October 1950. Nicknamed the "American Bulldog" by Winston Churchill, Smith was a tough-minded, hard-driving, often intimidating military careerist.

Smith came to the position of DCI as one of the most highly regarded and most senior-ranking military officers in the government. During World War II, he had served as Chief of Staff of the Allied Forces in North Africa and the Mediterranean, and later became Dwight Eisenhower's Chief of Staff, after Eisenhower's appointment as Commander of the European theater. Following the war, Smith served as U.S. Ambassador to the Soviet Union.

---

[2] For a full discussion of these changes, see pp. 13, 14.

[3] CIG's acquisition of nominal authority in Latin America may have been a symbolic gain, but the organization faced institutional obstacles in the assumption of its mission there. In mid-1946, jurisdiction for Latin America was reassigned to the CIG. The process by which the transfer occurred is unknown, but it is clear that FBI Director Hoover had conceded his authority grudgingly. A formal agreement between the two agencies (presumably initiated by Hoover) stipulated that no FBI Latin American files were to be turned over to the CIG.

The Korean War placed enormous pressures on the Agency during Smith's term, and had a major impact on the size and direction of the CIA. Although by the time of Smith's appointment the Agency's functions had been established—overt and clandestine collection, covert operations, intelligence analysis, and coordination of departmental activities—Smith supervised sweeping administrative changes which created the basic structure that remains in effect to this day. As DCI, Smith easily outranked the service intelligence chiefs with whom he had to deal. His stature and personality made him one of the strongest Directors in the Agency's history.

IV. The Evolution of the Central Intelligence Function, 1946-1949

A. The Pattern Established, 1946-1949

The CIG had been established to rectify the duplication among the military intelligence services and to compensate for their biased analyses. The rather vaguely conceived notion was that a small staff would assemble and review the raw data collected by the departmental intelligence services and produce objective estimates for the use of senior American policymakers. Although in theory the concept was reasonable and derived from real informational needs, institutional resistance made implementation virtually impossible. The military intelligence services jealously guarded both their information and what they believed were their prerogatives in providing policy guidance to the President, making CIG's primary mission an exercise in futility.

Limited in the execution of its coordinating responsibility, the organization gradually emerged as an intelligence producer, generating current intelligence summaries and thereby competing with the Departments in the dissemination of information. The following section will explore the process by which CIG, and later the CIA, created by the National Security Act of 1947, drifted from its original purpose of producing coordinated national estimates to becoming primarily a current intelligence producer.

In January 1946, Souers assumed direction over a feeble organization. Its personnel had to be assigned from other agencies, and its budget was allocated from other departments. Clearly, the Departments were not inclined to relinquish manpower and money to a separate organization, even if that organization was little more than an adjunct of their own. Postwar personnel and budget cuts further limited the support which the Departments were willing to provide. Those who were assigned could not remain long; some were of mediocre ability. By U.S. Government standards, CIG was a very small organization. In June 1946, professional and clerical personnel numbered approximately 100.

CIG had two overt collection components. The Domestic Contact Service (DCS) solicited domestic sources, including travelers and businessmen for foreign intelligence information on a voluntary and witting basis.[4] The Foreign Broadcast Information Service (FBIS), an element of OSS, monitored overseas broadcasts. There were two staffs, the Interdepartmental Coordinating and Planning Staff

---

[4] The term "witting" is used by intelligence professionals to indicate an individual's knowledgeable association with an intelligence service.

(ICAPS), which dealt with the Departments, and the Central Reports Staff (CRS), which was responsible for correlation and evaluation. A Council, comprised of three Assistant Directors, dealt with internal matters.

In March 1946, the Central Reports Staff consisted of 29 professionals, 17 "on loan" from the Departments of State, War, and Navy, and 12 full-time analysts. The crucial element in the conception of CRS was Souers' plan to have four full-time representatives from the Departments and the JCS who would participate in the estimates production process and speak for the chiefs of their agencies in presenting departmental views. The plan never developed. The departmental representatives were eventually assigned, but they were not granted the requisite authority for the production of coordinated intelligence. Only one was physically stationed with CIG. The Departments' failure to provide personnel to CIG was only the first indication of the resistance which they posed on every level.

The military particularly resented having to provide a civilian agency with military intelligence data. The services regarded this as a breach of professionalism, and more importantly, believed that civilians could not understand, let alone analyze, military intelligence data. The intensity of the military's feelings on the issue of civilian access is indicated by the fact that CIG could not receive information on the capabilities and intentions of U.S. armed forces.

Almost immediately the State Department challenged CIG on the issue of access to the President. Truman had requested that CIG provide him with a daily intelligence summary from the Army, Navy, and State Departments. However, Secretary of State Byrnes asserted his Department's prerogative in providing the President with foreign policy analyses. While CIG did its summary, the State Department continued to prepare its own daily digest. Truman received both.

The United States' first major postwar intelligence evaluation project further revealed the obstruction which the Departments posed to CIG's mission. In March 1946, the Army, Navy, and Air Force intelligence services were directed to join with CIG "to produce the highest possible quality of intelligence on the U.S.S.R. in the shortest possible time." Intended to be broadly focused, the study began in an atmosphere of urgency. Recent events had aroused alarm over the growing belligerency of the Soviet Union and had revealed the United States' relative ignorance of Soviet military strength in relation to its own.

The project was ridden with contention from the start. The military regarded the project as their own and did not expect or want CIG to review and process their raw intelligence materials for evaluation. Security restrictions prevented assignment of work to interdepartmental task forces and required that subject areas be assigned Department by Department. Each agency was interested in the project only as it served its individual purposes. For example, the Air Force regarded the study exclusively as a means of evaluating the U.S.S.R.'s air capability. CIG's intended role as an adjudicator between Departments was quickly reduced to that of an editor for independent departmental estimates. The report was actually published in March 1948, two years after it had been commissioned.

In the spring of 1946 the NIA, probably at the request of Vandenberg, authorized CIG to carry out independent research and analysis "not being presently performed" by the other Departments. The authorization led to a rapid increase in the size and functions of CIG's intelligence staff. In August 1946, DCI Vandenberg established the Office of Research and Evaluation (ORE) to replace the Central Reports Staff, which had been responsible for correlation. ORE's functions were manifold—the production of national current intelligence, scientific, technical, and economic intelligence, as well as interagency coordination for national estimates. At the same time, CIG was granted more money and personnel, and Vandenberg took full advantage of the opportunity to hire large numbers of people. One participant recalled Vandenberg as saying, "If I didn't fill all the slots I knew I'd lose them." By the end of 1946, Vandenberg took on at least 300 people for ORE.

With its own research and analysis capability, CIG could carry out an independent intelligence function without having to rely on the Departments for guidelines or for data. In effect, it made CIG an intelligence producer, while still assuming the continuation of its role in the production of coordinated national estimates. Yet acquisition of an independent intelligence role meant that production would outstrip coordinated analysis as a primary mission. Fundamentally, it was far easier to collect and analyze data than it had been or would be to work with the Departments in producing coordinated analysis. In generating its own intelligence, CIG could compete with the Departments without the problem of departmental obstruction.

The same 1946 directive which provided the CIG with an independent research and analysis capability also granted the CIG a clandestine collection capability. Since the end of the war, the remnant of the OSS clandestine collection capability rested with the Strategic Services Unit (SSU), then in the War Department. In the postwar dismantling of OSS, SSU was never intended to be more than a temporary body. In the spring of 1946, an interdepartmental committee, whose members had been chosen by the President, recommended that CIG absorb SSU's functions.

The amalgamation of SSU constituted a major change in the size, structure, and mission of CIG. Since 1945, SSU had maintained both personnel and field stations. Seven field stations remained in North Africa and the Near East. Equipment, codes, techniques, and communications facilities were intact and ready to be activated.

The transfer resulted in the establishment of the Office of Special Operations (OSO). OSO was responsible for espionage and counterespionage. Through SSU, the CIG acquired an infusion of former OSS personnel, who were experienced in both areas. From the beginning, the data collected by OSO was highly compartmented. The Office of Reports and Estimates did not draw on OSO for its raw information. Overt collection remained ORE's major source of data.[6]

The nature and extent of the requests made to ORE contributed to its failure to fulfill its intended role in national intelligence estimates. President Truman expected and liked to receive CIG's daily summary of international events. His known preference meant that work on the

---

[6] The acquisition of a clandestine collection capability and authorization to carry out independent research and analysis enlarged CIG's personnel strength considerably. As of December 1946, the total CIG staff numbered approximately 1,816. Proportionately, approximately one-third were overseas with OSO. Of those stationed in Washington, approximately half were devoted to administrative and support functions, one-third were assigned to OSO, and the remainder to intelligence production.

Daily, as it was called, assumed priority atte᷉
justification for the *Daily* as an addition to ot᷉
maries was that CIG had access to all informat᷉
ments that had only their own. This was not t᷉
1949, CIG and later CIA received almost all i᷉
from State. Although CIG had been created to᷉
tive efforts of the Departments, its acquisition o᷉
ligence production capability was now contribu᷉

The pressures of current events and the conse᷉
formation within the government generated ᷉
official requests to ORE. Most were concerned with events of the
moment rather than with national intelligence, strictly defined. ORE,
in turn, tended to accept any and all external requests—from State,
from the JCS, from the NSC. As ORE attempted to satisfy the wide-
ranging demands of many clients, its intelligence became directed to
a working-level audience rather than to senior policymakers. As such,
it lost the influence it was intended to have. Gradually, ORE built up
a series of commitments which made it less likely and less able to direct
its efforts to estimate production.

The passage of the National Security Act in July 1947 legislated
the changes in the Executive branch that had been under discussion
since 1945. The Act established an independent Air Force; provided
for coordination by a committee of service chiefs, the Joint Chiefs of
Staff (JCS), and a Secretary of Defense; and created the National
Security Council (NSC).[7] The CIG became an independent department and was renamed the Central Intelligence Agency.

Under the Act, the CIA's mission was only loosely defined, since
efforts to thrash out the CIA's duties in specific terms would have
contributed to the tension surrounding the unification of the services.
The five general tasks assigned to the Agency were (1) to advise
the NSC on matters related to national security; (2) to make recommendations to the NSC regarding the coordination of intelligence activities of the Departments; (3) to correlate and evaluate intelligence
and provide for its appropriate dissemination; (4) to carry out "service of common concern" and (5) "to perform such other functions and
duties related to intelligence affecting the national security as the
NSC will from time to time direct . . . ." The Act did not alter the
functions of the CIG. Clandestine collection, overt collection, production of national current intelligence, and interagency coordination
for national estimates continued, and the personnel and internal structure remained the same.[7a]

As the CIA evolved between 1947 and 1950, it never fulfilled its
estimates function, but continued to expand its independent intelligence production. Essentially, the problems that had developed in the
CIG continued. Since its creation in 1946, incentives existed within
ORE for the production of current rather than national coordinated

---

[7] Not until the Act was amended in 1949 was provision made for a statutory
chairman for the JCS or for a Department of Defense. It then took a series of
presidential reorganization decrees in the 1950's to give the Secretary of Defense
the power he was to have by the 1960's. As of 1947, the positions of the Secretary
of Defense and the DCI were not dissimilar, but the DCI was to remain a mere
coordinator.

[7a] For chart showing CIA organization as of 1947, see p. 96.

ce. ORE was organized into regional branches, comprised of s in specialized areas, and a group of staff editors who were re-ible for reviewing and editing the branches' writing for inclusion ne ORE summaries. Since the President's daily summary quickly ecame ORE's main priority, contributions to the summary were visible evidence of good work. Individuals within each of the branches were eager to have their material included in the *Daily* and *Weekly* publications. To have undertaken a longer-term project would have meant depriving oneself of a series of opportunities for quick recognition. Thus, the route to personal advancement lay with meeting the immediate, day-to-day responsibilities of ORE. In doing so, individuals in ORE perpetuated and contributed to the current intelligence stranglehold.

The drive for individuals in the branches to have their material printed and the role of the staffs in reviewing, editing and often rejecting material for publication caused antagonism between the two groups. The branches regarded themselves as experts in their given fields and resented the staff's claims to editorial authority. A reorganization in 1947 attempted to break down the conflict between the reviewers and the producers but failed. By 1949, the regional branches, in effect, controlled the publications.

The branches' tenacious desire to maintain control over CIA publications frustrated successive efforts to encourage the production of estimates. Several internal studies conducted in 1949 encouraged the re-establishment of a separate estimates group within ORE, devoted exclusively to the production of national estimates. The branches resisted the proposed reorganizations, primarily because they were unwilling to resign their prerogatives in intelligence production to an independent estimates division.

A July 1949 study conducted by a senior ORE analyst stated that ORE's emphasis in production had shifted "from the broad long-term type of problem to a narrowly defined short-term type and from the predictive to the non-predictive type." The same year a National Security Council-sponsored study concluded that "the principle of the authoritative NIE [National Intelligence Estimate] does not yet have established acceptance in the government. Each department still depends more or less on its own intelligence estimates and establishes its plans and policies accordingly." [8] ORE's publications provide the best indication of its failure to execute its estimates function. In 1949, ORE had eleven regular publications. Only one of these, the ORE Special Estimate Series, addressed national intelligence questions and was published with the concurrence or dissent of the Departments comprising the Intelligence Advisory Committee. Less than one-tenth of ORE's products were serving the purposes for which the Office had been created.

B. The Reorganization of the Intelligence Function, 1950

By the time Walter Bedell Smith became DCI, it was clear that the CIA's record in providing national intelligence estimates had fallen far short of expectation. The obstacles presented by the departmental intelligence components, the CIA's acquisition of au-

---

[8] From the Dulles-Jackson-Correa Survey. See p. 17.

thority to carry out independent research and analysis, demands from throughout the government for CIA analyses, and internal organizational incentives had contributed to the failure of the coordinated national estimates function and to ORE's current intelligence orientation. In 1950 ORE did little more than produce its own analyses and reports. The wholesale growth had only confused ORE's mission and led the organization into attempting analysis in areas already being serviced by other department.[8a]

These problems appeared more stark following the outbreak of the Korean War in June 1950. Officials in the Executive branch and members of Congress criticized the Agency for its failure to predict more specifically the timing of the North Korean invasion of South Korea. Immediately after his appointment as DCI in October 1950, Smith discovered that the Agency had no current coordinated estimate of the situation in Korea. Under the pressure of war, demands for information were proliferating, and it was apparent that ORE could not meet those demands.

The immediacy of the war and the influence of William H. Jackson, who served with him as Deputy Director for Central Intelligence (DDCI), convinced Smith of the necessity for changes. After taking office, Smith and Jackson defined three major problems in the execution of the CIA's intelligence mission: the need to ensure consistent, systematic production of estimates; the need to strengthen the position of the DCI relative to the departmental intelligence components; and the need to delineate more clearly CIA's research and analysis function. Within three months the two men had redefined the position of the DCI; had established the Office of National Estimates, whose sole task was the production of coordinated "national estimates"; and had limited the Agency's independent research and analysis to economic research on the "Soviet Bloc" nations. Nevertheless, these sweeping changes and the strength of leadership which Smith and Jackson provided did not resolve the fundamental problems of jurisdictional conflicts among departments, duplication, and definition of a consumer market continued.

Jackson, a New York attorney and investment banker, had gained insight into the intelligence function through wartime service with Army intelligence and through his participation in the Dulles-Jackson-Correa Survey.[9] Commissioned by the National Security Council in 1948, the Survey examined the U.S. intelligence establishment, focusing principally on the CIA. The report enumerated the problems in the Agency's execution of both its intelligence and operational missions, and made recommendations for reorganization. Virtually all of the changes which Smith made during his term were drawn from the Survey in which Jackson participated.[10]

[8a] For chart showing CIA organization as of 1950 prior to the reorganization and including the clandestine operational component discussed on pp. 25 ff., See p. 97.

[9] Matthias Correa, a New York lawyer and a wartime assistant to Secretary Forrestal, was not an active participant in the Survey. Allen W. Dulles, later to become DCI, and Jackson were its principal executors.

[10] There is some indication that Jackson assumed his position with the understanding that he and Smith would act on the Survey's recommendations.

The IAC and the Office of National Estimates

In an August 1950 memorandum to Smith, CIA General Counsel Lawrence R. Houston stressed that the Intelligence Advisory Committee had assumed an advisory role to the NSC and functioned as a supervisory body for the DCI—contrary to the initial intention.[10a] The IAC's inflated role had diminished the DCI's ability to demand departmental cooperation for the CIA's national estimates responsibility. Houston advised that the DCI would have to exert more specific direction over the departmental agencies, if coordinated national intelligence production was to be achieved. Smith acted on Houston's advice and informed the members of the IAC that he would not submit to their direction. At the same time, Smith encouraged their participation in the discussion and approval of intelligence estimates. Basically, Smith cultivated the good will of the IAC only to avoid open conflict. His extensive contacts at the senior military level and his pervasive prestige freed him from reliance on the IAC to accomplish his ends.

Smith's real attempt to establish an ongoing process for the production of national estimates focused on the Office of National Estimates (ONE). At the time Smith and Jackson took office, there were at least five separate proposals for remedial action in ORE, all of which recommended the establishment of a separate, independent office for the production of national estimates.[11] Jackson himself had been the strongest advocate of such an office during his participation in the Dulles-Jackson-Correa Survey, and he was prepared to act quickly to implement a separation of the research and reporting function from the estimates function. As a first step, ORE was dismantled.

To organize the Office of National Estimates, Smith called on William Langer, the Harvard historian who had directed the Research and Analysis Branch of OSS during the war. In addition to his intellectual capacities, Langer possessed the bureaucratic savvy and personal dynamism to carry out the concept of ONE. He was determined to keep the organization small and loosely run to avoid bureaucratic antagonisms.[12]

As organized in 1950, the Office of National Estimates had two components, a group of staff members who drafted the estimates and a senior body, known as the Board, who reviewed the estimates and coordinated the intelligence judgments of the several Departments. Jackson envisioned the Board members as "men of affairs," experienced in government and international relations who could make sage, pragmatic contributions to the work of the analysts. At first all staff members were generalists, expected to write on any subject, but gradually the staff broke down into generalists, who wrote the estimates and regional specialists, who provided expert assistance.

With the help of recommendations from Ludwell Montague, an historian and a senior ORE analyst, and others, Langer personally selected each of the ONE staff members, most of whom were drawn

---

[10a] See p. 25 for more discussion of the Intelligence Advising Committee.

[11] The individuals who advanced the recommendation included John Bross of the Office of Policy Coordination, General Magruder of SSU, Ludwell Montague of ORE, and William Jackson in the Dulles-Jackson-Correa Survey.

[12] One story, perhaps apocryphal, has Bedell Smith offering Langer 200 slots for ONE, to which Langer snapped back, "I can do it with twenty-five."

from ORE. By the end of November, ONE had a staff of fifty professionals. Seven Board members were also hired. They included four historians. one former combat commander, and one lawyer.[13]

As a corrective to what he regarded as the disproportionate number of academics on the Board, Jackson devised the idea of an outside panel of consultants who had wide experience in public affairs and who could bring their practical expertise to bear on draft estimates. In 1950 the "Princeton consultants",[14] as they came to be called, included George F. Kennan, Hamilton Fish Armstrong, the editor of *Foreign Affairs*, and Vannevar Bush, the atomic scientist.[15]

As ONE was conceived in 1950. it was to be entirely dependent on departmental contributions for research support. Although Langer found the arrangement somewhat unsatisfactory for the predictable reasons and considered providing ONE with its own research capability, the practice continued. However, as a result of the CIA's gradual development of its own independent research capabilities over the next twenty years, ONE increasingly relied on CIA resources. The shift in ONE's sources meant that the initial draft estimates—the estimates over which the Departments negotiated—became more CIA products than interdepartmental products.

The process of coordinating the Departments' judgments was not easy. A major problem was the nature of IAC representation and interaction between the IAC and the Board. At first, the IAC members as senior officers in their respective agencies were too removed from the subjects treated in the estimates to provide substantive discussions. An attempt to have the Board meet with lower-ranking officers meant that these officers were not close enough to the policy level to make departmental decisions. This problem of substantive background vs. decisionmaking authority was never really resolved and resulted in a prolonged negotiating process.

Almost immediately the military challenged ONE on the nature of the estimates, demanding that they be factual and descriptive. Montague, however, insisted that they be problem-oriented in order to satisfy the needs of the NSC. Jackson, Langer, Montague and others viewed the NIEs as providing senior policymakers with essential information on existing problems.

ONE's link to policymakers existed through the NSC, where meetings opened with a briefing by the DCI. Bedell Smith's regular attendance and his personal stature meant that the Agency was at least listened to when briefings were presented. Former members of ONE have said that this was a period when they felt their work really was making its way to the senior level and being used. The precise way in

---

[13] The historians: Sherman Kent, Ludwell Montague, DeForrest Van Slyck, and Raymond Sontag. General Clarence Huebner, retired U.S. Commander of all U.S. forces in Europe, represented the military. Maxwell Foster, a Boston lawyer, and Calvin Hoover, a professor of economics at Duke University, were the other two members. Both resigned within a few months, however.

[14] They met at the Gun Club at Princeton University.

[15] ONE's practice of using an outside group of senior consultants for key estimates continued into the 1960's, although the consultants' contribution became less substantial as the ONE analysts developed depth of background and understanding in their respective fields.

which these NIEs were used is unclear. Between 1950 and 1952 ONE's major effort dominated by production of estimates related to the Korea War, particularly those involving analyses of Soviet intentions.

The Office of Research and Reports

The estimates problem was only symptomatic of the Agency's broader difficulties in intelligence production. By 1950 ORE had become a directionless service organization, attempting to answer requirements levied by all agencies related to all manner of subjects—politics, economics, science, technology. ORE's publications took the form of "backgrounders," country studies, surveys, and an occasional estimate. In attempting to do everything, it was contributing almost nothing. On November 13, 1950, the same order that created ONE also renamed ORE the Office of Research and Reports (ORR), and redefined the Agency's independent intelligence production mission.

The Dulles-Jackson-Correa Survey had recommended that out of ORE a division be created to perform research services in fields of common concern that might be usefully performed centrally. Specifically, the report suggested the fields of science, technology, and economics. The report pointedly excluded political research, which it regarded as the exclusive domain of the State Department's Office of Intelligence Research. Once again, having participated in the Survey group, Jackson was disposed to implement its recommendations.

The issue of responsibility for political research had been a source of contention between ORE and State, which objected to the Agency's use of its data to publish "Agency" summations on subjects which State believed were appropriately its own and which were covered in State's own publications. Jackson had already accepted State's claims and was more than willing to concede both the political research and coordination functions to the Department. In return, the Office of Research and Reports was to have responsibility for economic research on the "Soviet Bloc."

There were three components of ORR: the Basic Intelligence Division and Map Division, both of which were maintained intact from ORE, and the newly created Economic Research Area (ERA). Basic Intelligence had no research function. It consisted of a coordinating and editing staff in charge of the production of National Intelligence Surveys, compendia of descriptive information on nearly every country in the world, which were of primary interest to war planning agencies.[16] The Map Division consisted of geographers and cartographers, most of whom were veterans of OSS. As the only foreign map specialists in the government, the division provided government-wide services.

The Economic Research Area became the focus of the Agency's research and analysis effort, and the Agency's development of this capability had a major impact on military and strategic analysis of the Soviet Union in the decade of the 1950's. ERA benefitted enormously from Jackson's appointment of Max Millikan as Assistant Director of ORR. A professor of economics at the Massachusetts Institute of Technology, Millikan had participated in the Office of Price

---

[16] ORE had assumed this function in 1948.

Administration and War Shipping Administration during the war and later served in the State Department's Office of Intelligence Research.

Millikan came to ORR in January 1951 and devoted his exclusive attention to organizing ORR's economic intelligence effort. He divided ERA into five areas: Materials, Industrial, Strategic, Economic Services, and Economic Analysis, and embarked on an extensive recruitment program among graduate students in corresponding specialties. In July 1951, ORR personnel numbered 461, including the Map and Basic Intelligence Divisions and some ORE personnel who had been retained. By January 1952, when Millikan left to return to MIT, ORR's strength had increased to 654, with all of that growth in ERA. ORR continued to grow, and in February 1953, it employed 766 persons.

This remarkable and perhaps excessive escalation was a result of the redefinition of the Agency's research and analysis mission and the immediate pressures of the Korean War. Although the Agency was limited to economic research, its intelligence had to service virtually all levels of consumers. Unlike ONE, ORR's intelligence was never intended to be directed to senior policymakers alone. Instead, ORR was to respond to the requests of senior and middle-level officials throughout the government, as well as serving a coordinating function. The breadth of ORR's clientele practically insured its size. In addition, the fact that ORR was created at the height of the Korean War, when the pressure for information was at a consistent peak, and when budgetary constraints were minimal, meant that personnel increases could be justified as essential to meet the intelligence needs of the war. After the war there was no effort to reduce the personnel strength.

Despite ORR's agreement with State regarding jurisdiction for political and economic intelligence, there remained in 1951 *twenty-four government departments and agencies producing economic intelligence.* Part of ORR's charge was to coordinate production on the "Soviet Bloc." In May 1951 the Economic Intelligence Committee (EIC) was created as a subcommittee of the IAC. With interdepartmental representation, the EIC, under the chairmanship of the Assistant Director, ORR, was to insure that priority areas were established among the agencies and that, wherever possible, duplication was avoided.[17] The EIC also had a publication function. It was to produce reports providing "the best available foreign economic intelligence" from U.S. Government agencies. The EIC papers were drafted in ORR and put through the EIC machinery in much the same way that ONE produced NIEs. Because of ORR's emerging expertise in economic intelligence, it was able to exert a dominant role in the coordination process and more importantly, on the substance of EIC publications.

The Agency's assumption of the economic research function and the subsequent creation of the EIC is a prime example of the ill-founded attempts to exert control over the departmental intelligence components. While the Agency was given primary responsibility for eco-

---

[17] The EIC included representatives from State, Army, Navy, Air Force, CIA, and the JCS sat on the EIC.

nomic research on the "Soviet Bloc," other departments still retained their own intelligence capabilities to meet what they regarded as their specific needs. Senior officials, particularly the military, continued to rely on their departmental staffs to provide them with information. The EIC thus served primarily as a publication body. Yet the assignment of a publication role to the EIC only contributed to the already flooded intelligence paper market within the government.

The fundamental problem was one of accretion of additional functions without dismantling existing capabilities. To assume that a second-level committee such as the EIC would impose real control and direction on the entrenched bureaucratic interests of twenty-four government agencies was at best misplaced confidence and at worst foolhardy optimism. The problem grew worse over the next decade as developments in science and technology created a wealth of new intelligence capabilities.

The Office of Current Intelligence

Completely contrary to its intended functions, ORE had developed into a current intelligence producer. The Dulles-Jackson-Correa Survey had sharply criticized CIA's duplication of current intelligence produced by other Departments, principally State. After his appointment as Deputy Director of Central Intelligence, Jackson intended that CIA would completely abandon its current political intelligence function. State's Office of Intelligence Research would have its choice of personnel not taken into ONE and ORR, and any former ORE staff members not chosen would leave.

In spite of Jackson's intention, all former ORE personnel stayed on. Those who did not join State, ONE, or ORR were first reassigned the task of publication of the *Daily*. Subsequently, they joined with the small COMINT (communications intelligence) unit which had been established in 1948 to handle raw COMINT data from the Army. The group was renamed the Office of Current Intelligence (OCI) on January 12, 1951. Drawing on COMINT and State Department information, OCI began producing the *Current Intelligence Bulletin* which replaced the *Daily*. As of January 1951 this was to be its only function—collating data for the daily CIA publication.

Internal demands soon developed for the Agency to engage in current political research. Immediately following the disbandment of CIA's current politicial intelligence functions, the Agency's clandestine components insisted on CIA-originated research support. They feared that the security of their operations would be jeopardized by having to rely on the State Department. As a result of their requests, OCI developed into an independent political research organization. Although OCI began by providing research support only to the Agency's clandestine components, it gradually extended its intelligence function to service the requests of other Departments. Thus, the personnel which Jackson never intended to rehire and the organization which was not to exist had survived and reacquired its previous function.

The Office of Scientific Intelligence

The Office of Scientific Intelligence (OSI) had been created in 1949, and like other CIA components, had confronted military resistance to the execution of its coordination role.[18] OSI's real conflict with the military lay with the division of responsibility for the production of scientific and technical intelligence. The chief issue was the distinction between intelligence relating to weapons and means of warfare already reduced to known prototypes and intelligence at the pilot-plant stage, anterior to prototypes. The military resisted OSI's intrusion into the first area and fundamentally, wished to restrict OSI to research in the basic sciences.

In August 1952 the military succeeded in making the distinction in an agreement which stipulated that the services would have primary responsibility for the production of intelligence on all weapons, weapons systems, military equipment and techniques in addition to intelligence on research and development leading to new military material and techniques. OSI assumed primary responsibility for research in the basic sciences, scientific resources and medicine. Initially, this order had a devastating effect on the morale of OSI analysts. They regarded the distinction which the military-had drawn as artificial, since it did not take into account the inextricable links between basic scientific research and military and weapons systems research. Ultimately, the agreement imposed few restraints on OSI. With technological advances in the ensuing years, OSI developed its own capability for intelligence on weapons systems technology and continued to challenge the military on the issue of basic science-technology research.

The OSI-military agreement included a provision for the creation of the Scientific Estimates Committee (SEC) which, like the EIC, was to serve as a coordinating body as well as a publication source for interagency scientific intelligence. Like the EIC, the SEC represented a feeble effort at coordination and a source for yet another publication.

In January 1952, CIA's intelligence functions were grouped under the Directorate for Intelligence (DDI). In addition to ONE, the DDI's intelligence production components included: the Office of Research and Reports (ORR), the Office of Scientific Intelligence (OSI), and the Office of Current Intelligence (OCI). Collection of overt information was the responsibility of the Office of Operations (OO). The Office of Collection and Dissemination (OCD) engaged in the distribution of intelligence as well as storage and retrieval of unevaluated intelligence.

The immediate pressures for information generated by the Korean War resulted in continued escalation in size and intelligence production. Government-wide demands for the Agency to provide information on Communist intentions in the Far East and around the world justified the increases. By the end of 1953 DDI personnel numbered 3,338. Despite the sweeping changes, the fundamental problem of duplication among the Agency and the Departments remained. Smith and Jackson had painstakingly redefined the Agency's intelligence functions, yet the Agency's position among the departmental intelligence services was still at the mercy of other intelligence producers.

---

[18] OSI's creation was prompted by the Dulles-Jackson-Correa Survey's evaluation of the poor state of scientific intelligence in the CIA.

C. Departmental Intelligence Activities

Apart from their role in the production of coordinated national estimates CIG and CIA were intended to exercise some direction over the intelligence activities of the State Department and the military— determining which collection and production functions would most appropriately and most efficiently be conducted by which Departments to avoid duplication.

The intention of CIA's responsibility in this area was essentially a management function. The extent to which Souers, Hillenkoetter, Vandenberg and Bedell Smith saw this as a primary role is difficult to determine. Each DCI was concerned with extracting the cooperation of the Departments in the production of national intelligence. That was a difficult enough task.

A major problem related to the coordination of departmental activities was the role of the Director of Central Intelligence, specifically his relationship to the military intelligence chiefs. The Director had no designated authority over either the departmental intelligence components or over the departmental intelligence chiefs.[18a] Thus, he could not exert any real pressure on behalf of the Agency and its objectives. Confronted with objections or a challenge from the Army G-2 chief, for example, the Director had no basis on which to press his arguments or preferences except in terms of the Agency's overall mission. This give him little or no leverage, for the intelligence chiefs could appeal to their Department heads, who served as the DCI's supervisors. The military chiefs of intelligence and the military staffs acted in a way which assumed that the DCI was one among equals— or less.

By the end of his term Vandenberg had become convinced that the only means by which CIG could accomplish its coordination mission was through control of the departmental intelligence agencies. Approaching the Intelligence Advisory Board, Vandenberg asked that they grant the DCI authority to act as "executive agent" for the departmental secretaries in matters related to intelligence. In effect, the DCI was to be given authority for supervision of the departmental intelligence components. The IAB approved Vandenberg's request and drafted an agreement providing for the DCI's increased authority. However, Hillenkoetter preferred not to press for its enactment and instead, hoped to rely on day-to-day cooperation. By failing to act on Vandenberg's initiative, Hillenkoetter undermined the position of the DCI in relation to the Departments.

Consideration of the 1947 National Security Act by the Congress was accompanied by active deliberation in the Executive about the newly constituted Central Intelligence Agency. The DCI's relationship to the departmental intelligence components, the Departments' authority over the Agency, and the Departments' roles in the production of national intelligence continued to be sources of contention. The fundamental issue remained one of control and jurisdiction: how much would the CIA gain and how much would the Departments be willing to concede?

[18a] Through the 1947 Act the DCI was granted the right to "inspect" the intelligence components of the Departments, but the bureaucratic value of that right was limited and DCIs have traditionally not invoked it.

As the bill took shape, the Departments resented the DCI's stated role as intelligence advisor to the NSC, thereby responsible to the President. The military intelligence chiefs, Inglis of the Navy and Chamberlin of the Army, favored continuation of the Intelligence Advisory Board. They advocated providing it with authority to grant approval or dissent for recommendations before they reached the NSC. If enacted, this arrangement would have given the Departments veto power over the Agency and, in effect, would have made the IAB the advisory body to the NSC.

Robert Lovett, Acting Secretary of State, made a similar recommendation. He proposed an advisory board to insure "prior consideration by the chiefs of the intelligence services" for matters scheduled to go before the NSC. The positions of both Lovett and the military reflected the reluctance of the Departments to give the CIA the primary intelligence advisory role for senior policymakers.

More specifically, the Departments themselves resisted conceding a direct relationship between the President and the DCI. Such an arrangement was perceived as limiting and threatening the Secretaries' own advisory relationships to the President.

Between 1946 and 1947, in an effort to curb the independence of the DCI, the military considered successive pieces of legislation restricting the Director's position to military careerists. Whether the attempted legislation was prompted by the concern over civilian access to military intelligence or by a desire to gain control of the Agency is unknown. In either case, the Departments were tenaciously protecting what they perceived to be their best interests.

In spite of continued resistance by the Departments the National Security Act affirmed the CIA's role in coordinating the intelligence activities of the State Department and the military. In 1947 the Intelligence Advisory Committee (IAC) was created to serve as a coordinating body in establishing intelligence requirements [19] among the Departments. Chaired by the DCI, the IAC included representatives from the Department of State, Army, Air Force, the Joint Chiefs of Staff, and the Atomic Energy Commission.[20] Although the DCI was to "establish priorities" for intelligence collection and analysis, he did not have the budgetary or administrative authority to control the departmental components. Moreover, no Department was willing to compromise what it perceived as its own intelligence needs to meet the collective needs of policymakers as defined by the DCI.

V. Clandestine Activities

A. Origins of Covert Action

The concept of a central intelligence agency developed out of a concern for the quality of intelligence analysis available to policymakers. The 1945 discussion which surrounded the creation of CIG focused on the problem of intelligence coordination. Two years later debates on the CIA in the Congress and the Executive assumed only the coordination role along with intelligence collection (both overt and clandestine) and analysis for the newly constituted Agency.

---

[19] Requirements constitute the informational objectives of intelligence collection, e.g., in 1947 determining Soviet troop strengths in Eastern Europe.

[20] Note: With the creation of the CIA and NIA and the IAB were dissolved.

Yet, within one year of the passage of the National Security Act, the CIA was charged with the conduct of covert psychological, political, paramilitary, and economic activities.[21] The acquisition of this mission had a profound impact on the direction of the Agency and on its relative stature within the government.

The precedent for covert activities existed in OSS. The clandestine collection capability had been preserved through the Strategic Services Unit, whose responsibilities CIG absorbed in June 1946. The maintenance of that capability and its presence in CIA contributed to the Agency's ultimate assumption of a covert operational role.

The United States, initiation of covert operations is usually associated with the 1948 Western European elections. It is true that this was the first officially recorded evidence of U.S. covert political intervention abroad. However, American policymakers had formulated plans for covert action—at first covert psychological action—much earlier. Decisions regarding U.S. sponsorship of clandestine activities were gradual but consistent, spurred on by the growing concern over Soviet intentions.

By late 1946, cabinet officials were preoccupied with the Soviet threat, and over the next year their fears intensified. For U.S. policymakers, international events seemed to be a sequence of Soviet incursions. In March 1946, the Soviet Union refused to withdraw its troops from the Iranian province of Azerbaijan; two months later civil war involving Communist rebel forces erupted in Greece. By 1947, Communists had assumed power in Poland, Hungary, and Rumania; and in the Phillipines the government was under attack by the Hukbalahaps, a communist-led guerrilla group.

For U.S. officials, the perception of the Soviet Union as a global threat demanded new modes of conduct in foreign policy to supplement the traditional alternatives of diplomacy and war. Massive economic aid represented one new method of achieving U.S. foreign policy objectives. In 1947, the United States embarked on an unprecedented economic assistance program to Europe with the Truman Doctrine and the Marshall Plan. By insuring economic stability, U.S. officials hoped to limit Soviet encroachments. Covert operations represented another, more activist departure in the conduct of U.S. peacetime foreign policy. Covert action was an option that was something more than diplomacy but still short of war. As such, it held the promise of frustrating Soviet ambitions without provoking open conflict.

The suggestion for the initiation of covert operations did not originate in CIG. Sometime in late 1946, Secretary of War Robert Patterson suggested to Forrestal that military and civilian personnel study this form of war for future use. What prompted Patterson's suggestion is unclear. However, from Patterson's suggestion policymakers proceeded to consider the lines of authority for the conduct of psychological operations. Discussion took place in the State-War-Navy Coordinating Committee (SWNCC), whose members included the Secretaries of the

---

[21] Psychological operations were primarily media-related activities, including unattributed publications, forgeries, and subsidization of publications; political action involved exploitation of dispossessed persons and defectors, and support to political parties; paramilitary activities included support to guerrillas and sabotage; economic activities consisted of monetary operations.

three Departments, Byrnes, Patterson and Forrestal.[22] In December 1946, a SWNCC subcommittee formulated guidelines for the conduct of psychological warfare in peacetime and wartime.[23] The full SWNCC adopted the recommendation later that month.

Discussion continued within the Executive in the spring and summer of 1947. From all indications, only senior-level officials were involved, and the discussions were closely held. From establishing guidelines for the possibility of psychological warfare, policymakers proceeded to contingency planning. On April 30, 1947, a SWNCC subcommittee was organized to consider and actually plan for a U.S. psychological warfare effort. On June 5, 1947, the subcommittee was accorded a degree of permanency and renamed the Special Studies and Evaluations Subcommittee. By this time, the fact that the U.S. would engage in covert operations was a given; what remained were decisions about the organizational arrangements and actual implementation. Senior officials had moved from the point of conceptualization to determination of a specific need. Yet it is not clear whether or not they had in mind specific activities geared to specific countries or events.

In the fall of 1947 policymakers engaged in a series of discussions on the assignment of responsibility for the conduct of covert operations. There was no ready consensus and a variety of opinions emerged. DCI Hillenkoetter had his own views on the subject. Sometime in October 1947 he recommended "vitally needed psychological operations"—again in general terms without reference to specific countries or groups—but believed that such activities were military rather than intelligence functions and therefore belonged in an organization responsible to the JCS. Hillenkoetter also believed congressional authorization would be necessary both for the initiation of psychological warfare and for the expenditure of funds for that purpose. Whatever Hillenkoetter's views on the appropriate authorization for a psychological warfare function, his opinions were undoubtedly influenced by the difficulties he had experienced in dealing with the Departments. It is likely that he feared CIA's acquisition of an operational capability would precipitate similar problems of departmental claims on the Agency's operational functions. Hillenkoetter's stated preferences had no apparent impact on the outcome of the psychological warfare debate.

Within a few weeks of Hillenkoetter's statement, Forrestal, the Secretaries of the Army, Navy, and Air Force, along with the JCS, advanced their recommendations regarding the appropriate organization to conduct covert psychological warfare. In a proposal dated November 4, they held that propaganda of all kinds was a function of the State Department and that an Assistant Secretary of State in consultation with the DCI and a military representative should be responsible for the operations.

---

[22] SWNCC was established late in 1944 as an initial attempt at more centralized decisionmaking.

[23] In peacetime, psychological warfare would be directed by an interdepartmental subcommittee of SWNCC with the approval of the JCS and the National Intelligence Authority. During war, a Director of Psychological Warfare would assume primary responsibility under a central committee responsible to the President. The committee would consist of representatives from the SWNCC and from CIG.

On November 24, President Truman approved the November 4 recommendation, assigning psychological warfare coordination to the Secretary of State. Within three weeks, the decision was reversed. Despite the weight of numbers favoring State Department control, the objections of Secretary of State George Marshall eliminated the option advanced by the other Secretaries. Marshall opposed State Department responsibility for covert action. He was vehement on the point and believed that such activities, if exposed as State Department actions, would embarrass the Department and discredit American foreign policy both short-term and long-term.

Apart from his position as Secretary of State, the impact of Marshall's argument derived from the more general influence he exerted at the time. Marshall had emerged from the war as one of America's "silent heroes." To the public, he was a quiet, taciturn, almost unimpressive figure, but as the Army Chief of Staff during the war, he had gained the universal respect of his civilian and military colleagues for his commitment, personal integrity, and ability.

In the transition from military officer to diplomat, he had developed a strong sense that the United States would have to adopt an activist role against the Soviet Union. Immediately after his appointment as Secretary in February 1947, he played a key role in the decision to aid Greece and Turkey and quickly after, in June 1947, announced the sweeping European economic recovery program which bore his name. It was out of concern for the success and credibility of the United States' recently articulated economic program that Marshall objected to State Department conduct of covert action. Marshall favored placing covert activities outside the Department, but still subject to guidance from the Secretary of State.

Marshall's objections prevailed, and on December 14 the National Security Council adopted NSC 4/A, a directive which gave the CIA responsibility for covert psychological operations. The DCI was charged with ensuring that psychological operations were consistent with U.S. foreign policy and overt foreign information activities. On December 22 the Special Procedures Group was established within the CIA's Office of Special Operations to carry out psychological operations.

Although Marshall's position prevented State from conducting psychological warfare, it does not explain why the CIA was charged with the responsibility. The debate which ensued in 1947 after the agreement on the need for psychological warfare had focused on control and responsibility. At issue were the questions of who would plan, direct, and oversee the actual operations.

State and the military wanted to maintain control over covert psychological operations, but they did not want to assume operational responsibility. The sensitive nature of the operations made the Departments fear exposure of their association with the activities. The CIA offered advantages as the organization to execute covert operations. Indeed, in 1947 one-third of the CIA's personnel had served with OSS. The presence of former OSS personnel, who had experience in wartime operations, provided the Agency with a group of individuals who could quickly develop and implement programs. This, coupled with its overseas logistical apparatus, gave the Agency a ready capability. In addition, the Agency also possessed a system of unvouchered funds for its clandestine collection mission, which meant that there was no need to approach Congress for separate appropriations. With the Departments unwilling to assume the risks involved in covert activities, the CIA provided a convenient mechanism.

During the next six months psychological operations were initiated in Central and Eastern Europe. The activities were both limited and amateur and consisted of unattributed publications, radio broadcasts, and blackmail. By 1948 the Special Procedures Group had acquired a radio transmitter for broadcasting behind the Iron Curtain, had established a secret propaganda printing plant in Germany, and had begun assembling a fleet of balloons to drop propaganda materials into Eastern European countries.

Both internally and externally the pressure continued for an expansion in the scope of U.S. covert activity. The initial definition of covert action had been limited to covert psychological warfare. In May 1948, George F. Kennan, Director of the State Department's Policy Planning Staff, advocated the development of a covert political action capability. The distinction at that time was an important and real one. Political action meant direct intervention in the electoral processes of foreign governments rather than attempts to influence public opinion through media activities.

International events gave force to Kennan's proposal. In February 1948, Communists staged a successful coup in Czechoslovakia. At the same time, France and Italy were beleaguered by a wave of Communist-inspired strikes. In March 1948, near hysteria gripped the U.S. Government with the so-called "war scare." The crisis was precipitated by a cable from General Lucius Clay, Commander in Chief, European Command, to Lt. General Stephen J. Chamberlin, Director of Intelligence, Army General Staff, in which Clay said, "I have felt a subtle change in Soviet attitude which I cannot define but which now gives me a feeling that it [war] may come with dramatic suddenness."

The war scare launched a series of interdepartmental intelligence estimates on the likelihood of a Soviet attack on Western Europe and the United States. Although the estimates concluded that there was no evidence that the U.S.S.R. would start a war, Clay's cable had articulated the degree of suspicion and outright fear of the Soviet Union that was shared by policymakers at this time. Kennan proposed that State, specifically the Policy Planning Staff, have a "directorate" for overt and covert political warfare. The director of the Special Studies Group, as Kennan named it, would be under State Department control, but not formally associated with the Department. Instead, he would have concealed funds and personnel elsewhere, and his small staff of eight people would be comprised of representatives from State and Defense.

Kennan's concept and statement of function were endorsed by the NSC. In June 1948, one month after his proposal, the NSC adopted NSC 10/2, a directive authorizing a dramatic increase in the range of covert operations directed against the Soviet Union, including political warfare, economic warfare, and paramilitary activities.

While authorizing a sweeping expansion in covert activities, NSC 10/2 established the Office of Special Projects, soon renamed the Office of Policy Coordination (OPC), within the CIA to replace the Special Procedures Group. As a CIA component OPC was an anomaly. OPC's budget and personnel were appropriated within CIA allocations, but the DCI had little authority in determining OPC's activities. Responsibility for the direction of OPC rested with the Office's director, designated by the Secretary of State. Policy guidance—decisions on the need for specific activities—came to the OPC director from State and Defense, bypassing the DCI.

The organizational arrangements established in 1948 for the conduct of covert operations reflected both the concept of covert action as defined by U.S. officials and the perception of the CIA as an institution. Both the activities and the institution were regarded as extensions of State and the military services. The Departments (essentially the NSC) defined U.S. policy objectives; covert action represented one means of attaining those objectives; and the CIA executed the operations.

In a conversation on August 12, 1948, Hillenkoetter, Kennan, and Sidney Souers discussed the implementation of NSC 10/A. The summary of the conversation reveals policymakers firm expectation that covert political action would serve strictly as a support function for U.S. foreign and military policy and that State and the services would define the scope of covert activities in specific terms. The summaries of the participants' statements as cited in a CIA history bear quoting at length:

> Mr. Kennan made the point that as the State Department's designated representative he would want to have specific knowledge of the objectives of every operation and also of the procedures and methods employed in all cases where those procedures and methods involved political decisions.
>
> Mr. Souers indicated his agreement with Mr. Kennan's thesis and stated specifically that it has been the intention of the National Security Council in preparing the document that it should reflect the recognition of the principle that the Departments of State and the National Military Establishment are responsible for the conduct of the activities of the Office of Special Projects, with the Department of State taking preeminence in time of peace and the National Military Establishment succeeding the pre-eminent position in wartime.
>
> Admiral Hillenkoetter agreed with Mr. Kennan's statement that the political warfare activity should be conducted as an instrument of U.S. foreign policy and subject in peacetime to direct guidance by the State Department.
>
> Mr. Kennan agreed that it was necessary that the State Department assume responsibility for stating whether or not individual projects are politically desirable and stated that as the State Department's designated representative he would be accountable for providing such decisions.

Likewise, reflecting on his intentions and those of his colleagues in 1948, Kennan recently stated:

. . . we were alarmed at the inroads of the Russian influence in Western Europe beyond the point where the Russian troops had reached. And we were alarmed particularly over the situation in France and Italy. We felt that the Communists were using the very extensive funds that they then had in hand to gain control of key elements of life in France and Italy, particularly the publishing companies, the press, the labor unions, student organizations, women's organizations, and all sort of organizations of that sort, to gain control of them and use them as front organizations. . . .

That was just one example that I recall of why we thought that we ought to have some facility for covert operations. . . .

. . . It ended up with the establishment within CIA of a branch, an office for activities of this nature, and one which employed a great many people. It did not work out at all the way I had conceived it or others of my associates in the Department of State. We had thought that this would be a facility which could be used when and if an occasion arose when it might be needed. There might be years when we wouldn't have to do anything like this. But if the occasion arose we wanted somebody in the Government who would have the funds, the experience, the expertise to do these things and to do them in a proper way.[24]

Clearly, in recommending the development of a covert action capability in 1948, policymakers intended to make available a small contingency force that could mount operations on a limited basis. Senior officials did not plan to develop large-scale continuing covert operations. Instead, they hoped to establish a small capability that could be activated at their discretion.

B. The Office of Policy Coordination, 1948–1952

OPC developed into a far different organization from that envisioned by Forrestal, Marshall, and Kennan in August 1948. By 1952, when it merged with the Agency's clandestine collection component, the Office of Special Operations, OPC had expanded its activities to include worldwide covert operations, and it had achieved an institutional independence that was unimaginable at the time of its inception.

The outbreak of the Korean War in the summer of 1950 had a significant effect on OPC. Following the North Korean invasion of South Korea, the State Department as well as the Joint Chiefs of Staff recommended the initiation of paramilitary activities in Korea and China. OPC's participation in the war effort contributed to its transformation from an organization that was to provide the capability for a limited number of *ad hoc* operations to an organization that conducted continuing, ongoing activities on a massive scale. In concept, manpower, budget, and scope of activities, OPC simply skyrocketed. The comparative figures for 1949 and 1952 are staggering. In 1949 OPC's total personnel strength was 302; in 1952 it was 2,812 plus 3,142 overseas contract personnel. In 1949 OPC's budget figure was $4,700,-000; in 1952 it was $82,000,000. In 1949 OPC had personnel assigned

---

[24] George F. Kennan testimony, October 28, 1975, pp. 8–10.

to seven overseas stations; in 1952 OPC had personnel at forty-seven stations.

Apart from the impetus provided by the Korean War several other factors converged to alter the nature and scale of OPC's activities. First, policy direction took the form of condoning and fostering activity without providing scrutiny and control. Officials throughout the government regarded the Soviet Union as an aggressive force, and OPC's activities were initiated and justified on the basis of this shared perception. The series of NSC directives which authorized covert operations laid out broad objectives and stated in bold terms the necessity for meeting the Soviet challenge head on. After the first 1948 directive authorizing covert action, subsequent directives in 1950 and 1951 called for an intensification of these activities without establishing firm guidelines for approval.

On April 14, 1950, the National Security Council issued NSC 68, which called for a non-military counter-offensive against the U.S.S.R., including covert economic, political, and psychological warfare to stir up unrest and revolt in the satellite countries. A memo written in November 1951 commented on the fact that such broad and comprehensive undertakings as delineated by the NSC could only be accomplished by the establishment of a worldwide structure for covert operations on a much grander scale than OPC had previously contemplated. The memo stated:

> It would be a task similar in concept, magnitude and complexity to the creation of widely deployed military forces together with the logistical support required to conduct manifold, complex and delicate operations in a wide variety of overseas locations.

On October 21, 1951 NSC 10/5 replaced NSC 10/2 as the governing directive for covert action. It once again called for an intensification of covert action and reaffirmed the responsibility of the DCI in the conduct of covert operations. Each of these policy directives provided the broadest justification for large-scale covert activity.

Second, OPC operations had to meet the very different policy needs of the State and Defense Departments. The State Department encouraged political action and propaganda activities to support its diplomatic objectives, while the Defense Department requested paramilitary activities to support the Korean War effort and to counter communist-associated guerrillas. These distinct missions required OPC to develop and maintain different capabilities, including manpower and support material.

The third factor contributing to OPC's expansion was the organizational arrangements that created an internal demand for projects. The decision to undertake covert political action and to lodge that responsibility in a group distinct from the Departments required the creation of a permanent structure. OPC required regular funding to train and pay personnel, to maintain overseas stations (and provide for the supporting apparatus), and to carry out specific projects. That funding could not be provided on an *ad hoc* basis. It had to be budgeted for in advance. With budgeting came the need for ongoing activities to justify future allocations—rather than leaving the flexibility of responding to specific requirements.

To fulfill the different State and Defense requirements OPC adopted a "project" system rather than a programmed financial system. This meant that operations were organized around projects—individual activities, e.g. funding to a political candidate—rather than general programs or policy objectives, and that OPC budgeted in terms of anticipated numbers of projects. The project system had important internal effects. An individual within OPC judged his own performance, and was judged by others, on the importance and number of projects he initiated and managed. The result was competition among individuals and among the OPC divisions to generate the maximum number of projects. Projects remained the fundamental units around which clandestine activities were organized, and two generations of Agency personnel have been conditioned by this system.

The interaction among the OPC components reflected the internal competition that the project system generated. OPC was divided between field personnel stationed overseas and Headquarters personnel stationed in Washington. Split into four functional staffs (dealing with political warfare, psychological warfare, paramilitary operations and economic warfare) and six geographical divisions, Headquarters was to retain close control over the initiation and implementation of projects to insure close policy coordination with State and Defense. Field stations were to serve only as standing mechanisms for the performance of tasks assigned from Washington.

The specific relationship between the functional staffs, the geographical divisions and the overseas stations was intended to be as follows: With guidance from the NSC, the staffs would generate project outlines for the divisions. In turn, the divisions would provide their respective overseas stations with detailed instructions on project action. Very soon, however, each of the three components was attempting to control project activities. Within the functional staffs proprietary attitudes developed toward particular projects at the point when the regional divisions were to take them over. The staffs were reluctant to adopt an administrative support role with respect to the divisions in the way that was intended. Thus, the staffs and the divisions began to look upon each other as competitors rather than joint participants. In November 1949 an internal study of OPC concluded that:

> . . . the present organization makes for duplication of effort
> and an extensive amount of unnecessary coordination and
> competition rather than cooperation and teamwork. . . .

A reorganization in 1950 attempted to rectify the problem by assigning responsibility for planning single-country operations to the appropriate geographical division. This meant that the divisions assumed real operational control. The staffs were responsible for coordinating multiple country operations as well as providing the guidance function. In principle the staffs were to be relegated to the support role they were intended to serve. However, the break was never complete. The distinctions themselves were artificial, and staffs seized on their authority over multiple country activities to maintain an operational role in such areas as labor operations. This tension between the staffs and the divisions continued through the late 1960's as some staffs achieved maximum operational independence. The situation is a commentary on the project orientation which originated with OPC and the recognition that promotion and rewards were derived from project management—not from disembodied guidance activities.

The relationship between Washington and the field was subject to pressures similar to those that influenced the interaction between the divisions and the staffs. Predictably, field personnel began to develop their own perspective on suitable operations and their mode of conduct. Being "there", field personnel could and did argue that theirs was the most realistic and accurate view. Gradually, as the number of overseas personnel grew and as the number of stations increased, the stations assumed the initiative in project development.

The regional divisions at Headquarters tended to assume an administrative support role but still retained approval authority for projects of particular sensitivity and cost. The shift in initiative first from the staffs to the divisions, then to the stations, affected the relative desirability of assignments. Since fulfillment of the OPC mission was measured in terms of project development and management, the sought-after places were those where the projects originated. Individuals who were assigned those places rose quickly within the Directorate.

C. Policy Guidance

Responsibility for coordination with the State and Defense Departments rested with Frank G. Wisner, appointed Assistant Director for Policy Coordination (ADPC) on September 1, 1948. Described almost unanimously by those who worked with him as "brilliant," Wisner possessed the operational instincts, the activist temperament, and the sheer physical energy required to develop and establish OPC as an organization. Wisner also had the advantages of independent wealth and professional and social contacts which he employed skillfully in advancing OPC's position within the Washington bureaucracy.

Wisner was born into a prominent Southern family and distinguished himself as an undergraduate and a law student at the University of Virginia. Following law school, Wisner joined a New York law firm where he stayed for seven years. After a brief stint in the Navy, Wisner was assigned to OSS and spent part of his time serving under Allen Dulles in Wiesbaden, Germany. At the end of the war he returned to law practice, but left again in 1947 to accept the post of Deputy to the Assistant Secretary of State for Occupied Areas. It was from this position that Wisner was tapped to be ADPC.

Although the stipulation of NSC 10/2 that the Secretary of State designate the ADPC was intended to insure the ADPC's primary identification with State, that did not occur. Wisner quickly developed an institutional loyalty to OPC and its mission and drew on the web of New York law firm connections that existed in postwar Washington as well as on his State Department ties to gain support for OPC's activities.

The guidance that State and Defense provided OPC became very general and allowed the maximum opportunity for project development. Approximately once a week Wisner met with the designated representatives of State and Defense. Given that Kennan had been a prime mover in the establishment of OPC, it was unlikely that as the State Department's designated representative from 1948 to 1950 he would discourage the overall direction of the organization he had helped create. From 1948 to 1949 Defense was represented by General

Joseph T. McNarney, the former Commander of U.S. Forces in Europe. Having stood "eyeball to eyeball" with the Russians in Germany, McNarney was highly sympathetic to the OPC mission.

With the broad objectives laid out in NSC 10/2, the means of implementation were left to OPC. The representatives were not an approval body, and there was no formal mechanism whereby individual projects had to be brought before them for discussion. Because it was assumed that covert action would be exceptional, strict provisions for specific project authorization were not considered necessary. With minimal supervision from State and Defense and with a shared agreement on the nature of the OPC mission, individuals in OPC could take the initiative in conceiving and implementing projects. In this context, operational tasks, personnel, money and material tended to grow in relation to one another with little outside oversight.

In 1951, DCI Walter Bedell Smith took the initiative in requesting more specific high-level policy direction. In May of that year, after a review of NSC 68, Smith sought a clarification of the OPC mission from the NSC.[26] In a paper dated May 8, 1951, entitled the "Scope and Pace of Covert Operations" Smith called for NSC restatement or redetermination of the several responsibilities and authorities involved in U.S. covert operations. More importantly, Smith proposed that the newly created Psychological Strategy Board provide CIA guidance on the conduct of covert operations.[27]

The NSC adopted Smith's proposal making the Psychological Strategy Board the approval body for covert action. The body that had been responsible for exercising guidance over the CIA had received it from the DCI. Whatever the dimensions of the growth in OPC operations, the NSC had not attempted to limit the expansion.

D. OPC Activities

At the outset OPC activities were directed toward four principal operational areas: refugee programs, labor activities, media development, and political action. Geographically, the area of concentration was Western Europe. There were two reasons for this. First, Western Europe was the area deemed most vulnerable to Communist encroachment; and second, until 1950 both CIA (OSO) and OPC were excluded from the Far East by General Douglas MacArthur, who refused to concede any jurisdiction to the civilian intelligence agency in the Pacific theater—just as he had done with OSS during the war.

OPC inherited programs from both the Special Procedures Group (SPG) and the Economic Cooperation Administration (ECA). After the issuance of NSC 10/2 SPG turned over to OPC all of its resources, including an unexpended budget of over $2 million, a small staff, and its communications equipment. In addition to SPG's propaganda activities OPC acquired the ECA's fledgling labor projects as well as the accompanying funds. Foreign labor operations continued and be-

---

[26] Soon after his appointment as DCI in October 1950, Smith succeeded in having OPC placed directly under the jurisdiction of the DCI, making Wisner responsible to him rather than to the Department of State and Defense. See pp. 37–38.

[27] The Psychological Strategy Board (PSB) was an NSC subcommittee established on April 4, 1951 to exercise direction over psychological warfare programs. Its membership included departmental representatives and PSB staff members.

came a major focus of CIA activity on a worldwide basis throughout the 1950's and into the mid-1960's.

The national elections in Europe in 1948 had been a primary motivation in the establishment of OPC. By channeling funds to center parties and developing media assets, OPC attempted to influence election results—with considerable success. These activities formed the basis for covert political action for the next twenty years. By 1952 approximately forty different covert action projects were underway in one central European country alone. Other projects were targeted against what was then referred to as the "Soviet bloc."

During his term in the State Department Wisner had spent much of his time on problems involving refugees in Germany, Austria and Trieste. In addition, his service with OSS had been oriented toward Central Europe. The combination of State's continuing interest and Wisner's personal experience led to OPC's immediate emphasis on Central European refugee operations. OPC representatives made contact with thousands of Soviet refugees and emigrés for the purpose of influencing their political leadership. The National Committee for Free Europe, a group of prominent American businessmen, lawyers, and philanthropists, and Radio Free Europe were products of the OPC program.

Until 1950 OPC's paramilitary activities (also referred to as preventive direct action) were limited to plans and preparations for stay-behind nets in the event of future war. Requested by the Joint Chiefs of Staff, these projected OPC operations focused, once again, on Western Europe and were designed to support NATO forces against Soviet attack.

The outbreak of the Korean War significantly altered the nature of OPC's paramilitary activities as well as the organization's overall size and capability. Between fiscal year 1950 and fiscal year 1951, OPC's personnel strength jumped from 584 to 1531. Most of that growth took place in paramilitary activities in the Far East. In the summer of 1950, following the North Korean invasion of South Korea, the State Department requested the initiation of paramilitary and psychological operations on the Chinese mainland. Whatever MacArthur's preferences, the JCS were also eager for support activities in the Far East. This marked the beginning of OPC's active paramilitary engagement. The Korean War established OPC's and CIA's jurisdiction in the Far East and created the basic paramilitary capability that the Agency employed for twenty years. By 1953, the elements of that capability were "in place"—aircraft, amphibious craft, and an experienced group of personnel. For the next quarter century paramilitary activities remained the major CIA covert activity in the Far East.

E. OPC Integration and the OPC–OSO Merger

The creation of OPC and its ambiguous relationship to the Agency precipitated two major administrative problems, the DCI's relationship to OPC and antagonism between OPC and the Agency's clandestine collection component, the Office of Special Operations. DCI Walter Bedell Smith acted to rectify both problems.

As OPC continued to grow, Smith's predecessor, Admiral Hillenkoetter, resented the fact that he had no management authority over OPC, although its budget and personnel were being allocated through the CIA. Hillenkoetter's clashes with the State and Defense Departments as well as with Wisner, the Director of OPC, were frequent. Less than a week after taking office Smith announced that as DCI he would assume administrative control of OPC and that State and Defense would channel their policy guidance through him rather than through Wisner. On October 12, 1950, the representatives of State, Defense and the Joint Chiefs of Staff formally accepted the change. The ease with which the shift occurred was primarily a result of Smith's own position of influence with the Departments.

OPC's anomalous position in the Agency revealed the difficulty of maintaining two separate organizations for the execution of varying but overlapping clandestine activities. The close "tradecraft" relationship between clandestine collection and covert action, and the frequent necessity for one to support the other was totally distorted with the separation of functions in OSO and OPC. Organizational rivalry rather than interchange dominated the relationship between the two components.

On the operating level the conflicts were intense. Each component had representatives conducting separate operations at each station. Given the related missions of the two, OPC and OSO personnel were often competing for the same agents and, not infrequently, attempting to wrest agents from each other. In 1952 the outright hostility between the two organizations in Bangkok required the direct intervention of the Assistant Director for Special Operations, Lyman Kirkpatrick. There an important official was closely tied to OPC, and OSO was trying to lure him into its employ.

The OPC–OSO conflict was only partially the result of overseas competition for assets. Salary differentials and the differences in mission were other sources of antagonism. At the time of its creation in 1948 OPC was granted liberal funding to attract personnel quickly in order to get its operation underway. In addition, the burgeoning activities enabled people, once hired, to rise rapidly. The result was that OPC personnel held higher-ranking, better-paid positions than their OSO counterparts.

Many OSO personnel had served with OSS, and their resentment of OPC was intensified by the fact that they regarded themselves as the intelligence "purists," the professionals who engaged in collection rather than action and whose prewar experience made them more knowledgeable and expert than the OPC recruits. In particular, OSO personnel regarded OPC's high-risk operations as a threat to the maintenance of OSO security and cover. OPC's favored position with State and Defense, its generous budget, and its visible accomplishments all contrasted sharply with OSO's silent, long-term objectives in espionage and counterespionage. By June 1952 OPC had overtaken OSO in personnel and budget allocation. Soon after his appointment as DCI, Smith addressed the problem of the OPC–OSO conflict. Lawrence Houston, the CIA's General Counsel, had raised the issue with him and recommended a merger of the two organizations.[28] Sentiment in OSO and OPC

---

[28] The Dulles-Jackson-Correa survey had also advised a merger of OPC, OSO and the Office of Operations, the Agency's overt collection component.

favored the principle of a merger. Lyman Kirkpatrick, the Executive Assistant to the DCI, Major General W. G. Wyman, Assistant Director for Special Operations, Wisner, and William Jackson all appeared to have favored a merger—although there was disagreement on the form it should take.

Between 1951 and 1952 Smith made several cosmetic changes to foster better coordination between OPC and OSO. Among them was the appointment of Allen W. Dulles as Deputy Director for Plans in January 1951.[29] Dulles was responsible for supervising both OPC and OSO, although the two components were independently administered by their own Directors. During this period of "benign coordination" Smith consulted extensively with senior officials in OPC and OSO. OPC's rapid growth and its institutional dynamism colored the attitude of OSO toward a potential merger. In the discussions which Bedell Smith held, senior OSO personnel, specifically Lyman Kirkpatrick and Richard Helms, argued for an integration of OPC functions under OSO control rather than an integrated chain of command down to station level. Fundamentally, the OSO leadership feared being engulfed by OPC in both operations and in personnel. However, by this time Bedell Smith was committed to the idea of an integrated structure.

Although some effort was made to combine the OSO and OPC Western Hemisphere Divisions in June 1951, real integration at the operations level did not occur until August 1952, when OSO and OPC became the Directorate of Plans (DDP). Under this arrangement, Wisner was named Deputy Director for Plans and assumed the command functions of the ADSO and ADPC. Wisner's second in command, Chief of Operations, was Richard Helms, drawn from the OSO side to strike a balance at the senior level. At this time Dulles replaced Jackson as DDCI.

The merger resulted in the maximum development of covert action over clandestine collection. There were several reasons for this. First was the orientation of Wisner himself. Wisner's OSS background and his OPC experience had established his interests in the operational side of clandestine activities. Second, for people in the field, rewards came more quickly through visible operational accomplishments than through the silent, long-term development of agents required for clandestine collection. In the words of one former high-ranking DDP official, "Collection is the hardest thing of all; it's much easier to plant an article in a local newspaper."

F. Congressional Review

The CIA was conceived and organized as an agent of the Executive branch. Traditionally, Congress' only formal relationship to the Agency was through the appropriations process. The concept of Congressional oversight in the sense of scrutinizing and being fully informed of Agency activities did not exist. The international atmosphere, Congress relationship to the Executive branch and the Congressional committee structure determined the pattern of interaction between the Agency and members of the legislature. Acceptance of the

---

[29] Dulles had been serving as an advisor to successive DCIs since 1947. Smith and Jackson prevailed upon him to join the Agency on a full-time basis.

need for clandestine activities and of the need for secrecy to protect those activities contributed to Congress' relatively unquestioning and uncritical attitude regarding the CIA, as did the Executive branch's ascendancy in foreign policy for nearly two decades following World War II. The strong committee system which accorded enormous power to committee chairmen and limited the participation of less senior members in committee business resulted in informal arrangements whereby selected members were kept informed of Agency activities primarily through one-to-one exchanges with the DCI.

In 1946, following a Joint Committee review Congress enacted the Legislative Reorganization Act which reduced the number of committees and realigned their jurisdictions.[30] The prospect of a unified military establishment figured into the 1946 debates and decisions on Congressional reorganization. However, Congress did not anticipate having to deal with the CIA. This meant that after the passage of the National Security Act in 1947 CIA affairs had to be handled within a committee structure which had not accommodated itself to the existence of a central intelligence agency.

In the House and Senate the Armed Services and Appropriations Committees were granted jurisdiction over the Agency. No formal CIA subcommittees were organized until 1956. Until then small *ad hoc* groups composed of a few senior committee members reviewed the budget, appropriated funds, and received annual briefings on CIA activities. The DCIs kept senior committee members informed of large-scale covert action projects at the approximate time of implementation. There was no formal review or approval process involved; it was simply a matter of courtesy to the senior members. The initiative in gaining information on specific activities rested with the members.

For nearly twenty years a small group of ranking members dominated these relationships with the Agency. As Chairman of the House Armed Services Committee, Representative Carl Vinson, a Democrat from Georgia, presided over CIA matters from 1949 to 1953 and from 1955 to 1965. Clarence Cannon served as chairman of the House Appropriations Committee from 1949 to 1953 and from 1955 to 1964 and chaired the Defense Subcommittee which had supervising authority over CIA appropriations. Cannon organized a special group of five members to meet informally on CIA appropriations. In the Senate between 1947 and 1954 chairmanship of the Armed Services Committee was held by Chan Gurney, Millard Tydings, Richard Russell and Leverett Saltonstall. In 1955 Russell assumed the chairmanship and held the position until 1968.

Because the committee chairmen maintained their positions for extended periods of time, they established continuing relationships with DCIs and preserved an exclusivity in their knowledge of Agency activities. They were also able to develop relationships of mutual trust and understanding with the DCIs which allowed informal exchanges to prevail over formal votes and close supervision.

Within the Congress procedures governing the Agency's budget assured maximum secrecy. The DCI presented his estimate of the

---

[30] The Act limited members' committee assignments, provided for professional staffing, tried to regularize meetings, and made some changes in the appropriations process as well as legislating other administrative modifications.

budget for the coming fiscal year broken down into general functional categories. Certification by the subcommittee chairmen constituted approval. Exempt from floor debate and from public disclosure, CIA appropriations were and are concealed in the Department of Defense budget. In accordance with the 1949 Act the DCI has only to certify that the money as appropriated has been spent. He does not have to account publicly for specific expenditures, which would force him to reveal specific activities.

To allow greater flexibility for operational expenditures the Contingency Reserve Fund was created in 1952. The Fund provided a sum independent of the regular budget to be used for unanticipated large projects. For example, the initial funding for the development of the U-2 reconnaissance aircraft was drawn from the Contingency Reserve Fund. The most common use of the Fund was for covert operations.

Budgetary matters rather than the specific nature of CIA activities were the concern of Congressional members, and given the perception of the need for action against the Soviet Union, approval was routine. A former CIA Legislative Counsel characterized Congressional attitudes in the early 1950s in this way:

> In the view of the general public, and of the Congress which in the main reflected the public attitude, a national intelligence service in those days was more or less a part and parcel of our overall defense establishment. Therefore, as our defense budget went sailing through Congress under the impact of the Soviet extension of power into Eastern Europe, Soviet probes into Iran and Greece, the Berlin blockade, and eventually the Korean War, the relatively modest CIA budget in effect got a free ride, buried as it was in the Defense and other budgets. When Directors appeared before Congress, which they did only rarely, the main concern of the members was often to make sure that we [the CIA] had what we needed to do our job.

Limited information-sharing rather than rigorous oversight characterized Congress relationship to the Agency. Acceptance of the need for secrecy and Congressional procedures would perpetuate what amounted to mutual accommodation.

By 1953 the Agency had achieved the basic structure and scale it retained for the next twenty years.[30a] The Korean War, United States foreign policy objectives, and the Agency's internal organizational arrangements had combined to produce an enormous impetus for growth. The CIA was six times the size it had been in 1947.

Three Directorates had been established. In addition to the DDP and the DDI, Smith created the Deputy Directorate for Administration (DDA). Its purpose was to consolidate the management functions required for the burgeoning organization. The Directorate was responsible for budget, personnel, security, and medical services Agency-wide. However, one quarter of DDA's total personnel strength was assigned to logistical support for overseas operations. The DDP commanded the major share of the Agency's

[30a] For chart showing CIA organization as of 1953, see p. 98.

budget, personnel, and resources; in 1952 clandestine collection and covert action accounted for 74 percent of the Agency's total budget; [31] its personnel constituted 60 percent of the CIA's personnel strength. While production rather than coordination dominated the DDI, operational activities rather than collection dominated the DDP. The DDI and the DDP emerged at different times out of disparate policy needs. There were, in effect, separate organizations. These fundamental distinctions and emphases were reinforced in the next decade.

---

[31] This did not include DDA budgetary allocations in support of DDP operations.

PART TWO

THE DULLES ERA, 1953–1961

INTRODUCTION

During the years 1953 to 1961 the Agency emerged as an integral element in high-level United States policymaking. The CIA's covert operational capability provided the Agency with the stature it acquired. Rather than functioning in a strict support role to the State and Defense Departments, the CIA assumed the initiative in defining the ways covert operations could advance U.S. policy objectives and in determining what kinds of operations were suited to particular policy needs. The force of Allen Dulles' leadership and his recognition throughout the government as the quintessential case officer accounted in large part for the enhancement of and shift in the Agency's position. The reason for Dulles' influence extended well beyond his personal qualities and inclinations. The composition of the United States Government, international events, and senior policymakers' perception of the role the Agency could play in United States foreign policy converged to make Dulles' position in the government and that of the Agency unique in the years 1953 to 1962.

The 1952 election brought Dwight D. Eisenhower to the presidency. Eisenhower had been elected on a strident anti-Communist platform, advocating an aggressive worldwide stance against the Soviet Union to replace what he described as the Truman Administration's passive policy of containment. Eisenhower cited the Communist victory in China, the Soviet occupation of Eastern Europe, and the Korean War as evidence of the passivity which had prevailed in the United States Government following World War II. He was equally strong in calling for an elimination of government corruption and for removal of Communist sympathizers from public office.

This was not simply election rhetoric. The extent to which the urgency of the Communist threat had become a shared perception is difficult to appreciate. By the close of the Korean War, a broad consensus had developed about the nature of Soviet ambitions and the need for the United States to respond. In the minds of government officials, members of the press, and the informed public, the Soviets would try to achieve their purposes by penetrating and subverting governments all over the world. The accepted role of the United States was to prevent that expansion.

Washington policymakers regarded the Central Intelligence Agency as a major weapon—both offensive and defensive—against communism. By 1953, the Agency's contributions in the areas of political action and paramilitary warfare were recognized and respected. The CIA alone could perform many of the activities seemingly required to meet the Soviet threat. For senior government officials, covert operations had become a vital tool in the pursuit of United States foreign policy objectives.

During the 1950's the CIA attracted some of the most able lawyers, academicians, and young, committed activists in the country. They brought with them professional associations and friendships which extended to the senior levels of government. This informal network of contacts enhanced the stature of the Agency considerably. Men such as Frank Wisner, Desmond FitzGerald, then in the Far East Division of DDP and later Deputy Director for Plans, C. Tracy Barnes, the Special Assistant to Wisner for Paramilitary and Psychological Operations, William Bundy, an analyst in the Office of National Estimates, Kingman Douglass, former investment banker and head of OCI, and Loftus Becker, then Deputy Director for Intelligence, had developed a wide array of contacts which bridged the worlds of government, business law, journalism, and politics, at their highest levels. The fact that senior Agency officials had shared similar wartime experiences, came from comparable social backgrounds, and served in positions comparable in those of other government officials contributed significantly to the legitimacy of and confidence in the Agency as an instrument of government. Moreover, these informal ties created a shared consensus among policymakers about the role and direction of the Agency.

At the working level, these contacts were facilitated by the Agency's location in downtown Washington. Housed in a sprawling set of buildings in the center of the city—along the Reflecting Pond at the Mall and elsewhere—Agency personnel could easily meet and talk with State and Defense officials throughout the day. The CIA's physical presence in the city gave it the advantage of seeming an integral part of, rather than a separate element of, the government.

No one was more convinced than Allen Dulles that the Agency could make a special contribution to the advancement of United States foreign policy goals. Dulles came to the post of DCI in February 1953 with an extensive background in foreign affairs and foreign espionage. By the time of his appointment his interests and his view of the CIA had been firmly established. The son of a minister, Dulles was raised in a family which combined a strong sense of moral purpose with a long tradition of service at senior levels of government. This background gave Allen Dulles and his older brother, John Foster, the opportunity to participate in international affairs and brought a dimension of conviction to their ideas and opinions.[1]

Before becoming DCI, Dulles' background included ten years in the Foreign Service with assignments to the Versailles Peace Conference, Berlin, and Constantinople. Law practice in New York followed. After the outbreak of World War II William Donovan called on Dulles to serve in OSS. Dulles was assigned to Bern, the center for OSS activities against the Germans, where he developed a dazzling array of operations against the Germans and Italians. After the war Dulles returned to law practice in New York. He served as a consult-

---

[1] Dulles' paternal grandfather had been Secretary of State under Benjamin Harrison; his maternal grandfather had served as United States Minister (then the equivalent of Ambassador) in Mexico, Russia, and Spain; and his uncle, Robert Lansing, had been Secretary of State under Woodrow Wilson.

ant to DCIs Vandenberg and Hillenkoetter, and in 1948 President Truman and Secretary Forrestal asked him to participate in the NSC Survey of the CIA. He joined the Agency in January 1951 as the Deputy Director for Plans. Later that year he replaced William Jackson as DDCI, a position he held until February 1953, when he was named Bedell Smith's successor.

Dulles' experience in the Foreign Service, OSS, and the law coupled with his naturally gregarious personality had won him a vast array of domestic and international contacts in government, law, and the press. As DCI Dulles used and cultivated these contacts freely to enhance the Agency's stature. He made public speeches, met quietly with members of the press, and socialized constantly in Washington society. Dulles' own unofficial activities were indicative of the web of associations which existed among senior Agency personnel and the major sectors of Washington society. By the early 1950's the CIA had gained a reputation among United States Government agencies as a young, vital institution serving the highest national purpose.

In 1953, Dulles took a dramatic stand against Senator Joseph Mc-Carthy, and his action contributed significantly to the Agency's reputation as a liberal institution. At a time when the State Department and even the military services were cowering before McCarthy's preposterous charges and attempting to appease the Wisconsin Senator, Dulles openly challenged McCarthy's attacks on the Agency. He denied McCarthy's charges publicly, had Senate subpoenas quashed, and demanded that McCarthy make available to him any evidence of Communist influence or subversion in the Agency. Within a month, McCarthy backed off. The episode had an important impact on agency morale and on the public's perception of the CIA. As virtually the only government agency that had successfully resisted McCarthy's allegations and intrusions, the CIA was identified as an organization that fostered free and independent thinking.

A crucial factor in securing the Agency's place within the government during this period was the fact that the Secretary of State, John Foster Dulles, and the DCI were brothers. Whatever the formal relationships among the State Department, the NSC, and the CIA, they were superseded by the personal and working association between the brothers. Most importantly, both enjoyed the absolute confidence of President Eisenhower. In the day-to-day formulation of policy, these relationships were crucial to the Executive's support for the Agency and more specifically, for Allen Dulles personally in defining his own role and that of the Agency.

Dulles' role as DCI was rooted in his wartime experience with OSS. His interests and expertise lay with the operational aspects of intelligence, and his fascination with the details of operations persisted. Perhaps the most important effect of Dulles' absorption with operations was its impact on the Agency's relationship to the intelligence "community"—the intelligence components in the Department of State and Defense. As DCI, Dulles did not assert his position or the Agency's in attempting to coordinate departmental intelligence activities.

For the Agency, this constituted a lost opportunity. Throughout the 1950's, the CIA was in the forefront of technological innovation and developed a strong record on military estimates. Conceivably, Dulles could have used these advances as bureaucratic leverage in exerting some control over the intelligence community. He did not. Much of the reason was a matter of personal temperament. Jolly and extroverted in the extreme, Dulles disliked and avoided confrontations at every level. In so doing, he failed to provide even minimal direction over the intelligence agencies at a time when intelligence capabilities were undergoing dramatic changes. Dulles was equally inattentive to the administration of the Agency itself, and the real internal management responsibility fell to his able Deputy Director, General Charles P. Cabell, who served throughout Dulles' term.

I. The Clandestine Service [2]

It is both easy to exaggerate and difficult to appreciate the position which the Clandestine Service secured in the CIA during the Dulles administration and, to a large extent, retained thereafter. The number and extent of the activities undertaken are far less important than the impact which those activities had on the Agency's institutional identity—the way people within the DDP, the DDI, and the DDA perceived the Agency's primary mission, and the way policymakers regarded its contribution to the process of government.

Covert action was at the core of this perception, and its importance to the internal and external evaluation of the Agency was derived largely from the fact that only the CIA could and did perform this function. Moreover, in the international environment of the 1950's Agency operations were regarded as an essential contribution to the attainment of United States foreign policy objectives. Political action, sabotage, support to democratic governments, counterintelligence—all this the Clandestine Service could provide.

The Agency also benefitted from what were widely regarded as its operational "successes" in this period. In 1953 and 1954 two of the Agency's boldest, most spectacular covert operations took place—the overthrow of Premier Mohammed Mossadegh in Iran and the coup against President Jacobo Arbenz Guzman of Guatemala. Both were quick and virtually bloodless operations that removed from power two allegedly communist-associated leaders and replaced them with pro-Western officials. Out of these early acclaimed achievements both the Agency and Washington policymakers acquired a sense of confidence in the CIA's capacity for operational success.

The popular perception was an accurate reflection of the Agency's internal dynamics. The Clandestine Service occupied a preeminent position within the CIA. First, it had the constant attention of the DCI. Dulles was absorbed in the day-to-day details of operations. Working closely with Wisner and his key subordinates, Dulles conceived ideas for projects, conferred with desk officers, and delighted in the smallest achievements. Dulles never extended comparable time and attention to the DDI.

The DDP continued to command the major portion of Agency resources. Between 1953 and 1961, clandestine collection and covert action absorbed an average of 54 percent of the Agency's total annual budget.[3] Although this percentage represented a reduction from the

---

[2] The term "Clandestine Service" is used synonymously with the Deputy Directorate for Plans.
[3] This did not include DDA budgetary allocations in support of DDP operations.

period of the Korean War, the weight of the Agency's expenditures still fell to the DDP. During the same period, the DDP gained nearly 2,000 personnel. On its formal table or organization, the DDP registered an increase of only 1,000 personnel. However, increases of nearly 1,000 in the logistics and communications components of the DDA represented growth in support to Clandestine Service operations.

A. Internal Procedures; Secrecy and Its Consequences

Within the Agency the DDP was a Directorate apart. Because of presumed security needs the DDP was exempt from many of the review procedures that existed within the Agency. Secrecy was deemed essential to the success and protection of DDP activities.

The demands of security—as defined by individuals within the DDP—resulted in capricious administrative procedures. Wisner and Dulles condoned and accepted exceptional organizational arrangements. Neither man was a strong manager, and neither had the disposition to impose or to adhere to strict lines of authority. Both men believed that the functional dynamics of clandestine activities required the absence of routinization, and it was not unusual for either of them to initiate projects independent of the staffs and divisions that would ordinarily be involved.

Although the Comptroller's Office was responsible for tracking budgetary expenditures in the DDP on a project-by-project basis, special activities were exempt from such review. For example, foreign intelligence projects whose sensitivity required that they be authorized at the level of the Assistant Deputy Director for Plans or above were not included in the Comptroller's accounting. Records on the costs of such projects were maintained within the Directorate by the Foreign Intelligence Staff.[4] Often political projects which had a highly sensitive classification were implemented without full information being provided to the DDA or to the Comptroller.

The Office of the Inspector General was formally established in 1951 to serve as an intra-agency monitoring unit. Its range of duties included surveys of agency components and consideration of grievances. Until 1957 there were restrictions on the Office's authority to investigate the DDP components and to examine specific operational problems within the Directorate. The DDP maintained its own inspection group, staffed by its own careerists.

The DDP became a highly compartmented structure in which information was limited to small groups of individuals. Throughout the Directorate information was subject to the "need to know" rule. This was particularly true of highly sensitive political action and paramilitary operations, but it was also routine practice to limit the routing of cable traffic from the field to Headquarters. Within the DDP exceptions to standard guidelines for project approval and review were frequent. In certain cases an operation or the identity of an agent was known only to the Deputy Director for Plans and the two or three officers directly involved. In the words of a former high-rank-

---

[4] The Foreign Intelligence Staff was one of the several functional staffs in the DDP. Among its responsibilities were checking the authenticity of sources and information, screening clandestine collection requirements, and reviewing the regional divisions' projects, budget information, and operational cable traffic.

ing DDP official, "Flexibility is the name of the game." A forceful case can be made in support of these procedures, for reasons of counterespionage, maximum creativity, etc. However, the arrangements placed enormous premiums on the professional integrity of the individuals involved and left many decisions subject to the strains and lapses of personal judgments.

The Agency's drug testing program is a clear example of the excesses that resulted from a system that allowed individuals to function with the knowledge that their actions would not be subject to scrutiny from others either within or outside the DDP. Testing and experiments were conducted without the participants' prior knowledge and without medical screening, and drugs were administered without participation of trained medical or scientific personnel. One person is known to have died as a result of Agency experimentations. Those responsible for the drug testing programs were exempt from routine Agency procedures of accountability and approval.

Blurred lines of authority continued to characterize relationships among the DDP components. As discussed earlier, the intended roles of the functional staffs and the geographical divisions (administrative support vs. operational control) had broken down under the incentives to generate and manage projects. During this period both the Covert Action (CA) Staff and the Counterintelligence (CI) Staff ran field operations while also serving as advisory and coordinating bodies for the operations conducted by the geographical divisions.[5]

The CI staff actually monopolized counterintelligence operations and left little latitude to the divisions to develop and implement their own counterintelligence activities. The staff maintained their own communications channels with the field, and CI operations were frequently conducted without the knowledge of the respective DDP Division Chiefs or Station Chiefs. The example of the CI Staff is the extreme. It was derived from the personal influence that CI chief, James Angleton, exercised for nearly twenty years. Nonetheless, the CI Staff is indicative of the compartmentation within the Directorate that created pockets of privilege for specific operations.

An important consequence of the degree of compartmentation that existed in the Clandestine Service was the impact on the intelligence process. Theoretically, the data collected by the DDP field officers could have served as a major source for DDI analysis. However, strict compartmentation prevented open contact between the respective DDP divisions and DDI components.

The overriding element in the distant relationship between the DDP and the DDI was the so-called "sources and methods" rule. DDI analysts seldom had access to raw data from the field. In the decade of the 1950's information collected from the field was transmitted to Headquarters and summarized there for dissemination to all of the analytic components throughout the government, including the DDI.[6]

The DDP adhered strictly to its principle of not revealing the identity of its assets. Reports gave only vague descriptions of assets

---

[5] The Covert Action Staff was involved with a full range of political, propaganda, and labor activities.

[6] More recently, reports officers in the field draft intelligence summaries which receive minimal review at Headquarters before dissemination.

providing information. Intelligence analysts found this arrangement highly unsatisfactory, since they could not judge the quality of information they were receiving without some better indication of the nature and reliability of the source. Analysts therefore tended to look upon DDP information—however limited their access to it—with reservations and relied primarily on overt materials and COMINT for their production efforts.

Throughout Dulles' term desk-to-desk contact between DDP officers and DDI analysts was practically nonexistent. The rationale for this was to prevent individual analysts from imposing requirements on the collectors. The DDP viewed itself as serving the community's clandestine collection needs subject to government-wide requirements. The DDI leadership, on the other hand, believed that the DDP should respond primarily to its requirements. The DDP's definition prevailed. The Clandestine Service maintained control over determining which requests it accepted from the community.

Intelligence requirements were established through a subcommittee of the Intelligence Advisory Committee.[7] After the intelligence priorities were defined, the DDP's Foreign Intelligence Staff reviewed them and accepted or vetoed the requirements unilaterally. Moreover, because the requirements were very general the DDP had considerable latitude in interpreting and defining the specific collection objectives. The most significant consequence of this process was that the DDP itself essentially controlled the specific requirements for its collectors without ongoing consultation with the DDI.

The existence of this enforced isolation between the two Directorates negated the potential advantages of having collectors and analysts in the same agency. Despite efforts in the 1960's to break down the barriers between the Directorates, the lack of real interchange and interdependence persisted.

The tolerance of flexible procedures within the DDP, the Directorate's exemption from accountability to outside components and the DCI's own patronage gave the DDP a considerable degree of freedom in undertaking operations. In addition, the loose process of external review, discussed later in this section, contributed to the Directorate's independence. The DDP's relative autonomy in the Agency also affected the mission and functions of the other two Directorates. In the case of the DDI the consequences were significant for the execution of the intelligence function. These patterns solidified under Dulles and shaped the long-term configuration of the Agency.

B. Clandestine Activities, 1953–1961

Covert action expanded significantly in the 1953 to 1961 period. Following the Korean War and the accompanying shift in the perception of the Soviet threat from military to political, the CIA concentrated its operations on political action, particularly support to electoral candidates and to political parties. The Agency also continued

---

[7] Later through the United States Intelligence Board (USIB). See p. 63.

to develop its paramilitary capability, employing it in Guatemala in 1954, the Far East, and in the ill-fated Bay of Pigs landing in Cuba in 1961. Relative to the paramilitary operations in Laos and Vietnam in the 1960's, the scale of these activities was minimal.

Geographically, the order of priorities was Western Europe, the Far East, and Latin America. With the Soviets in Eastern Europe and Communist parties still active in France and Italy, Europe appeared to be the area most vulnerable to Communist encroachments. The CIA station in West Berlin was the center of CIA operations against Eastern Europe, and the German Branch of the European Division was the Agency's largest single country component. By 1962 the Western Hemisphere Division had experienced considerable success in penetrating the major Communist Parties in Latin America.

Just as the Agency's activities reflected certain geographical patterns, they also displayed functional patterns. In the period 1952 to 1963 the Agency acquired most of its clandestine information through liaison arrangements with foreign governments. Both Wisner and Dulles cultivated relations with foreign intelligence officials and because of the United States' predominant postwar position, governments in Western Europe, in particular, were very willing to cooperate in information sharing. Liaison provided the Agency with sources and contacts that otherwise would have been denied them. Information on individuals, on political parties, on labor movements, all derived in part from liaison. Certainly, the difficulty and long-term nature of developing assets was largely responsible for the CIA's initial reliance on liaison.

The existence of close liaison relationships inhibited developing independent assets. First, it was simply easier to rely on information that had already been gleaned from agents. Regular meetings with local officials allowed CIA officers to ask questions and to get the information they needed with minimal effort. It was far easier to talk to colleagues who had numerous assets in place than to expend the time required merely to make contact with an individual whose potential would not be realized for years. Second, maintenance of liaison became an end in itself, against which independent collection operations were judged. Rather than serving as a supplement to Agency operations it assumed primary importance in Western Europe. Often, a proposal for an independent operation was rejected because a Station Chief believed that if the operation were exposed, the host government's intelligence service would be offended.

Reliance on liaison did not mean that the Agency was not developing its own capability. Liaison itself enhanced the Agency's political action capability through the information it provided on the domestic situation in the host country. With the Soviet Union and communist parties as the targets the Agency concentrated on developing anti-Communist political strength. Financial support to individual candidates, subsidies to publications including newspapers and magazines, involvement in local and national labor unions—all of these interlocking elements constituted the fundamentals of a typical political action program. Elections, of course, were key operations, and the Agency involved itself in electoral politics on a continuing basis. Likewise, case officers groomed and cultivated individuals who could provide strong pro-Western leadership.

Beyond the varying forms of political action and liaison the Agency's program of clandestine activities aimed at developing an international anti-Communist ideology. Within the Agency the International Organizations Division coordinated this extensive organizational propaganda effort. The Division's activities included operations to assist or to create international organizations for youth, students, teachers, workers, veterans, journalists, and jurists. This kind of activity was an attempt to lay an intellectual foundation for anticommunism around the world. Ultimately, the organizational underpinnings could serve as a political force in assuring the establishment or maintenance of democratic governments.

C. Executive Authorization of Covert Action

During the Dulles period there were several attempts to regularize and improve the process of Executive coordination and authorization of covert action. Although the changes provided a mechanism for Agency accountability to the Executive, none of the arrangements significantly restricted CIA activities. The perception of American foreign policy objectives encouraged the development of anti-Communist activities; the Agency held the advantage in its ability to introduce project proposals based on detailed knowledge of internal conditions in a given foreign country; Dulles' personal influence and the fact of his brother's position lent enormous weight to any proposal that originated with the Agency.

Until 1955 no formal approval mechanism existed outside the Agency for covert action projects. Since 1948, when covert action was first authorized, senior State Department and Defense Department officials were designated to provide only loose policy guidance to CIA—with the assumption that covert operations would be infrequent. As covert activities proliferated, loose understandings rather than specific review formed the basis for CIA's accountability for covert operations.

Following the Korean War, the Defense Department's role in relation to covert action became more one of providing physical support to the Agency's paramilitary operations. Liaison between DOD and CIA was not channelled through lower levels but was handled by a designated DOD representative. For several years there was some tension between the two agencies because the Defense Department official who was responsible for liaison was not trusted by senior agency personnel. In 1957 he was dismissed, and his replacement was able to ease relations between the two agencies.

Apart from day-to-day liaison at the working level, a series of senior bodies developed over the years to provide guidance for the initiation of covert operations. The Psychological Strategy Board (PSB), an NSC subcommittee, had been established in 1951. Since both departmental representatives and PSB staff members sat on the Board, it was too large and too widely representational to function as a senior policymaking body. The Board's definition of covert activity was also faulty, since it assumed a neat distinction between psychological operations and political and paramilitary operations. With the proliferation of activities in the latter two categories there was a need to include these programs in the policy guidance mechanism. Where the initiative for change originated is unclear, but in September 1953 the Operations Coordinating Board (OCB) was established to replace the PSB. Although the new Board's membership was restricted to Deputy-level officials,[8] it never served in an approval capacity. Moreover, its interdepartmental composition made Dulles reluctant to discuss secret operations with OCB members. Dulles employed the OCB primarily to gain backing for requests to the Bureau of the Budget for reserve releases to meet unbudgeted expenses.

In March and November 1955 two NSC policy directives, NSC 5412/1 and NSC 5412/2 were issued, outlining revised control procedures. They established a group of "designated representatives" of the President and Secretaries of State and Defense to review and approve covert action projects. Irregular procedures characterized the group's functioning. The actual membership of the 5412 Committee or "Special Group" as it came to be known, varied as *ad hoc* task forces were organized for different situations. Neither the CIA nor the Group established clearly defined criteria for submitting projects to the NSC body, and until 1959 meetings were infrequent. In that year regular weekly meetings began, but the real initiative for projects continued to rest with the Agency. Special Group members frequently did not feel confident enough to judge Agency capabilities or to determine whether a particular project was feasible.

After the Bay of Pigs failure President Kennedy requested a review of U.S. paramilitary capabilities. The President's request assumed the necessity for continued, indeed, expanded operations, and the purpose of the report was to explore ways of insuring successful future paramilitary actions—as well as determining why the Bay of Pigs landing had failed. Directed by General Maxwell Taylor, the report recommended strengthening the top-level direction for operations by establishing a review group with permanent membership. As a result of the report, the standing members of the Special Group included McGeorge Bundy, the Special Assistant for National Security Affairs as Chairman, U. Alexis Johnson, Under Secretary of State, Roswell Gilpatric, Deputy Secretary of Defense, the DCI, and General Lyman Lemnitzer, Chairman of the Joint Chiefs of Staff. This group assumed a more vigorous role in planning and reviewing covert operations.

D. Congressional Review

During the term of Allen Dulles the Congressional committee structure and the perception of the Agency as a first line defense against Communism remained the determinants in the relationship between the CIA and the Congress. Dulles himself reinforced the existing procedures through his casual, friendly approach to Congress, and he secured the absolute trust of senior ranking members. While Dulles was DCI Richard Russell continued as Chairman of the Senate Armed Services Committee, Carl Vinson remained as Chairman of the

---

[8] OCB members included the Under Secretary of State, the Deputy Secretary of Defense, the Special Assistant to the President for Cold War affairs, and the Director of the Mutual Security Administration (the designation for the foreign aid program at that time).

House Armed Services Committee, and from 1955 to 1964 Clarence Cannon held the chairmanship of the House Appropriations Committee. Dulles' appearance before a group consisted of a *tour d'horizon* on the basis of which members would ask questions. Yet the procedure was more perfunctory than rigorous. Likewise, members often preferred not knowing about Agency activities. Leverett Saltonstall, the former Massachusetts Senator and a ranking member of the Senate Armed Services and Appropriations Committees stated candidly:

> Dominated by the Committee chairmen, members would ask few questions which dealt with internal Agency matters or with specific operations. The most sensitive discussions were reserved for one-to-one sessions between Dulles and individual Committee chairmen.

In spite of the appearance of a comfortable relationship between Congress and the Agency, there were serious efforts to alter the nature of the procedures. During the Dulles administration there were two strong but unsuccessful attempts to strengthen Congress' oversight role and to broaden the participation of members in the execution of the Committees' responsibilities. The failure of these attempts derived principally from the strength of the Committee system and from the adroit tactics of the Executive branch in deflating the impetus for change.

In 1955 Senator Mike Mansfield introduced a Resolution for a Joint Oversight Committee. The Mansfield Resolution resulted from a congressional survey of the Executive branch. The Hoover Commission, chaired by former President Herbert Hoover, was established in 1954 to evaluate the organization of Executive agencies. A small task force under General Mark Clark was assigned responsibility for the intelligence community. The prospect of a survey of the Clandestine Service, information from which would be reported to the full Congress, led President Eisenhower, presumably in consultation with Allen Dulles, to request a separate, classified report on the DDP to be delivered to him personally. The group charged with the investigation was the Doolittle Committee, so named after its Chairman, General James Doolittle, a distinguished World War II aviator. In turn, the Clark Task Force agreed not to duplicate the activities of the Doolittle Committee. Essentially, the arrangement meant that the Congress was prevented from conducting its own investigation into the Clandestine Service.[9]

---

[9] The orientation and composition of the Doolittle Committee did not encourage criticism of the Agency's activities or of the existing framework of decision-making. Early drafts of instructions to General Doolittle were prepared by the Agency. The four members of the Committee were well known in the Agency and had affiliations with the Executive. Doolittle himself was a friend of Wisner's; Morris Hadley, a New York lawyer, was an old friend of Allen Dulles; William Pawley was a former ambassador; and William Franke had been an Assistant Secretary of the Navy. Although the Doolittle report did call for better coordination between the CIA and the military and better cooperation between the DDP and the DDA, the report was principally an affirmation of the need for a clandestine capability. The prose was chilling:

"It is now clear that we are facing an implacable enemy whose avowed objective is world domination by whatever means and at whatever cost. There are no

Among the members of the Clark Task Force, Clark and Admiral Richard L. Connolly were responsible for the CIA.[9a] The Task Force found an excessive emphasis on covert action over intelligence analysis and in particular criticized the quality and quantity of the Agency's intelligence on the Soviet Union. With regard to the Congress the Task Force recommended the establishment of an oversight group, a mixed permanent body including members of Congress and distinguished private citizens. The full Hoover Commission did not adopt the Task Force proposal but instead recommended two bodies: a joint congressional oversight committee and a group comprised of private citizens.

It was on the basis of the Commission's recommendation that Senator Mansfield introduced his resolution on January 14, 1955. Debated for over a year, the resolution had thirty-five co-sponsors. However, fierce opposition existed among senior members, including Russell, Hayden and Saltonstall, who were reluctant to concede their Committees' respective jurisdictions over the Agency. An exchange between Mansfield and Saltonstall during the floor debate is indicative of the pespective existing in the Senate at the time:

> Mr. MANSFIELD. Mr. President, I know the Senator from Massachusetts speaks from his heart, but I wonder whether the question I shall ask now should be asked in public; if not, let the Senator from Massachusetts please refrain from answering it: How many times does the CIA request a meeting with the particular subcommittees of the Appropriations Committee and the Armed Services Committee, and how many times does the Senator from Massachusetts request the CIA to brief him in regard to existing affairs?

> Mr. SALTONSTALL. I believe the correct answer is that at least twice a year that happens in the Armed Services Committee, and at least once a year it happens in the Appropriations Committee. I speak from my knowledge of the situation during the last year or so; I do not attempt to refer to previous periods. Certainly the present administrator and the former administrator, Gen. Bedell Smith, stated that they were ready at all times to answer any questions we might wish to ask them. The difficulty in connection with asking

---

rules in such a game. Hitherto acceptable norms of human conduct do not apply. If the United States is to survive, long-standing American concepts of "fair play" must be reconsidered. We must develop effective espionage and counterespionage services and must learn to subvert, sabotage and destroy our enemies by more clever, more sophisticated, and more effective methods than those used against us. It may become necessary that the American people be made acquainted with, understand and support this fundamentally repugnant philosophy."

[9a] The report called for a separation of the Clandestine Service into what was virtually the old OPC–OSO division. Its criticism was sharp and pointed:

"It appears that the clandestine collection of raw intelligence from the USSR has been overshadowed by the concentration of the DCI and others of an inordinate amount of their time and efforts on the performance of the Agency's cold war functions. The Task Force therefore is of the opinion that the present internal organization of the CIA for the performance of the DDP types of functions has had a decidedly adverse effect on the accomplishment of the Agency's espionage and counterespionage functions."

questions and obtaining information is that we might obtain information which I personally would rather not have, unless it was essential for me as a Member of Congress to have it.

Mr. MANSFIELD. Mr. President, I think the Senator's answer tells the whole story, for he has informed us that a subcommittee of the Senate Armed Services Committee has met only twice a year with members of the CIA, and that a subcommittee of the Senate Appropriations Committee has met only once a year with members of the CIA. Of course, it is very likely that the meetings in connection with the Appropriations Committee occurred only at a time when the CIA was making requests for appropriations. That information from the Senator from Massachusetts does not indicate to me that there is sufficiently close contact between the congressional committees and the CIA, as such.

Mr. SALTONSTALL. In reply, let me state—and I should like to discuss this point more fully when I present my own views on this subject—that it is not a question of reluctance on the part of the CIA officials to speak to us. Instead, it is a question of our reluctance, if you will, to seek information and knowledge on subjects which I personally, as a Member of Congress and as a citizen, would rather not have, unless I believed it to be my responsibility to have it because it might involve the lives of American citizens.

Mr. MANSFIELD. I see. The Senator is to be commended.

Opposition to the Resolution also existed in the Executive branch. After its introduction, the NSC requested Dulles' analysis. The DCI responded with a long memorandum analyzing the problems such a committee would create. Although the memo did not express outright objection, the effect of enumerating the problems was to recommend against its establishment. Dulles expressed concern about the possible breaches of security on the part of committee staff members. In particular he stated that foreign intelligence services would object to information sharing and that U.S. liaison relationships would be jeopardized. Dulles ably convinced the senior members of the Executive that an oversight committee was undesirable. Although the Administration's objections were undoubtedly known by the congressional leadership, the decisive factor in the defeat of the Mansfield Resolution was the opposition of the senior-ranking members. In addition to the objections of Russell, Hayden, and Saltonstall, Senator Alben Barkley, the former Vice President, and Senator Stuart Symington spoke strongly against the bill when it came to the floor. On April 11, 1956 the resolution was defeated by a vote of 59 to 27 with more than a dozen of the original co-sponsors voting against.

One change did result from the protracted debate on an oversight committee: formal CIA subcommittees were created in the Armed Services and Appropriations Committees. Yet the same small group of individuals continued to be responsible for matters related to the Agency. In the Armed Services Committee Russell appointed Senators Saltonstall and Byrd, both of whom had been meeting informally with Russell on Agency activities, to a CIA subcommittee. Subsequently, Senators Lyndon Johnson and Styles Bridges were appointed to the subcommittee. In 1957 the Senate Appropriations Committee formalized a CIA subcommittee for the first time. The members of the subcommittee were, again, Russell, Bridges and Byrd. Essentially, these three men held full responsibility for Senate oversight of the CIA. They frequently conducted the business of the two subcommittees at the same meeting.[10] Despite attempts to regularize the subcommittee meetings, the most frequent form of interchange with the CIA remained personal communications between the subcommittee's chairman, Richard Russell, and Allen Dulles. In 1961, following the Bay of Pigs, Senator Eugene McCarthy attempted to revive the idea of a formally designated CIA oversight committee, but his effort failed.

In the House, under Chairman Carl Vinson, the Armed Services Committee formally established a CIA subcommittee, chaired by Vinson. The Subcommittee reviewed the CIA's programs, budget and legislative needs. Briefings on CIA operations were more regularized than in the Senate and the House Armed Services staff maintained almost daily contact with the Agency. The House Appropriations Committee did not establish a formal subcommittee. Instead Cannon continued to rely on his special group of five members. As part of the security precautions surrounding the functioning of the special group, its membership never became public knowledge.

II. Intelligence Production

In the decade of the 1950's, the CIA was the major contributor to technological advances in intelligence collection. At the same time DDI analysts were responsible for methodological innovations in strategic assessments. Despite these achievements, CIA's intelligence was not serving the purpose for which the organization had been created—informing and influencing policymaking.

The size and structure of the Deputy Directorate for Intelligence remained constant during the Dulles Administration, retaining the composition it had acquired in 1950. ORR, OSI, OCI and ONE were the centers of DDI's intelligence analysis. The Office of Current Intelligence continued to pump out its daily, weekly and monthly publications and in terms of volume produced dominated the DDI's output. OCI continued to compete with the other intelligence components of the government in providing up-to-the-minute summaries of worldwide events.

The 1951 State Department-CIA agreement had given ORR exclusive responsibility for economic research and analysis on the Soviet Union and its satellites, and it was in this area that the Agency distinguished itself during the 1950's. ORR was divided into four principal components: the Office of the Assistant Director, the Economic Research Area (ERA), the Geographic Research Area (GRA), and the Coordination Staff. The Economic Research Area was the focus of the research and analysis effort. Each ERA division (Analysis, Industrials, Materials, and Service) had two responsibilities: the production of all-source economic intelligence on the Soviet Union and the production of material for the NIEs.[10a] Day-to-day responsibility for coordination rested with the respective divisions, but

---

[10] Between 1955 and 1969 when Carl Hayden served as Chairman of the Senate Appropriations Committee, he usually sat in on the subcommittee meetings.

[10a] ERA had gone through several reorganizations since 1950.

most ERA publications were based on CIA data alone and did not represent coordinated interdepartmental intelligence.

The quality of ERA's work benefitted enormously from research and analysis done by outside consultants between 1953 and 1955. The Center for International Studies (CENIS) at the Massachusetts Institute of Technology made the principal contribution in this category. When Max Millikan left the directorship of ORR in 1953, he arranged for an ongoing consultancy relationship between the Agency and CENIS. The CENIS effort contributed substantially to ORR's innovations in the analysis of Soviet strategic capabilities.

Although at the insistence of the military the Agency was officially excluded from military analysis, ORR's immediate emphasis became Soviet strategic research. There were two reasons for ORR's concentration in this area. First, the prevailing fear of the Soviet threat made knowledge of Soviet strategic capabilities a priority concern for civilian policymakers as well as the military. Second, and more importantly, military analysis was the area where the Agency had to establish itself if it was to assume legitimacy as an intelligence producer in competition with the services. The military services constituted the Agency's greatest threat in the execution of its mission and only by generating strategic intelligence could CIA analysts begin to challenge the military's established position as intelligence producers.

By introducing economic production capacities into assessments of Soviet strategic capabilities the Agency challenged the basic premises of the military's judgments. For example, the Air Force mission required that it be informed about Soviet advances in nuclear weapons and air technology. The Air Force justified its budgetary claims in part on the basis of the projected size and capabilities of Soviet strategic forces. Air Force intelligence based its estimates on knowledge of Soviet technology and laboratory research, which by 1953 were well advanced. ORR based its estimates of Soviet deployments on Soviet economic production capabilities, which were severely limited as a result of the war. Consequently, ORR's methodology attributed lower strategic deployments, i.e., long-range bombers and missiles, to the Russians.

ORR's contribution to the area of strategic assessments came quickly. In the mid-1950's a major controversy developed over the Soviet Union's long-range bomber capability. The issue was complicated and intensified because the military services were then suffering post-Korean War budget cuts and were vying with one another for marginal resources. Air Force estimates that the Russians were making a substantial investment in intercontinental bombers argued for disproportionate allocations to the United States Strategic Air Command and air defense systems also belonging to the Air Force. The Navy and Army both questioned the Air Force case.

In the midst of this controversy the Office of National Estimates, drawing heavily on work done by ORR and by CENIS at MIT, produced its estimates of Soviet bomber production. The ONE assessments were more moderate than those of the Air Force. ONE analysts argued that because of production difficulties, the U.S.S.R. could not operate as large a long-range bomber force as the Air Force was predicting. The Agency's contribution to military estimates at this time marked the beginning of its gradual ascendancy over the military in strategic analysis. The real take-off point for the Agency occurred in the early 1960's with the data supplied by sophisticated overhead reconnaissance systems.

Despite the Agency's analytic advances, the extent to which the CIA estimates actually influenced policy was limited. The CIA had been created to provide high-quality national intelligence estimates to policymakers. However, the communication and exchange necessary for analysts to calibrate, anticipate and respond to policymakers' needs never really developed.

Although the NIEs were conceived and drafted with senior policymakers in mind, the estimates were not consistently read by high-level officials. Between 1955 and 1956, a senior staff member of the Office of National Estimates surveyed the NIE readership by contacting Executive Assistants and Special Assistants of the President and Cabinet officers, asking whether or not the NIEs were actually placed on their superiors' desks. The survey revealed that senior policymakers were not reading the NIEs. Instead, second and third level officials used the estimates for background information in briefing senior officials.

Of all the products of the intelligence community NIEs represented the broadest, most informed judgments available. The process of coordinating NIEs was laborious, involving protracted painstaking negotiations over language and nuance. In those instances where a department held views very different from those of the other agencies, a dissenting footnote in the estimate indicated the difference of opinion. The necessity to accommodate the views of numerous participants meant that conclusions were frequently hedged judgments rather than firm predictions. To obtain the broadest possible consensus the specificity of the evaluations had to be compromised. This indefinite quality in the estimates limited the NIEs' utility for policymakers.

The failure of the NIEs to serve their fundamental purpose as basic information for senior officials was indicative of the overall failure of intelligence to intersect with policy. Even in an office as small as the Office of National Estimates, where the staff never exceeded fifty-four professionals, close interchange did not exist between staff specialists and senior "consumer" officials, whose policy decisions depended on specific expert information.

The problem was magnified throughout the DDI. The Directorate's size constituted a major obstacle to the attainment of consistent interchange between analysts and their clients. In 1955 there were 466 analysts in ORR, 217 in OCI, and 207 in OSI. The process of drafting, reviewing and editing intelligence publications involved large numbers of individuals each of whom felt responsible for and entitled to make a contribution to the final product. Yet without access to policymakers analysts did not have an ongoing accurate notion of how the form and substance of the intelligence product might best serve the needs of senior officials. The product itself—as defined and arbitrated among DDI analysts—rather than the satisfaction of specific policy needs became the end.

_____

By the 1960's the CIA had achieved significant advances in its strategic intelligence capability. The development of overhead reconnaissance, beginning with the U–2 aircraft and growing in scale and

sophistication with follow-on systems, generated information in greater quantity and accuracy than had ever before been contemplated.
Basic data on the Soviet Union beyond the reach of human collection,
such as railroad routes, construction sites, and industrial concentra-
tions became readily available. At the same time, CIA analysts began
reevaluating assumptions regarding Soviet strategic capabilities.
Largely at the initiative of the ONE Soviet staff, a different sorting
of estimates developed. The general estimate of Soviet military intentions and capabilities had become unwieldly and took an inordinate-
ly long time to produce. Gradually a series of separate estimates were
drafted dealing with such subjects as strategic attack, air and missile
defense, and general purpose forces. These estimates resulted in a shift
from "worst case" assessments to projections on the most likely assort-
ment of weapons. The military services tended to credit Soviet missiles
with maximum range and payload and to assume that as many as possible were targeted on the United States for a possible first-strike. The
Agency advanced the proposition that the U.S.S.R. was not putting all
or most of its resources into maximum payload intercontinental ballistic missiles (ICBMs) but had priorities for "sizes and mixes" of
weapons, including substantial numbers of intermediate-range ballistic
missiles (IRBMs) and medium-range ballistic missiles (MRBMs). In
the short run the Agency proved to be more nearly correct than the
services, though in the longer run, the Soviets were to develop much
larger ICBM capabilities than ONE predicted.

An additional factor working to the CIA's advantage in the
early 1960's was material supplied by Colonel Oleg Penkovsky. Well-
placed in Soviet military circles, Penkovsky turned over a number of
classified documents relating to Soviet strategic planning and capabilities. Having an agent "in place," i.e., a Soviet official who was providing information from within the Soviet Government, represented
the ultimate achievement in the Agency's clandestine collection mission. These three factors—technological breakthrough, analytic innovation, and the single most valuable Soviet agent in CIA history—
converged to make the Agency seem the government's most reliable
source of intelligence on Soviet strategic capabilities.

Of the three achieveemnts in the late 1950's and the early 1960's,
overhead reconnaissance was by far the most significant. The development of the U–2 and its follow-on systems had an enormous impact
on intelligence collection capabilities and on the Agency's relative
standing in the intelligence community.

Richard M. Bissell, whom Dulles named his Special Assistant for
Planning and Coordination in 1954, organized a small group of
Agency personnel to shepherd the project through. Bissell's background was in economics, and he combined academic experience with
extensive government service, first during World War II in the Department of Commerce and the War Shipping Administration and
later with the Economic Cooperation Administration, among other
positions. Bissell was an innovator above all, quick to seize new ideas
and to sponsor their development. For the next six years he maintained
virtually exclusive control over the development of the U–2 program,
its management, and the initiation of follow-on reconnaissance systems.

The Agency's sponsorship and deployment of the U–2 reconnaissance aircraft was a technical achievement nothing short of spectacular. The U–2 represented dramatic advances in aircraft design and production as well as in camera and film techniques. In July 1955, only eighteen months after contracting the U–2 became operational, and a fleet of 22 airplanes was deployed at a cost $3 million below the original cost estimate.

The U–2 marked the beginning of the Agency's emergence as the intelligence community's leader in the area of technical collection capability. Soon after the first U–2 flight in 1955 Bissell moved quickly to organize the research and development of follow-on systems. The Agency never attempted to establish its own technological R&D capability. Instead, it continued to utilize the best private industrial manpower available. In large part this arrangement accounts for the consistent vitality and quality of the Agency's technical R&D capability, which remains unsurpassed to this day.[10b]

The deployment of the U–2's follow-on systems coincided with the growing controversy over United States defense policy and the alleged Soviet advances in intercontinental missile deployment. The services, in particular the Air Force, produced estimates on Soviet missile capability which stated that the U.S.S.R. was superseding the United States in long-range missile production. By 1959 the issue involved Congress and became a subject of heated political debate in the 1960 Presidential campaign. Democrats, led by former Secretary of the Air Force, Senator Stuart Symington of Missouri, charged the Eisenhower Administration with permitting the U.S.S.R. to exceed the United States in bomber and missile strength. Data generated by the CIA's photographic reconnaissance systems produced evidence that these charges were ill-founded. The U.S.S.R. had not approached the United States in missile production. It is unclear to what extent Eisenhower relied directly on ONE estimates in taking his position on this issue. The controversy was largely a political one, dividing along party lines. However, it is likely that Eisenhower's stance, if not actually determined by, was at least reinforced by ONE intelligence analysis, which was never made public.

The development of overhead reconnaissance systems created a need for another group of intelligence specialists: photographic interpreters. The Agency had established a photographic center in the DDI in 1953. As a result of the U–2 deployment that group formed the nucleus of a quickly expanding specialty among intelligence analysts. In 1961 the National Photographic Interpretation Center (NPIC) was established under the DCI's direction. Staffed by CIA and military personnel, NPIC was a DDI component until 1973, when it was a component transferred to the Directorate for Science and Technology (DDS&T).

[10b] In 1955 to coordinate collection requirements for the U–2 program Bissell arranged for an informal Ad Hoc Requirements Committee (ARC), comprised initially of representatives of CIA, Army, Navy, and Air Force. Subsequently, representatives of NSA, the Joint Chiefs of Staff, and the State Department were included. In 1960, after the deployment of the U–2's follow-on system, a formal USIB (see pp. 62–63 for a discussion of USIB) subcommittee, the Committee on Overhead Reconnaissance (COMOR), succeeded the ARC. COMOR was responsible for the development and operation of all overhead reconnaissance systems.

These technological developments in the late 1950's constituted the beginning of an important expansion in the CIA's functions and capabilities. Technical collection was to have a significant effect on the Agency's relationship to the departmental intelligence services and on the allocation of resources within the intelligence community.

III. The Coordination Problem

Dulles' neglect of the community management or coordination aspect of his role as DCI was apparent to all who knew and worked with him. During a period when the Agency was responsible for numerous innovations, analytic and technical, Dulles might have seized the opportunity to strengthen the DCI's position relative to the military services. As the community became larger and as technical systems required larger budgetary allocations, the institutional obstacles to coordination increased.

Two episodes in Dulles' term illustrate his lack of initiative in coordination. One involved the Economic Research Area in ORR and the other, the Office of Scientific Intelligence. Both represented opportunities that, if taken, would have enhanced the DCI's capacity to manage the community's intelligence activities.

By 1956 the major portion of ERA's work was devoted to Soviet strategic analysis. The work was scattered throughout the four ERA divisions, making production unwieldy and inefficient. In that year senior ERA personnel advanced a proposal to establish a Military Economics Branch which would combine the fragmented military intelligence efforts then being conducted in ERA. Dulles rejected the recommendation on the grounds that the services might interpret such a move as a unilateral attempt by the Agency to assume large responsibilities in their fields of primary concern. In effect, Dulles' reluctance to challenge the military services limited the Agency's own work effort. More importantly, it allowed the Agency's production of strategic intelligence to go without formal recognition in the community. A decision by Dulles to establish the Agency's authority in the field of national military intelligence would have required a confrontation and a bureaucratic battle—neither of which Dulles was inclined to pursue.

The second example involved the establishment of the interdepartmental Guided Missiles Intelligence Committee (GMIC), an Intelligence Advisory Committee subcommittee created in 1956. Since 1949 the Office of Scientific Intelligence had wrangled with the military services over the division of responsibility for producing scientific and technical intelligence. DCID 3/4, issued in 1952, stipulated that OSI's primary mission was research for basic scientific intelligence, leaving research for technical intelligence with the military. Despite the restrictions of DCID 3/4, the inseparable links between basic science and technology allowed OSI to branch into technical science. By 1955 OSI had five divisions in the technical sciences area, including a Guided Missiles Intelligence Division.

The growing community-wide emphasis on guided missiles intelligence raised the issue of interagency coordination. Discussions on the subject provoked a split between the State Department and the CIA, on the one hand, and the services on the other. State and the Agency, specifically OSI, favored an interdepartmental committee with overall responsibility for coordinating and producing guided missiles intelligence. The services and the Joint Staff favored exclusive Defense Department control. It took two years to resolve the issue. Between 1954 and 1956 Dulles hedged on the problem and was unwilling to press OSI's claims. Finally in 1956 he took the matter to Secretary of Defense Charles Wilson, who supported the creation of a committee over the objections of the Joint Staff and Navy and Army intelligence.[11] The services, however, retained the right to appoint the chairman.

In both these instances, the organization of OSI and the formation of the GMIC, Dulles had an opportunity in the first stages of new areas of intelligence production to establish a pattern of organization for the community and to assert the DCI's position. By not acting, Dulles allowed departmental procedures to become more entrenched and routinized, making later coordination attempts all the more difficult.

At the time of its 1954 survey the Clark Task Force of the Hoover Commission [12] recognized the need for more efficient intelligence community management. The Task Force members recommended the appointment of a Deputy Director to assume internal management responsibilities for the Agency, leaving the DCI free for his coordination role. Dulles turned the recommendation around and appointed General Lucien Truscott his deputy for community affairs. Clearly, Truscott lacked even the DCI's limited authority in his coordinating task.

Most of Truscott's efforts were directed at resolving jurisdictional conflicts between the Agency and the military intelligence services. The most persistent and troublesome operational problem in intelligence community coordination involved the Army's espionage activities, particularly in Western Europe. The Army, Air Force, and to a lesser extent, the Navy, had continued their independent clandestine collection operations after the war. Among the services, the Army had been the most active in the field and grossly outnumbered the CIA in manpower. The services' justification for their operations had been that during wartime they would need clandestine collection support. That capability required long-term development. Service activities, in particular the Army's, resulted in excessive duplication of the CIA effort and frequently, competition for the same agents.

In 1958 Truscott succeeded in working out an arrangement with the services, which attempted to rationalize clandestine collection activities. A National Security Council Intelligence Directive assigned CIA the primary responsibility for clandestine activities abroad. An accompanying directive gave the DCI's designated field representatives a modified veto over the services' field activities, by requiring that disagreements be referred to Washington for arbitration by the DCI and the Secretary of Defense. Although issuing these directives theoretically provided the DCI with authority over espionage activities, in practice the directives only created a means of adjudicating disputes. Military commanders continued to rely on service intelligence personnel to satisfy their intelligence requirements. To some extent the difficulties were eased after 1959 but this was not as a result of Truscott's efforts. The principal reason was that the development

---

[11] The Air Force had come to support the idea of an IAC subcommittee.
[12] See p. 52–53 for a discussion of the Hoover Commission.

of technical collection systems made heavy drains on service intelligence budgets and reduced the funds available for human collection. After 1959 Air Force activities declined sharply as the service began developing overhead reconnaissance systems. Likewise, the availability of photographic data made the Army less able to justify large budgetary allocations for human collection.

Within the Executive branch there were efforts to strengthen the direction of the intelligence community. In January 1956, President Eisenhower created the President's Board of Consultants on Foreign Intelligence Activities (PBCFIA). Composed of retired senior government officials and members of the professions, the PBCFIA was to provide the President with advice on intelligence matters.[13] The Board was a deliberative body and had no authority over either the DCI or the community. Accordingly, it had little impact on the administration of the CIA or on the other intelligence services. The Board did identify the imbalance in Dulles' role as DCI and in December 1956 and in December 1958 recommended the appointment of a chief of staff for the DCI to carry out the CIA's internal administration. In 1960 the Board suggested the possibility of separating the DCI from the Agency, having him serve as the President's intelligence advisor and as coordinator for community activities. Nothing resulted from these recommendations. In part the failure to implement these proposals was a reflection of PBCFIA's impotence. However, Dulles' personal standing had a major influence on policymakers' acceptance of his limited definition of the role. President Eisenhower, who himself repeatedly pressed Dulles to exert more initiative in the community, indicated his fundamental acceptance of Dulles' performance in a statement cited in a CIA history:

> I'm not going to be able to change Allen. I have two alternatives, either to get rid of him and appoint someone who will assert more authority or keep him with his limitations. I'd rather have Allen as my chief intelligence officer with his limitations than anyone else I know.

On another level the PBCFIA did try to create a stronger institutional structure for the community. In 1957 the Board recommended merging the United States Communications Intelligence Board with the IAC. PBCFIA's proposal was directed at improving the community's overall direction. The USCIB was established in 1946 to advise and make recommendations on communications intelligence to the Secretary of Defense.[14] The PBCFIA's recommendation for the IAC–USCIB merger was intended to strengthen the DCI's authority and to improve intelligence coordination, by making the DCI chair-

---

[13] The original PBCFIA members, all of whom were recommended by Dulles, included: General Doolittle, Sidney Souers, General Omar Bradley, Admiral Richard Connolly, General John E. Hull, Morris Hadley, a New York lawyer, William B. Francke, former Secretary of the Navy, David Bruce, Former Ambassador, Henry Wriston, former president of Brown University, and Donald Russell, a member of the Clark Task Force and former Assistant Secretary of State.

[14] USCIB's membership included the Secretaries of State, Defense, the Directors of the FBI, and representatives of the Army, Navy, Air Force, and CIA. USCIB votes were weighted. Representatives of State, Defense, the FBI, and CIA each had two votes; other members had one. Although the DCI sat on the Committee, he had no vote.

man of the newly established body. The services objected to the creation of the Board, since it meant that in the area of electronic intelligence they would be reduced to an advisory role *vis à vis* the DCI and would lose the representational dominance they held in USCIB. Despite the services' objections, in 1958 the United States Intelligence Board (USIB) was created to assume the duties of the IAC and USCIB. As with the IAC, USIB worked mostly through interdepartmental subcommittees in specialized areas.

Like the IAC, USIB was little more than a superstructure. It had no budgetary authority, and did not provide the DCI with any direct control over the components of the intelligence community. The separate elements of the community continued to function under the impetus of their own internal drives and mission definitions. Essentially, the problem that existed at the time of the creation of CIG remained.

From 1953 to 1961 a single Presidential administration and consistent American policy objectives which had wide public and governmental support contributed to a period of overall stability in the CIA's history.[15] Allen Dulles' orientation and policymakers' operational reliance on the Agency made clandestine activities the dominant CIA mission. The ethos of secrecy within the DDP allowed the Directorate exemption from the usual accountability procedures resulting in a large degree of independence in the conduct of operations.

The Agency's intelligence production, though distinguished by advances in technical collection and in analysis, had not achieved the consistent policy support role that had been the primary purpose for the CIA's creation. While Dulles may have served as the briefing officer during NSC meetings, in the day-to-day conduct of foreign policy policymakers did not look to the Agency for information and analyses.

The Agency was equally unsuccessful in fulfilling its interdepartmental coordination function. The inherent institutional obstacles to management of the community's intelligence activities combined with Dulles' indifference to this area of responsibility allowed the perpetuation of a fragmented government-wide intelligence effort.

---

[15] For chart showing CIA organization as of 1961, see p. 99.

PART THREE

CHANGE AND ROUTINIZATION, 1961–1970

INTRODUCTION

In the 1960's as in the previous decade the CIA's covert operational capability dominated Agency activities. Policymakers' reliance on covert action fostered the CIA's utilization of its existing operational capabilities as well as an increase in paramilitary activities in support of counterinsurgency and military programs. In intelligence production the Agency expanded its areas of specialization, but senior government officials still did not consistently draw on the DDI's intelligence analysis or on the DCI for policy support.

The most significant development for the Agency during this period was the impact of technological capabilities on intelligence production. These advances resulted in internal changes and necessitated increased attention to coordinating the activities of the intelligence community. The large budgetary resources involved and the value of technical collection systems precipitated major bureaucratic battles and pointed up the increasing, rather than diminishing, problems surrounding interagency participation in the intelligence process. Despite the Agency's internal adjustments and a sustained effort in the early 1960's to effect better management in the community, the CIA's fundamental structure, personnel, and incentives remained rooted in the early 1950's.

Beginning in the fall of 1961 the CIA vacated its scattered array of buildings in downtown Washington and moved to its present structure in Langley, Virginia. Allen Dulles had lobbied long and hard to acquire a single building for the Agency. Reasons of efficiency and the need for improved security dictated the move. Several locations were considered, including a building in the city. However, no single downtown structure could accommodate all the Agency employees stationed in Washington and also provide the requisite security for the clandestine component. The availability of land in Langley, eight miles from the city, made a new building there seem the ideal solution.

The effects of the move are difficult to gauge. Some have argued that the building has encouraged interchange between the DDI and the DDP, making the Agency a more integrated organization. That benefit seems marginal, given the procedural and institutional barriers between the two directors. A more significant effect may be on the negative side, specifically the physical isolation of the Agency from the policymakers it was created to serve.

In 1961, Cold War attitudes continued to shape the foreign policy assumptions of United States officials. One need only recall the militant tone of John F. Kennedy's January 1961 inaugural address to appreciate the accepted definition of the United States role. The Soviet pronouncement ending the moratorium on nuclear testing in July 1961 and the erection of the Berlin Wall a month later reinforced existing attitudes. In the early years of the decade, American confidence and conviction were manifested in an expansive foreign policy that included the abortive Bay of Pigs invasion, a dramatic confrontation with the Soviet Union over the installation of Soviet missiles in Cuba, increased economic assistance to underdeveloped countries in Latin America and Africa, and rapidly escalating military activities in Southeast Asia.

Although the American presence in Vietnam, beginning in 1963, symbolized U.S. adherence to the strictures of the Cold War, perceptions of the Soviet Union had begun to change. The image of an international communist monolith began breaking down as differences between the U.S.S.R. and the People's Republic of China emerged. Moreover, the strategic arms competition assumed increased importance in Soviet-American relations. By the mid-1960's the Soviet Union possessed a credible, but minimal, nuclear deterrent against the United States; by the end of the decade the two nations were approaching strategic parity. Soviet advances provided the impetus for efforts at arms control and for attempts at greater cooperation in cultural and economic areas. The CIA was drawn into each of these major developments in United States policy.

1. The Directors of Central Intelligence, 1961–1970

In the 1950's Allen Dulles had given his personal stamp to the Agency and in large measure independently defined his role as DCI. In the next decade the successive Presidents, John F. Kennedy, Lyndon B. Johnson, and Richard M. Nixon, had a greater influence on the role of the DCI—his stature and his relative position among policymakers.

John A. McCone, November 1961–April 1965

John McCone came to the Central Intelligence Agency as an outsider. His background had been in private industry, where he had distinguished himself as a corporate manager. Trained as an engineer, McCone entered the construction business and rose to become Executive Vice President of Consolidated Steel Corporation. Later in his career, he founded his own engineering firm, and during World War II became involved in shipbuilding and aircraft production. Following the war, he served on several government committees and held the position of Under Secretary of the Air Force. In 1958, McCone was named to the Atomic Energy Commision, and later that year he took over as its chairman.

The Bay of Pigs failure precipitated President Kennedy's decision to replace Allen Dulles and to appoint a DCI who had a more detached view of the Agency's operational capability. McCone brought a quick, sharp intellect to his job as DCI, and he devoted much of his attention to sorting out management problems at the community level. His political independence as a staunch Republican in a Democratic administration as well as his personal confidence made him a strong and assertive figure among policymakers.

Unquestionably, the missile crisis in October 1962 solidified McCone's place in the Kennedy Administration as an active participant in the policy process. The human and technical resources that the

Agency brought to bear—U-2 flights over Cuba, overhead reconnaissance over the U.S.S.R., supplemented by agents in both places—clearly identified the Agency's contribution in a period of crisis and enhanced McCone's position as DCI. McCone resigned in 1965 because Lyndon Johnson had not accorded him the stature and access he had enjoyed under Kennedy.

Vice-Admiral William Raborn, April 1965–June 1966

At the time of his appointment as DCI Vice-Admiral William Raborn had retired from the Navy and was employed in the aerospace industry. A graduate of Annapolis, Raborn had had a successful Naval career as an administrator and combat officer. His most significant accomplishment was his participation in the development of the Polaris missile system. Immediately prior to his retirement from the Navy in 1963, Raborn served as Deputy Chief of Naval Operations. He was Director of Central Intelligence for only a year, and his impact on the Agency was minimal.

Richard M. Helms, June 1966–February 1973

Richard Helms became DCI following nearly twenty-five years in the Clandestine Service. Just as Allen Dulles had identified himself with the intelligence professions, Helms identified himself with the Agency as an institution. Having served in a succession of senior positions since the early 1950's, Helms was a first-generation product of the CIA, and he commanded the personal and professional respect of his contemporaries.

Helms' international orientation began early. Most of his secondary education consisted of private schooling in Germany and Switzerland. After graduating from Williams College in 1935, he worked as a journalist. In 1942, he joined the service and was assigned to OSS. Helms remained an intelligence officer through the transitions to SSU and the Central Intelligence Group. As a member of the CIA's Office of Special Operations, he rose to become Deputy Assistant Director for Special Operations. An excellent administrator, he served as Assistant Deputy Director for Plans (ADDP) under both Wisner and Bissell. In 1963 Helms was named DDP and was appointed Deputy Director of Central Intelligence (DDCI) under Raborn.

As Director of Central Intelligence, Helms' interests remained on the operations side, and he did not display a strong interest in the management problems related to the intelligence community. One colleague stated that "during his term as Director, Helms ran the DDP out of his hip pocket." Helms labored under the difficulty of two Presidents who were not receptive to the DCI's function as senior intelligence officer. Lyndon Johnson was mired in Vietnam and bent on a military victory; Richard Nixon had an inherent distrust of the Agency and preferred to work within his White House staff. Neither President gave the DCI the opportunity to fulfill his role as chief intelligence advisor.

II. The Clandestine Service

A. Clandestine Activities, 1961–1970

The Clandestine Service dominated the Agency's activities during this period. In budget, manpower, and degree of DCI attention accorded the DDP, clandestine operations remained the CIA's most consuming mission. The DDP continued to function as a highly compartmented structure with small groups of individuals responsible for and privy to selected activities. That ethos unquestionably fostered and supported the development of such excessive operations as assassination plots against foreign leaders. Nonetheless, the policies and operational preferences of the Executive branch dictated the priorities in the Agency's activities.

Evidence of Communist guerrilla activities in Southeast Asia and Africa convinced President Kennedy and his closest advisors, including Robert Kennedy and General Maxwell Taylor, of the need for the United States to develop an unconventional warfare capability. "Counterinsurgency," as the U.S. effort was designated, aimed at preventing Communist-supported military victories without precipitating a major Soviet-American military confrontation. Simultaneously, the CIA was called on to develop and employ its paramilitary capabilities around the world. In the decade of the 1960's, paramilitary operations became the dominant CIA clandestine activity, surpassing covert psychological and political action in budgetary allocations by 1967.

Political action, propaganda, and operations involving international organizations continued. By the early 1960's the DDP had developed the infrastructure—assets in place—which allowed the development of continuing activities. The combination of the paramilitary surge and self-sustaining operations made the period 1964 to 1967 the most active for the execution of covert activities.

In the 1950's the administrative arrangements in the DDP were highly centralized. The DDP or his assistant, the ADDP, personally approved every project initiated either at Headquarters or in the field. By 1960 the delegation of approval authority became a bureaucratic necessity. Because the number of projects had proliferated, no one or two individuals could either efficiently act on or competently make judgments on the multitude of proposed activities. In 1960 a graduated approval process began to develop in the DDP, whereby Station Chiefs and Division Chiefs were authorized to approve projects, depending on cost and potential risk factors. The more sensitive projects were referred to the ADDP, the DDP, or the DCI. The extent to which the procedural changes affected the number and nature of projects approved is unclear.

Under the direction of the Kennedy Administration, paramilitary programs were initiated in Cuba, Laos, and Vietnam. The failure of the Bay of Pigs did not diminish senior officials' conviction that the U.S. had to take offensive action against the Cuban government. It is difficult to appreciate the near obsession that characterized attitudes toward Fidel Castro in the first two years of the Kennedy Administration. The presence of an avowed Communist leader ninety miles from the Florida coastline was regarded as an intrusion on U.S. primacy in the Western Hemisphere and as a direct threat to American security.

Between October 1961 and October 1962, the Agency conducted Operation MONGOOSE. The program consisted of collection, paramilitary, sabotage, and political propaganda activities, aimed at discrediting and ultimately toppling the Castro government. MONGOOSE was administered through a special Headquarters Task Force (Task Force W) that was comprised of some of the most able DDP "idea men" and operators. Describing the intensity of the Agency's effort and the breadth of activities that were generated, one former Task Force W member stated "It was very simple; we were at war with Cuba."

The Cuban effort coincided with a major increase in the Agency's overall Latin American program. The perception of a growing Soviet presence in the Western Hemisphere both politically and through guerrilla activity in Peru, Bolivia, and Colombia resulted in a 40% increase in the size of the Western Hemisphere Division between 1960 and 1965.[1]

In the early 1960's the decolonization of Africa sparked an increase in the scale of CIA clandestine activities on that continent. CIA actions paralleled growing interest on the part of the State Department and the Kennedy Administration in the "third world countries," which were regarded as a line of defense against the Soviet Union. The government-wide assumption was that the Soviet Union would attempt to encroach on the newly independent African states. Prior to 1960, Africa had been included in the European or Middle Eastern Division. In that year it became a separate division. Stations sprang up all over the continent. Between 1959 and 1963 the number of CIA stations in Africa increased by 55.5%. Apart from limiting Communist advances through propaganda and political action, the Agency's African activities were directed at gaining information on Communist China, the Soviet Union, and North Korea.

The Agency's large-scale involvement in Southeast Asia began in 1962 with programs in Laos and Vietnam. In Laos, the Agency implemented air supply and paramilitary training programs, which gradually developed into full-scale management of a ground war. Between 1962 and 1965, the Agency worked with the South Vietnamese Government to organize police forces and paramilitary units. After 1965, the CIA engaged in a full-scale paramilitary assistance program to South Vietnam. The CIA program paralleled the escalating U.S. military commitment to South Vietnam.

The Agency's extensive operational involvement in Southeast Asia had a tangible impact on the leadership within the DDP. By 1970, large numbers of individuals began retiring from the Agency. Essentially, these were the first-generation CIA professionals who had begun their careers in the late 1940's. Many were OSS veterans who had been promoted to senior positions early and remained. As these men began leaving the Agency, many of their positions were filled by individuals who had distinguished themselves in Southeast Asia-related activities. In the Clandestine Service—the present Deputy Director for Operations,[2] his predecessor, the Chief of the Counterintelligence Staff, and the Deputy Chief of the Soviet/East European Division all spent considerable time in the Far East at the height of the Agency's effort there.

By the end of the decade, the level of covert operations began to decline. Measured in terms of project numbers, budgetary expenditures

---

[1] Following the Bay of Pigs, an interagency inspection team recommended an increase in the Western Hemisphere Division to improve U.S. intelligence capabilities in Latin America.

[2] In 1973 DCI James Schlesinger changed the name of the Clandestine Service from the Directorate for Plans to the Directorate for Operations.

and personnel, the DDP's covert operations diminished between 1967 and 1971. The process of reduction extended over several years and derived principally from factors outside the Agency.

The most conspicuous intrusion into CIA operations was the 1967 *Ramparts* magazine article, which exposed CIA funding of international student groups, foundations, and private voluntary organizations that had begun in the 1950's. The revelations resulted in President Johnson's appointment of a three-person committee to examine the CIA's covert funding of American educational and private voluntary organizations operating abroad. Chaired by the Under Secretary of State, Nicholas Katzenbach, the Committee included DCI Richard Helms and Secretary of Health, Education and Welfare, John Gardner. After conducting its review, the Katzenbach Committee recommended that no federal agency provide covert financial assistance to American educational and voluntary institutions. The Katzenbach Report prompted an internal CIA examination of its domestic-based organizational activities. Although the Agency complied with the strict terms of the Katzenbach guidelines, funding and contact arrangements were realigned so that overseas activities could continue with little reduction. Overall, funding to educational or private voluntary organizations constituted a small proportion of covert activity, and the Katzenbach Report did not affect major operations in the areas of overseas political action, labor, and propaganda.

Government-wide personnel cutbacks had a wider impact on covert operations. In 1967 and 1969, concern over the U.S. balance of payments deficit prompted Executive Orders reducing the number of federal employees stationed overseas. Budgetary limitations imposed by the Office of Management and Budget and State Department restrictions on the number of cover positions made available to CIA personnel also contributed to significant reductions in DDP personnel.

By the end of the decade, internal concern developed over the problem of exposure for large-scale operations. It was this factor that determined Helms' 1970 decision to transfer the budgetary allocations for operations in Laos from the CIA to the Defense Department. Gradually, senior Agency personnel began to recognize the cumulative effects of long-term subsidies to and associations with political parties, media, and agents overseas—a large presence invited attention and was vulnerable to exposure.

During this period of escalation and decline in covert operations, clandestine collection was also undergoing some changes. As indicated in the preceding chapter, in the 1950's much of the DDP's clandestine information had, for a variety of reasons, come from liaison relationships with host governments. By the early 1960's the Clandestine Service had developed its own capability and was less dependent on liaison for executing its clandestine collection function. DDP case officers had had approximately ten years to engage in the long-range process of spotting, assessing, cultivating, and recruiting agents.

As Deputy Director for Plans from 1962 to 1965, Richard Helms attempted to upgrade the DDP's clandestine collection mission. Helms had been an OSO officer and, in contrast to both Wisner and Bissell, his professional identity had been forged on the "collection" side of the Clandestine Service. In the early 1960's, Helms embarked on a concerted effort to improve DDP training to produce officers who could recruit agents as well as maintain liaison relationships.

Technological developments had a major impact on clandestine collection "targets"—the specific objects of an agent's collection effort.[3] From at least the early 1950's, information related to Soviet strategic capabilities was a continuous priority for clandestine human source collection. However, the difficulties of access to the Soviet Union and Eastern Europe—the so-called "denied areas"—left even the most basic information out of the reach of human collection. Reconnaissance filled that gap, providing hard data on Soviet strategic deployments—locations of missile sites, production centers, and transport facilities. With the acquisition of these broad categories of information, human collection was redirected to more specific targets, including research and development.

B. Executive Authorization

During the 1962–1970 period, procedures for Executive authorization of covert action projects became more regularized, and criteria for approval became more strictly defined. In large part these procedural changes reflected a belated recognition that covert operations were no longer exceptional activities undertaken in extraordinary circumstances. Instead, covert operations had become an ongoing element in the conduct of U.S. foreign policy and required formalized channels of review and approval.

Although the approving bodies went through a number of name changes and adjustments in membership, fundamental assumptions governing review remained the same. Each group functioned in a way that blurred accountability for decisions; no participant was required to sign off on individual decisions; and the frequency of meetings was irregular. The absence of strict accountability was intentional. By shielding the President and senior officials from direct association with covert operations, it was possible for the Chief of State to publicly deny responsibility for an exposed operation. Such was the theory. In fact, as the Soviet attack on the U–2 in May 1960 illustrated, the President has historically assumed ultimate responsibility for U.S. actions.

During the Kennedy Administration the Special Group served as the review body for covert action. The Taylor Report in June 1961 redefined the membership of the Group in an effort to insure better review and coordination for the anticipated expansion in paramilitary activities. It was not until 1963 that formal criteria developed for submitting covert action projects to the Group. Until then, the judgment of the DCI had determined whether an Agency-originated project was submitted to the Group and its predecessor bodies for authorization. In 1963 project cost and risk became the general criteria for determining whether a project had to be submitted to the Special Group. Although the specific criteria were not established in writing, the Agency used $25,000 as the threshold amount, and all projects at that level and above were submitted for approval. Agency officials judged the relative risk of a proposed project—its potential for exposure, possibility for success, political sensitivity.

---

[3] "Target" refers to the specific source through which information may be obtained, e.g., a scientist or a research laboratory may be a target for Soviet technological innovation.

The Kennedy Administration's initiation of large-scale paramilitary activities resulted in the creation of two additional working groups, the Special Group on Counterinsurgency (CI), and the Special Group (Augmented). The Special Group (CI) had only three members, General Maxwell Taylor, the President's Military Advisor, McGeorge Bundy, the Assistant for National Security Affairs, and Attorney General Robert Kennedy. Established in January 1963, the Special Group (CI) was to provide coordination for counterinsurgency programs. The Special Group (Augmented) was responsible for supervising only one operation, MONGOOSE. The members of this body included McGeorge Bundy, Deputy Secretary of Defense, Roswell Gilpatric, Under Secretary of State, U. Alexis Johnson, Chairman of the JCS, Lyman Lemnitzer, McCone, Taylor and Robert Kennedy. The Special Group (Augmented) engaged in close supervision of and liaison with CIA officials regarding the execution of the MONGOOSE program. Following the disbandment of the operation in October 1962, the Special Group (Augmented) was dissolved.

The changes that occurred under Lyndon Johnson and Richard Nixon demonstrated that the review process remained subject to the working habits and preferences of individual Presidents. During the Johnson Administration, the Special Group was renamed the 303 Committee. However, the real forum for NSC-level decisions became the "Tuesday Lunches," a luncheon meeting at the White House that included President Johnson, Helms, McNamara, Bundy (later his successor Walt Rostow), the Chairman of the Joint Chiefs of Staff, and the Press Secretary to the President. These discussions were dominated by the subject of military operations in Vietnam, and the informality of the meetings fostered consensual fuzziness rather than hard choices.

In February 1970, the basic directive governing covert action authorization, NSC 5412/2, was replaced by National Security Decision Memorandum (NSDM) 40. That directive spelled out the duties of the newly-designated 40 Committee, which replaced the Special Group as the Executive decisionmaking body on covert operations.[4] NSDM 40 restated the DCI's responsibility for coordinating and controlling covert operations. Its only real modification from the 5412/2 directive was a provision that the 40 Committee annually review covert action projects previously approved.

A major shortcoming in the review process was the limited number of projects subject to external authorization. The vast majority of covert action projects were initiated and approved within the Agency. Moreover, whole categories of projects were exempt from outside authorization. Covert political action projects—those involving political parties, the press, media, and labor unions—are often made possible and supported by the existence of clandestine collection projects. The assets maintained through these projects provide access and information and serve as conduits for resources. Despite their importance to covert action projects and their frequently indistinguishable function, such projects were not defined as covert action and therefore were exempt from external authorization.

In the field covert action coordination between the State Department and the CIA was a continuing problem. Since the relationship between

---

[4] The 40 Committee members included the President's Assistant for National Security Affairs, the Deputy Secretary of Defense, the Under Secretary of State for Political Affairs, the Chairman of the Joint Chiefs of Staff, and the DCI.

Ambassadors and Chiefs of Station was not strictly defined, consultation between State and CIA was uneven. Ambassadors were generally informed of broad covert action programs undertaken in the host country but frequently did not know the details—identities of agents, methods of action, scope of the program. Some Ambassadors preferred not to know the extent of CIA activity, regarding it a diplomatic liability to be too closely identified with the CIA. Still, it was not unusual for Ambassadors themselves to recommend or request the initiation of covert intervention to bring about political conditions more favorable to U.S. policy. In each case, the kind of information an Ambassador received was dependent on his preference for being informed, his disposition to assert his prerogatives, and his relationship with the CIA Station Chief.

Efforts to improve coordination and to give the Ambassador a more formalized role were ineffective. In 1961 President Kennedy addressed a letter to all Ambassadors, indicating their responsibilities to oversee and coordinate all Embassy activities. A similar letter was addressed to Ambassadors by President Nixon in 1969. These Presidential initiatives did not fundamenetally alter relationships in the field. Having no direct authority over the Station Chief, an Ambassador could only make requests in his capacity as head of the "country team"—the ranking government agency representatives posted to the Embassy. He could not make demands or exercise formal control based on a position of recognized seniority. In terms of overall foreign policy coordination the situation was less than satisfactory.[4a]

C. Congressional Review

In the mid-1960's, international developments resulted in increased congressional demands for intelligence information. The 1967 Middle East War, advances in space technology, and nuclear proliferation contributed to heightened Congressional interest in the intelligence product. In response to Congressional requests DCI Richard Helms increased the number of briefings to committees, subcommittees and individual members. In 1967 thirteen Congressional committees, in addition to the four with oversight functions, received substantive intelligence briefings.

The increased Congressional demand for the intelligence product did not alter the closed, informal nature of Congressional oversight. Both John McCone and Richard Helms maintained good relationships with senior-ranking committee members, who were kept informed on an individual basis of important CIA activities. Cursory review of CIA activities continued to characterize the subcommittees' functions. In 1966 Senator Eugene McCarthy again sponsored a bill for the establishment of a CIA oversight committee, but the effort failed. Oversight had not progressed from information sharing to scrutiny.

III. The Effort at Management Reform

Technological developments forced attention to the problem of coordinating the collection activities of the departmental intelligence components. The costs of technical collection systems and competition for their deployment necessitated some working relationship to replace the undirected evolution that had marked the intelligence community

---

[4a] In 1974 the Ambassador's responsibilities for coordinating field activities were outlined by statute, but the same problems remain.

in the decade of the 1950's. During McCone's directorship, the problem was identified more specifically than it had been before, yet the obstacles to coordination were considerable. Later, the pressures of Vietnam, the changes in Executive decisionmaking, and the personal interests of the DCIs once again relegated community problems to a low priority.

The Bay of Pigs fiasco had a major impact on John F. Kennedy's thinking about the intelligence community. He felt he had been poorly served by the experts and sought to establish procedures that would better ensure his own acquisittion of intelligence judgments. In short, Kennedy defined a need for a senior intelligence officer and in so doing assured John McCone access and influence. The fact that McCone was known to have that access—he had a regular weekly meeting alone with the President—provided him with a degree of stature and leverage among the Departments which strengthened his role in the community.

Kennedy defined the DCI's role in a letter sent to McCone on January 16, 1962. In it Kennedy gave primary emphasis to the DCI's function as coordinator for the community and as principal intelligence officer for the President. The letter read, in part:

> In carrying out your newly assigned duties as DCI, it is my wish that you serve as the government's principal foreign intelligence officer, and as such that you undertake as part of your responsibility, the coordination and effective guidance of the total U.S. foreign intelligence effort. As the government's principal intelligence officer, you will assure the proper coordination, correlation, and evaluation of intelligence from all sources and its prompt dissemination to me and to other recipients as appropriate. In fulfillment of these tasks, I shall expect you to work closely with the heads of all departments and agencies having responsibilities in the foreign intelligence field. . . .
>
> As head of the CIA, while you will continue to have overall responsibility for the Agency, I shall expect you to delegate to your principal deputy, as you may deem necessary, so much of the direction of the detailed operation of the Agency as may be required to permit you to carry out your primary task as DCI. . . .

The letter drew a sharp distinction between McCone's responsibilities as head of the Agency and as coordinator for the community. Kennedy's action was in part an attempt to rectify Allen Dulles' conspicuous neglect of community affairs.[5] For any DCI, the demands of managing an organization with thousands of employees, overseeing a community nearly ten times the Agency's size, as well as keeping informed on substantive intelligence matters to brief the President, were excessive. Kennedy's instructions regarding the administration of the Agency were intended to relieve McCone of his internal responsibilities to allow him to better fulfill his roles in intelligence and interdepartmental coordination.

Although McCone agreed with Kennedy's concept of the DCI's job and vigorously pursued the President's objectives, the results were uneven. Following a 1961 study directed by Lyman B. Kirkpatrick,

---

[5] Between July and October 1961, PFIAB had, once again, recommended a redefinition of the role of the DCI.

the Agency Inspector General, several organizational changes were made in the Office of the Director. The most important change was the creation of a new position, Executive Director-Comptroller.[6] Kirkpatrick was appointed to the post, and his job was to assume most of the responsibility for internal management. In practice, the altered system did not significantly limit the DCI's involvement in Agency-related administrative matters. This was particularly true for issues involving the Clandestine Service. The fundamental nature of clandestine operations, the fact that they involved people in sensitive, complicated situations, demanded that the Agency's highest ranking official assume responsibility for decisions. A former member of McCone's staff stated that despite his community orientation, McCone spent 90 percent of his time on issues related to clandestine activities.[7]

From 1963 to 1966, much of the Agency's community effort was directed toward working out an agreement with the Air Force on overhead reconnaissance programs. The major issue was whether the CIA would continue to have an independent capability for the design and development of space systems. In 1961, the Agency and the Air Force had established a working relationship for overhead reconnaissance through a central administrative office, comprised of a small staff of CIA, Air Force, and Navy representatives. Its director reported to the Secretary of Defense, but accepted intelligence requirements through USIB. Budget appropriations for the central office came through the Air Force. Under the agreement, the Air Force provided the missiles, bases, and recovery capability for reconnaissance systems, and the CIA was responsible for research and development, contracting, and security. Essentially, this arrangement left the Agency in control of the collection program. Since a primary mission was at stake, the Air Force was not willing to relinquish control over development, production, and deployment to the Agency.

Two other factors magnified the reconnaissance program's importance to the Air Force. First, with the advent of intercontinental ballistic missiles (ICBMs), the manned bomber had lost its primacy in strategic planning. Second, when the civilian-controlled National Aeronautics and Space Administration (NASA) was created in 1958, the Air Force had been deprived of directing the overall U.S. areospace program. Because of these developments, the Air Force, particularly the Strategic Air Command, looked upon overhead reconnaissance as yet another mission that was being snatched away.

The Agency recognized that it could not assume management responsibility for reconnaissance systems, once developed. Missiles, launch sites, and recovery capabilities were not elements in the Agency's repertoire. Thus, whatever claims the CIA made for research and development, the Agency was dependent on the Air Force for administering the systems.[8]

---

[6] Other changes included placing the General Counsel's office, Audit Staff, Comptroller, Office of Budget, Program Analysis and Manpower directly under the DCI and establishing a separate Office of legislative counsel.

[7] An Agency employee characterized the three functional Directorates this way: "The DDI is a production outfit and can run itself, the DDS&T spends money, but the DDP always involves people problems."

[8] There were some within the Agency who favored CIA control over all phases of the reconnaissance program, but they were in the minority.

These factors complicated an already complex rivalry. Control by one agency or another involved more than budgets, manpower, and access to photography. A decision would affect the nature of the reconnaissance program itself. Given its mission, the Air Force was interested in tactical information, which required high resolution photography. The CIA, on the other hand, was committed to procuring national intelligence, essentially long-range strategic information. This required an area search capability, one with broad coverage but low resolution. Also at issue was the question of who would determine targeting and frequency of coverage, i.e., the establishment of requirements. If the Air Force assumed responsibility, its decisions would reflect its tactical orientation; if the Agency decided, national intelligence requirements would have precedence.

While the rivalry between the Air Force and the CIA was intense, the competition within the Department of Defense was equally acute. The Air Force determination to secure control of the reconnaissance program jeopardized the Secretary of Defense's capacity to utilize reconnaissance data. The information generated by photographic collection was crucial to the Secretary of Defense in making independent judgments on weapons procurement and strategic planning. If the Air Force controlled the reconnaissance program, the service would gain an enormous advantage in pressing its own claims. Secretary of Defense Robert McNamara was aware of the threat which the Air Force posed. In the protracted negotiations over the national reconnaissance program McNamara became McCone's ally against the Air Force in order to maintain the independence of his own position.

In August 1965, an agreement was reached that gave the Agency and the Secretary of Defense decisionmaking authority over the national reconnaissance program. A three-person Executive Committee (EXCOM) for the management of overhead reconnaissance was established. Its membership included the DCI, an Assistant Secretary of Defense, and the President's Science Advisor. The EXCOM reported to the Secretary of Defense, who was assigned primary administrative authority for overhead reconnaissance. The arrangement recognized the DCI's right as head of the community to establish collection requirements in consultation with USIB and gave him responsibility for processing and utilizing reconnaissance-produced data. To balance the Secretary of Defense's authority, the DCI could appeal to the President in the event he disagreed with the Secretary's decision.[9]

The agreement represented a compromise between military and Agency claims and provided substantive recognition of the DCI's national intelligence responsibility. As a decisionmaking structure, it has worked well. However, it has not rectified the inherent competition over technical collection systems that has come to motivate the intelligence process. The development of these systems has created in-

---

[9] In 1967, the Committee on Imagery Requirements and Exploitation (COMIREX) succeeded COMOR as the USIB subcommittee responsible for the management of collection planning. Unlike COMOR, COMIREX also had responsibility for the distribution of imagery obtained through photographic and aerial reconnaissance programs.

tense rivalry, principally between the Air Force and the Agency, over development. With so much money and manpower at stake with each new system, each Agency is eager to gain the benefits of successful contracting.

Beyond the interagency agreement on the reconnaissance program, McCone took other initiatives to develop better community-wide co-ordination. The establishment of the office of National Intelligence Programs Evaluation (NIPE) in 1963 was the first major DCI effort to ensure consistent contact with other intelligence components. The NIPE staff had three major responsibilities: reviewing and evaluating intelligence community programs as a whole; establishing an inventory of intelligence activities to facilitate judgments regarding the cost and effectiveness of particular programs; and assessing USIB committee actions to implement priority national intelligence objectives. In each area, the NIPE staff was limited by the absence of regularized procedures among intelligence agencies, by these agencies' resistance to any effort to impose external direction, and by the sheer magnitude of the task.

For example, in attempting to develop a consolidated intelligence budget the staff confronted four different program packages. Signals Intelligence (SIGINT) was prepared in a Consolidated Cryptological Program, consisting of the National Security Agency budget and the activities of the military services' cryptological agencies. The budget for the Defense Intelligence Agency [10] included DIA's allocations as well as those of the military intelligence services. The overhead reconnaissance program had its own budget, and the CIA program was formulated on the basis of categories different from those of any other program. These arrangements made it exceedingly difficult to break down the costs for categories of activities within the respective agencies or for major subordinate components of the community. The first national intelligence budget was compiled in 1965, when the approximation of intelligence expenditures was several billion dollars.

The preliminary budgetary work of the NIPE staff resulted in the establishment of the National Intelligence Resources Board (NIRB) in 1968. The NIRB was to advise the DCI in making judgments on foreign intelligence resource needs. NIRB was chaired by the Deputy Director of Central Intelligence, and its members included the Director of the State Department's Bureau of Intelligence and Research (INR) and the Director of the DIA. By 1970, a centralized reporting mechanism existed, capable of providing community-wide budgetary information in national foreign intelligence programs. Despite these advances in compiling budgetary and program information as well as other efforts at coordination through USIB subcommittees, a real process of centralized management and allocation of resources did not exist. Budgetary authority rested with the Departments, each of which defined its programs in terms of its specific needs.

---

[10] The Defense Intelligence Agency (DIA) was created by Secretary of Defense Robert McNamara in 1961. Staffed by representatives from each of the services, DIA was intended to limit the existing duplication among the military intelligence services and to provide more objective intelligence analysis than that being produced by the service intelligence components.

IV. The Directorate of Science and Technology (DDS&T)

Internally, the Agency was also adjusting to the impact of technical and scientific advances. The debate between the Air Force and the CIA over the national reconnaissance program coincided with the Agency's organization of an independent directorate for science and technology. The developments in technical collection programs, including overhead reconnaissance and ELINT (electronic intercepts), made plain the necessity for centralizing collection and analysis of scientific intelligence. As early as 1957, there had been suggestions that CIA's technical and scientific activities be combined under a new directorate. Richard Bissell's insistence on maintaining close control over the U–2 program and Allen Dulles' traditionalist definition of intelligence prevented the change.

Immediately after his appointment, John McCone made the issue of technical and scientific organizational arrangements a priority. McCone was convinced of the importance of technical collection programs and regarded the creation of a separate directorate essential to effective management and utilization of these capabilities. The 1961 Kirkpatrick study also recommended integration and reinforced the DCI's own preference.

In 1961, scientific and technical intelligence operations were scattered among the three Directorates. The reconnaissance component had been transferred to the DDI under the title Development Projects Division (DPD); in the DDI, the Office of Scientific Intelligence conducted basic scientific and technological research; the Technical Services Division of the DDP engaged in research and development to provide operational support for clandestine activities; and the Office of ELINT in the DDP was responsible for electronic intercepts. Organizing an independent directorate meant wresting manpower and resources from existing components. The resistance was considerable, and a year and half passed between the first attempt at creating the directorate and its actual establishment.

McCone's announcement of the Directorate for Research (DDR) in 1962 precipitated the two major controversies which surrounded the consolidation of the existing components—DDI's claim to OSI and DDP's claim to TSD.[11] Unwilling to relinquish their respective components, officials in both Directorates thwarted the initial effort to organize the Research Directorate. In August 1963, in the second attempt to integrate the scientific and technological functions, the Directorate for Science and Technology (DDS&T) was organized. As its first Deputy Director, Albert Wheelon aggressively supervised the organization of the new Directorate.[12] The component included OSI, the Data Processing Staff, the Office of ELINT, the Development Projects Division, and a newly created Office of Research and Development. Later in 1963, the Foreign Missile and Space Analysis

---

[11] Bissell's departure early in 1962 removed the major obstacle to transfer of the DPD.
[12] Wheelon joined OSI in the late 1950's from Thompson, Ramo-Wooldridge, the technical research firm.

Center was added. Significantly, the DDP retained TSD, which continued to carry out all technical research and development related to clandestine activities as well as administering aircraft support for covert operations.[12a]

The DDS&T was organized on the premise that close cooperation should exist between research and application, on the one hand, and technical collection and analysis, on the other. The Directorate's specific functions included, and continue to include, research, development, operations, data reduction, analysis, and contributions to estimates. This close coordination and the staffing and career patterns in the Directorate have contributed to the continuing vitality and quality of DDS&T's work.

The DDP began and remained a closed, self-contained component; the DDI evolved into a closed, self-contained component. However, the DDS&T was created with the assumption that it would continue to rely on expertise and advice from outside the Agency. A number of arrangements ensured constant interchange between the Directorate and the scientific and industrial communities. First, since all research and development for technical systems was done through contracting, DDS&T could draw on and benefit from the most advanced technical systems nationwide. Second, to attract high-quality professionals from the industrial and scientific communities, the Directorate established a competitive salary scale. The result has been personnel mobility between the DDS&T and private industry. It has not been unusual for individuals to leave private industry, assume positions with DDS&T for several years, then return to private industry. This pattern provided the Directorate with a constant infusion and renewal of talent. Finally, the Directorate established the practice of regularly employing outside advisory groups as well as fostering DDS&T staff participation in conferences and seminars sponsored by professional associations.

In the early 1960's, the Agency acquired tacit recognition of its technical achievements among the departmental intelligence components. Within the intelligence community, DDS&T began to exercise informal influence through the chairmanship of several USIB subcommittees. DDS&T representatives chair the Joint Atomic Energy Intelligence Committee (JAEIC), the Scientific Intelligence Committee (SIC), the Guided Missiles Astronautics Intelligence Committee (GMAIC), and periodically, the SIGINT (Signals Intelligence) Committee.

V. Intelligence Production

During the 1961–1970 period, the Agency expanded its finished intelligence production in two important areas, strategic and economic analysis. Although the Agency had engaged in research in both fields, its jurisdiction had been limited. According to the 1951 agreement with the State Department, the DDI could only pursue economic analysis on the "Soviet Bloc," while the State Department retained authority for economic reporting on the "Free World." In the mili-

---

[12a] For chart showing CIA organization as of 1964, see p. 100.

tary sphere, Dulles had accepted the services' claims to production of strategic intelligence and had restricted internal efforts to expand the CIA's coverage of military problems. By 1962, the international environment and bureaucratic factors in the Agency and the Pentagon converged to produce greater demands for economic and strategic intelligence and to support the expansion of the CIA's capabilities.

A. Economic Research and Analysis

In the early 1950's, the Economic Research Area of ORR had directed most of its efforts to long-term, strategic research and analysis on the Soviet Union. At that time, economic intelligence had a limited audience among policymakers, since international affairs were defined in political terms. Even in the mid-1950's, when the Agency extended its economic research to include the "Free World" countries, economic intelligence was subsumed in analyses of Soviet political objectives. Referring to the period of the 1950's, a former ERA analyst said, "Our biggest problem was whether or not anybody would read our product."

It was not until the mid-1960's that economic intelligence acquired an importance of its own. The emergence of independent African nations and the view that the Soviet Union would engage in economic penetration of the fledging governments resulted in more specific requests for information on these countries' economies. Approximately 15 percent of ERA's professional strength shifted from so-called Sino-Soviet Bloc research to what was formally designated "Free World" research. Still, the focus remained on countries that were Soviet targets.

Since ORR did not have specific authorization for research on non-Communist countries, McCone worked out an agreement with Secretary of State Dean Rusk in March 1965 whereby CIA's activities in this area were formally sanctioned. The combination of McCone's relative strength and ORR's recognized competence allowed the DCI to seize the initiative at a time when the State Department record on economic reporting was weak. This informal agreement gave the CIA a tacit charter to pursue economic intelligence worldwide.

In 1967, a major change occurred, when a market developed for policy-oriented non-Communist economic intelligence. The growing economic strength of Japan and of the countries of Western Europe produced a related decline in the U.S. competitive posture and reflected the growing inadequacy of the dollar-dominated international monetary system. Economic analysts found themselves called upon for more detailed research on "Free World" countries as trading partners and rivals of the United States. In 1967, the economic analysis function gained office status with the establishment of the Office of Economic Research (OER), which succeeded ORR. The devaluation of sterling at the end of 1967 and the international monetary crisis a few months later created additional demands for detailed analysis and reporting on international monetary problems. OER began receiving formal requirements from the Treasury Department in June 1968.

The increasing demands for information produced a current intelligence orientation in OER as each component struggled to meet the requests for timely analysis. Publication became the vehicle for individual recognition, and short-term research began to dominate OER's production output. In FY 1968 OER produced 47 long-term research studies, provided 800 responses to specific requests from U.S. Government departments, and published 1075 current intelligence articles.

B. Strategic Research and Analysis

The growing importance of the strategic arms competition between the United States and the Soviet Union had important effects on the Agency's military intelligence effort. Although in the decade of the 1950's the Agency had made some contributions to military intelligence, it had not openly challenged the military's prerogative in the area. That opportunity came in the early 1960's. The combination of Secretary of Defense Robert McNamara's reliance on the Agency for analysis and John McCone's insistence on the DCI's necessity to have independent judgments on military matters resulted in the expansion of the CIA's strategic intelligence effort and the acceptance of the Agency's role as a producer of military analysis.

By 1962, three separate Offices were engaged in military-related research : OCI, OSI, and ORR. Each had at least one division devoted to strategic analysis. In OCI, the Military Division reported on missions and functions in Soviet weaponry. OSI provided technological information through its Offensive and Defensive Divisions.[13] In mid-1962, ORR's military research effort was consolidated into the Military-Economic Division.

McNamara's initiatives to the Agency influenced the DDI's military intelligence capabilities in two ways. First, they legitimized the CIA effort, and second they upgraded the quality of the product. As Secretary of Defense, McNamara introduced innovative management and strategic planning programs. In particular, he sought to make long-range program decisions by projecting foreign policy needs, military strategy, and budgetary requirements against force structures. The kinds of questions which McNamara posed required increasingly sophisticated and detailed research and analysis. Dissatisfaction with the quality of service-produced military estimates contributed to his establishing the Defense Intelligency Agency (DIA), although the stated reason was to reduce duplication. McNamara also turned to the CIA to procure better quality analysis. He requested special studies and estimates on questions of strategic planning.

One of McNamara's priorities was to request comparative assessments on Soviet-American military programs. The Secretary's requests precipitated, once again, the conflict between the military and the Agency on the issue of CIA access to information on U.S. military capabilities. Given the military's longstanding objections to providing the Agency with data, senior officials in the DDI were reluctant to accept McNamara's requests. When the Secretary insisted on the estimates, the CIA had difficulty obtaining the necessary information. At the same time analysts in both the Pentagon and the Agency questioned whether the requisite ruble-dollar conversion costs could be

---

[13] When DDS&T was created in 1963, OSI became part of that Directorate.

made.[14] When the Agency made its first projections, the Air Force challenged the results.

The Cuban missile crisis in October 1962 contributed to the Agency's capacity to make comparative estimates and to its claim to engage in military analysis. Before the crisis, McCone had argued that the DCI had to be informed of U.S. strategic capabilities in order to give adequate intelligence support to the President. McCone was one of the key participants in the deliberations during October 1962, and the Agency's contribution to the verification of Soviet missile emplacements in Cuba was crucial. During the crisis, McCone obtained the data he requested on U.S. force dispositions. This was a wedge he needed. Following the crisis, with encouragement from McNamara, he continued to make the requests. By the mid-1960's the DDI was procuring information on U.S. strategic planning on a regular basis. Consistent access to this data increased the Agency's information base considerably and further established the CIA's claims to strategic research.

Early in 1965, CIA's work in military-economic intelligence was formally recognized through an exchange of letters between McCone and the Deputy Secretary of Defense, Cyrus Vance. The letters constituted recognition that the CIA had primary responsibility for studies related to the cost and resource impact of foreign military and space programs. Essentially, the Defense Department was agreeing formally to what the Agency had informally been doing for over a decade.

In addition to requesting special studies and estimates from the DDI, McNamara included Agency personnel in joint CIA–DIA exercises in long-term Soviet force projections. In 1962, McNamara established the Joint Analysis Group (JAG). Composed of military officers from DIA and representatives from OSI and ORR, JAG provided regular assessments on Soviet and beginning in 1966, Chinese future military strengths. These judgments were known as National Intelligence Projections for Planning (NIPP).

The Vietnam War absorbed a large share of the DDI's research strength. Following the initiation of the bombing campaign against North Vietnam in 1965, ORR was called on to provide regular bomb damage assessments, including information on the flow of supplies and men to South Vietnam, the recuperability of supply centers, and details of shipping and cargoes.

By 1966 both the Office of Research and Reports and the Office of Current Intelligence had established special staffs to deal with Vietnam. In addition, the Special Assistant for Vietnam Affairs (SAVA) staff was created under the direction of the DCI. While the DDP effort was increasing in proportion to the American military buildup, DDI estimates painted a pessimistic view of the likelihood of U.S. success with repeated escalations in the ground and air wars. At no time was the institutional dichotomy between the operational and analytical components more stark.

The increased volume of requests from the Pentagon pointed up the unwieldy nature of the DDI production effort. With two Offices per-

---

[14] Another issue involved the question of whether NIEs should take account of U.S. forces. Sherman Kent, the Director of ONE, opposed using data on U.S. capabilities, fearing that ONE would be drawn into debates about U.S. military programs.

forming closely related functions under greater demands and with the Defense Department—at least at the civilian level—having sanctioned the Agency's activity in this area, individuals closely involved with strategic analysis began to press for consolidation and the establishment of an office-level component. Although recommendations were advanced as early as 1964, opposition to the changes existed at senior levels in the DDI. In 1966, however, a series of personnel changes elevated several people who had long favored consolidation to senior Directorate positions. With the approval of DCI Helms, the military intelligence units in OCI and ORR were combined into a separate Office, the Office of Strategic Research (OSR).

The decade of the 1960's brought increased attention to the problem of coordinating intelligence activities in the community but illustrated the complex difficulties involved in effective management. Departmental claims, the orientation of the DCI, the role accorded him by the President, and the demands of clandestine operations all affected the execution of the interdepartmental coordination role. Although policymakers were inconsistent in their reliance on the Agency's intelligence analysis capability, all continued to rely heavily on the CIA's operational capability to support their policies. That fact established the Agency's own priorities. Despite the Agency's growing sophistication and investment in technological systems, clandestine activities continued to constitute the major share of the Agency's budget and personnel. Between 1962 and 1970 the DDP budget averaged 52 percent of the Agency's total annual budget.[15] Likewise, in the same period, 55 percent of full-time Agency personnel were assigned to DDP activities.[16] Essentially, the pattern of activity that had begun to emerge in the early 1950's and that had become firmly established under Dulles continued.

---

[15] This does not include the proportion of the DDA budget that supported DDP activities.

[16] This figure includes those individuals in the communications and logistics components of the DDA, whose activities were in direct support of the DDP mission.

PART FOUR

THE RECENT PAST, 1971–1975

INTRODUCTION

The years 1971 to 1975 were a period of transition and abrupt change for the CIA. The administrations of DCIs James R. Schlesinger and William E. Colby both reflected and contributed to shifts in the CIA's emphases. Spurred on by increased attention from the Executive branch, intelligence production, the problems of the community, and internal management changes became the primary concerns of the DCIs. Essentially, the diminishing scale of covert action that had begun in the late 1960's and continued in this period both required and provided the opportunity for a redefinition in the Agency's priorities.

The decline in covert action was indicative of the broad changes that had evolved in American foreign policy by the early 1970's. Détente rather than cold war characterized the U.S. posture toward the Soviet Union, and retrenchment rather than intervention characterized U.S. foreign policy generally. The cumulative dissension over Vietnam, the Congress' more assertive role in foreign policy, and shifts in the international power structure eroded the assumptions on which U.S. foreign policy had been based. The consensus that had existed among the press, the informed public, the Congress, and the Executive branch and that had both supported and protected the CIA broke down. As conflicting policy preferences emerged and as misconduct in the Executive branch was revealed, the CIA, once exempt from public examination, became subject to close scrutiny. The Congress and even the public began to seek a more active role in the activities that Presidents and the Agency had for so long controlled.

Foreign affairs were a continuing priority in the Nixon Administration. Until 1971, Vietnam absorbed most of the time and attention of the President and his Special Assistant for National Security Affairs, Henry Kissinger. After 1971, both turned to a redefinition of United States foreign policy. Sharing a global view of U.S. policy, the two men sought to restructure relationships with the Soviet Union and the People's Republic of China. It was Kissinger rather than Nixon who maintained regular contact with DCIs Helms and Colby, and in effect, it was Kissinger rather than the DCIs who served as Nixon's senior intelligence advisor. Under Kissinger's direction the NSC became an intelligence and policy staff, providing analysis on such key issues as missile programs. The staff's small size and close proximity to policymakers allowed it to calibrate the needs of senior officials in a way that made their information more timely and useful than comparable CIA analyses.

Both Kissinger's and Nixon's preferences for working with (and often independently of) small, tightly managed staffs is well known. However, both were genuinely interested in obtaining more and better quality intelligence from the CIA. In December 1970 Nixon requested a study of the intelligence community. Executed by James Schlesinger, then Assistant Director of the Bureau of the Budget, the study resulted in a Presidential Directive of November 5, 1971, assigning the DCI formal responsibility for review of the intelligence community budget.[1] The intention was that the DCI would advise the President on budgetary allocations by serving in a last review capacity. As a result of the Directive, the Intelligence Resources Advisory Committee (IRAC) was established to advise the DCI in preparing a consolidated intelligence budget for the President.[1a]

The effort faltered for two reasons. First, Nixon chose not to request Congressional enactment of revised legislation on the role of the DCI. This decision inherently limited the DCI's ability to exert control over the intelligence components. The DCI was once again left to arbitrate with no real statutory authority. Second, the implementation of the Directive was less energetic and decisive than it might have been. Helms did not attempt to make recommendations on budgetary allocations and instead, presented the President with the agreed views of the intelligence components. Furthermore, within the Agency the mechanism for assisting the DCI in community matters was weak. Early in 1972 Helms established the Intelligence Community (IC) staff as a replacement for the NIPE staff to assist in community matters. Between the time of the decision to create such a staff and its actual organization, the number of personnel assigned was halved. Moreover, the staff itself was composed only of CIA employees rather than community-wide representatives. This arrangement limited the staff's accessibility to other components of the community, and was a contributing factor to the disappointing results of the Nixon Directive.[1b]

1. The Directors of Central Intelligence, 1973–1975

James Schlesinger's tenure as DCI from February to July 1973 was brief but telling. An economist by training, Schlesinger brought an extensive background in national security affairs to his job as DCI. He came to the position with definite ideas on the management of the community and on improving the quality of intelligence.

He began his career as a member of the University of Virginia faculty. From 1963 to 1969 he served as Director of Strategic Studies at the Rand Corporation. He was appointed Assistant Director of the Bureau of the Budget in 1969 and continued as Assistant Director during the transition to the Office of Management and Budget. In 1971 President Nixon named him Chairman of the Atomic Energy Commission. He left that position to become DCI. Schlesinger had a clear sense of the purposes intelligence should serve, and during his six-

---

[1] The directive was addressed to the Secretaries of State, Defense, and Treasury, the Attorney General, the Director, Office of Science and Technology, the Chairman of the Joint Chiefs of Staff, PFIAB, and the Atomic Energy Commission.

[1a] IRAC members included representatives from the Departments of State, Defense, OMB, and CIA.

[1b] For chart showing CIA organization as of 1972, see p. 101.

month term he embarked on a series of changes that promised to alter the Agency's and the DCI's existing priorities.

William E. Colby succeeded Schlesinger. An OSS veteran and career DDP officer, Colby's background made him seem of the traditional operations school in the Agency. His overseas assignments included positions in Rome, Stockholm and Saigon, where he was Chief of Station. Yet Colby brought an Agency and community orientation to his term as DCI that was uncommon for DDP careerists. Colby saw himself first as a manager—for both the Agency and the community—rather than an operator.

His position as Executive Director under Schlesinger exposed him to Schlesinger's ideas of reform and reinforced his own disposition for innovation. Well before public disclosures and allegations regarding CIA activities, Colby was committed to reconciling the Agency's priorities with changing public attitudes and expectations. Soon after his appointment, the Agency became the focus of public and Congressional inquiries, and most of the DCI's time was absorbed in responding to these developments.

II. Attempts at Redirection

A. Internal Changes

It is likely that had Schlesinger remained as DCI, he would have assumed a vigorous role in the community and would have attempted to exercise the DCI's latitude in coordinating the activities of the departmental intelligence services. Schlesinger's overall objectives were to maximize his role as Director of Central Intelligence rather than as head of the Agency and to improve the quality of the intelligence product.

To strengthen efforts at better management Schlesinger altered the composition of the IC Staff by increasing the number of non-Agency personnel. In this way he hoped to facilitate the Staff's contacts with the other components of the community.

Schlesinger felt strongly that the Agency was too large. On the operations side, he believed the DDO [2] was overstaffed in proportion to the needs of existing activities. In the area of intelligence production he identified size as impeding the ability of analysts to interact with policymakers. Within six months he reduced personnel by 7 percent—with most of the cuts occurring in the DDO.

Under Colby attempts at innovation continued. Consistent with his management orientation, Colby attempted to alter existing patterns of decisionmaking within the Agency, specifically in the DDO and the Office of National Estimates. The DDO staff structure had created enormous problems of competing claims on operational areas and had fostered the development of small "duchies."

The counterintelligence function had become a separate entity, administered independently of the divisions and controlled by a small group of officers. Under this arrangement counterintelligence was not an integrated element in the Agency's clandestine capability. By breaking down the exclusive jurisdiction of the staff, Colby attempted to

---

[2] Schlesinger changed the name of the Clandestine Service from the Directorate for Plans to the Directorate for Operations.

incorporate counterintelligence into the day-to-day operations of the geographical divisions.

Colby sought to force the DDO to interact with other elements of the Agency. He supported the transfer of the Technical Services Division (TSD) from the DDO to the DDS&T. At the time of the creation of the DDS&T senior officials in the DDO (then DDP) had opposed the transfer of TSD to the new Directorate. That opposition continued. However, in 1973 Colby ordered the transfer. In addition to achieving management consolidation in the area of technology, Colby was attempting to break down the DDO's insularity.

Colby's enactment of the system of Management by Objectives (MBO) in 1973 tried to alter DDO administrative patterns in another way. The MBO system was instituted throughout the Agency, but it potentially affected the DDO the most by attempting to replace the project-based system with specific program objectives against which projects were to be developed. Under MBO, related projects are aggregated into "programs" aimed at a policy objective. As such, the system is primarily a means of evaluation to measure performance against stated objectives. Although the DDO directive establishing MBO in January 1974 ordered the elimination of the project system for purposes of planning, projects remain the basic units for approval procedures and for budgeting at the station and division levels. Thus, the internal demand created by the project system remains. MBO was not intended to rectify the incentives for the generation of projects, and has not succeeded in replacing the project system administratively. The nature of DDO operations makes it difficult to quantify results and therefore limits the utility of MBO. For example, recruitment of three agents over a given period may result in little worthwhile information, while a single agent may produce valuable results.

The changes that occurred on the intelligence side were at least in part a response to existing dissatisfaction with the intelligence product at the policymaking level. The Board of National Estimates had become increasingly insulated from the policymaking process. In 1950 Langer, Smith and Jackson had established the Board with the assumption that senior experts would serve as reviewers for estimates drafted by the ONE staff. Over time the composition of the Board had changed considerably. Rather than continuing to draw on individuals from outside the Agency, the Board became a source of senior staff positions for DDI careerists themselves. Promotion to the Board became the capstone to a successful DDI analyst's career. This meant that the Office and the Board became insular and lacked the benefit of views independent of the DDI intelligence process.

The Office and the Board had become more narrowly focused in other ways as well. ONE had a staff of specialists in geographic and functional areas. In the process of drafting estimates ONE analysts often failed to interact with other DDI experts in the same fields. As intelligence analysis became more sophisticated and specialized, particularly in the economic and strategic areas, Board members' expertise often did not equal the existing level of analysis. Consequently, the Board could not fulfill its function of providing review and criticism. Overall, the intelligence product itself suffered. With little direct contact between ONE and senior policymakers, there was no

continuing link between the NIEs and the specific intelligence needs
of United States officials. On occasion, Special NIEs (SNIEs) responded to questions specifically posed by policymakers, e.g., if the
United States does such and such in Vietnam will the Chinese inter-
vene. Even these documents, however, were seen by policymakers as
seldom meeting their real needs. NIEs were defined and produced by
a small group of individuals whose perspective was limited by both
their lack of access to consumers and by their inbred drafting process.

After his appointment in 1973, when approximately half the Board
positions were vacant, Colby abolished ONE and the Board and established in their place the National Intelligence Officers (NIOs).
A group of eleven senior specialists in functional and geographic
areas, the NIOs are responsible for intelligence collection and production in their designated fields. The senior NIO reports to the DCI.
The NIOs serve two specific functions. First, they are the DCI's senior
substantive staff officers in their designated specialties. Second, they
are coordinators of the intellgence production machinery and are to
make recommendations to the DCI on intelligence priorities and the
allocation of resources within the communnty. Their access is community-wide including the DDO. Their job is not to serve as drafters
of national intelligence estimates but to force the community's intelligence machinery to make judgments by assigning the drafting of
estimates to analysts. They do not collectively review estimates in the
way that the Board did. Essentially, they are intended to serve as
managers and facilitators of information.

Colby was responsible for another management innovation, the
Key Intelligence Questions (KIQs). A major problem in the DCI's
fulfillment of his role as nominal leader of the intelligence community
has been his inability to establish community-wide priorities for the
collection and production of national intelligence. As DCI Colby
addressed the problem in managerial terms and defined a set of Key
Intelligence Questions (KIQs). By establishing specific categories of
information needs and by utilizing the NIOs to activate the community's responses, Colby hoped to encourage better policy-related
performance. A year after issuance of the KIQs, the NIOs and the
Director evaluated the community's responsiveness to the guidelines.
The KIQ system has not altered the agencies' independent determination of intelligence collection and production priorities. This applies to
the CIA as well as to DIA and the service intelligence agencies.[3]
Although the limitations of the KIQ system are a commentary on the
DCI's limited authority with regard to the Departments, the system
also represents a larger misconception. The notion that control can be
imposed from the top over an organization without some effort to
alter internal patterns and incentives is ill-founded.

These changes were accompanied by shifts in emphasis in the DDO
and the DDI. In the Clandestine Service the scale of covert operations was reduced, and by 1972 the Agency's paramilitary program in
Southeast Asia was dissolved. Yet, the overall reduction did not affect
the fundamental assumptions, organization, and incentives governing

---

[3] NSA appears to have integrated its requirements more closely with the KIQ
system.

the DDO. The rationale remained the same, and the operational capability was intact—as CIA activities in Chile illustrated. Presidents could and did continue to utilize the Agency's covert action capability. CIA operations in Chile included a wide range of the Agency's clandestine repertoire—political action, propaganda, economic activities, labor operations, and liaison relations. In clandestine collection Soviet strategic capabilities remain the first priority. Responding to recent international developments, the DDO expanded its collection activities in other areas, notably international narcotics traffic—with considerable success.

In the DDI, economic intelligence continued to assume increased importance and to take on new dimensions. In sharp contrast to the British intelligence service, which has for generations emphasized international economics, the DDI only recently has begun developing a capability in such areas as international finance, the gold market, and international economic movements. A major impetus for this change came in August 1971 with the U.S. balance of payments crisis. Since that time, the demands for international economic intelligence have escalated dramatically.

In 1974 the Office of Political Research (OPR) was established to provide in-depth foreign political intelligence analysis. OPR is the smallest of the DDI Offices. For the most part, OPR analysts are insulated from day-to-day requests to allow them to concentrate on larger research projects. The Office's creation represented recognition of the need for long-term political research, which was not being fulfilled in the existing DDI structure.[4]

B. Outside Review

Increased Congressional interest in the CIA's intelligence analysis continued in this period. However, oversight of the CIA did not keep abreast of demands for the intelligence product. In 1971 the CIA subcommittee of the Senate Armed Services Committee did not hold one formal meeting to discuss CIA activity; it met only once in 1972 and 1973. One-to-one briefings between the DCI and the senior members continued to characterize the arrangements for Congressional review.

In 1973 Representative Lucien Nedzi made this comment on CIA-Congressional relations:

> Indeed, it is a bit unsettling that 26 years after the passage of the National Security Act the scope of real Congressional oversight, as opposed to nominal Congressional oversight, remains unformed and uncertain.

Nedzi was reflecting the fact that no formalized reporting requirements existed between the CIA and the Congress, particularly with regard to the initiation of covert action. Judgment and informal arrangements dictated the procedures.

Two changes in this period signalled growing Congressional concern with the oversight function. Yet the changes did not alter the fundamental relationship between the Agency and the Congress, which continued to be one of mutual accommodation. Although both the DCI and the Congressional members who were involved in the process appear to have been satisfied with the frequency of exchange and quality of information provided, in 1973 unrest developed among younger members of the House Armed Services Committee who de-

[4] For chart showing CIA organization as of 1975, see p. 102.

manded reform in intelligence oversight. Committee Chairman Edward Hébert responded by appointing Nedzi to chair the CIA subcommittee, thus replacing Hébert himself.

In 1975 the Hughes-Ryan Amendment to the Foreign Assistance Act formalized the reporting requirements on covert action. Fundamentally, it increased the number of committees to be informed of covert operations by requiring that the Senate Foreign Relations Committee and the House International Affairs Committee receive appropriate briefings in addition to the four CIA subcommittees. The Amendment did not provide for prior notification or approval of covert action, and as such, still left Congress in the role of passive recipient of information.

The Hughes-Ryan Amendment also altered procedures in the Executive branch somewhat. The Amendment specified that the President himself must inform the Congress of decisions to implement covert operations and must certify that the program(s) are essential to U.S. policy. Until 1974, 40 Committee decisions on covert action were not always referred to the President. Only if there was a disagreement within the Committee or if a member of the Committee thought the proposed operation was important enough or sensitive enough would the President become involved. Once again, these ambiguous arrangements were intentional, designed to protect the President and to blur accountability. The Amendment forced the President both to be informed himself and to inform the legislative branch of covert activities. Congress' action, though limited, reflected the growing momentum for change in the standards of conduct and procedures governing U.S. foreign intelligence activities.

Public disclosures between 1973 and 1974 of alleged CIA domestic programs had contributed to Congress' demand for broader and more regularized participation in decisions regarding CIA activities. Soon after Schlesinger's appointment the Watergate scandal exposed the Agency to charges of involvement with Howard Hunt, former CIA employee. As a result of repeated allegations concerning Agency acquiescence in White House demands related to Watergate revelations, Schlesinger requested that all Agency employees report any past or existing illegal activities to him or the Agency Inspector General. In response, Agency employees presented their knowledge and recollections of 693 possible CIA violations of internal directives. Known as the "Family Jewels," the file was reviewed by the Office of the Inspector General and by then DCI William Colby.

The review revealed the Agency's extensive involvement in domestic intelligence activities—in violation of its foreign intelligence charter. In response to requests from the Federal Bureau of Investigation and from Presidents Johnson and Nixon the Agency had participated in several programs designed to collect intelligence on domestic political groups. Operation CHAOS, whose purpose was to determine whether or not domestic political dissidents, including students, were receiving foreign support, resulted in the Agency's collection of information on thousands of Americans. The Agency's mail opening program, conducted in partial cooperation with the FBI, was directed against political activists, protest organizations, and subversive and extremist groups in the United States. Although the program had begun in the early 1950's as a means of monitoring foreign intelligence activities in the United States, by the late 1960's it had taken on the additional purpose of domestic surveillance. Following the internal Agency review, the mail opening program and Operation CHAOS were discontinued.

In December 1974 newspaper disclosures made further allegations regarding CIA domestic activities. What had been consensual acceptance of the CIA's right to secrecy in the interests of national security was rejected. The Agency's vulnerability to these revelations was indicative of the degree to which American foreign policy and the institutional framework that supported that policy were undergoing redefinition. The closed system that had defined and controlled U.S. intelligence activities and that had left decisions in the hands of a small group of individuals began to break down. The assumptions, procedures and actions that had previously enjoyed unquestionable acceptance began to be reevaluated.

PART FIVE

CONCLUSIONS

The CIA was conceived and established to provide high-quality intelligence to senior policymakers. Since 1947 the Agency—its structure, its place within the government and its functions—has undergone dramatic change and expansion. Sharing characteristics common to most large, complex organizations, the CIA has responded to rather than anticipated the forces of change; it has accumulated functions rather than redefining them; its internal patterns were established early and have solidified; success has come to those who have made visible contributions in high-priority areas. These general characteristics have affected the specifics of the Agency's development.

The notion that the CIA could serve as a coordinating body for departmental intelligence activities and that the DCI could orchestrate the process did not take into account the inherent institutional obstacles posed by the Departments. From the outset no Department was willing to concede a centralized intelligence function to the CIA. Each insisted on the maintenance of its independent capabilities to support its policy role. With budgetary and management authority vested in the Departments, the Agency was left powerless in the execution of interdepartmental coordination. Even in the area of coordinated national intelligence estimates the Departments did not readily provide the Agency with the data required.

It was not until John McCone's term as DCI that the Agency aggressively sought to assert its position as a coordinating body. That effort demonstrated the complex factors that determined the relative success of community management. One of the principal influences was the support accorded the DCI by the President and the cooperation of the Secretary of Defense. In a situation where the DCI commanded no resources or outright authority, the position of these two individuals was crucial. While Kennedy and McNamara provided McCone with consistent backing in a variety of areas, Nixon and Laird failed to provide Helms with enough support to give him the necessary bureaucratic leverage.

It is clear that the DCIs' own priorities, derived from their backgrounds and interests, influenced the relative success of the Agency's role in interdepartmental coordination. Given the limitations on the DCI's authority, only by making community activities a first order concern and by pursuing the problems assertively, could a DCI begin to make a difference in effecting better management. During Allen Dulles' term interagency coordination went neglected, and the results were expansion of competing capabilities among the Departments. For McCone, community intelligence activities were clearly a priority, and his definition of the DCI's role contributed to whatever advances were made. Helms' fundamental interests and inclinations lay within the Agency, and he did not push his mandate to its possible limits.

The DCI's basic problems have been competing claims on his time and attention and the lack of real authority for the execution of the central intelligence function. As presently defined, the DCI's job is burdensome in the extreme. He is to serve the roles of chief intelligence advisor to the President, manager of community intelligence activities, and senior executive in the CIA. History has demonstrated that the job of the DCI as community manager and as head of the CIA are competing, not complementary roles. In terms of both the demands imposed by each function and the expertise required to fulfill the responsibilities, the two roles differ considerably. In the future separating the functions with precise definitions of authority and responsibilities may prove a plausible alternative.

Although the Agency was established primarily for the purpose of providing intelligence analysis to senior policymakers, within three years clandestine operations became and continued to be the Agency's preeminent activity. The single most important factor in the transformation was policymakers' perception of the Soviet Union as a worldwide threat to United States security. The Agency's large-scale clandestine activities have mirrored American foreign policy priorities. With political operations in Europe in the 1950's, paramilitary operations in Korea, Third World activities, Cuba, Southeast Asia, and currently narcotics control, the CIA's major programs paralleled the international concerns of the United States. For nearly two decades American policymakers considered covert action vital in the struggle against international Communism. The generality of the definition or "threat perception" motivated the continual development and justification of covert activities from the senior policymaking level to the field stations. Apart from the overall anti-Communist motivation, successive Presidential administrations regarded covert action as a quick and convenient means of advancing their particular objectives.

Internal incentives contributed to the expansion in covert action. Within the Agency DDO careerists have traditionally been rewarded more quickly for the visible accomplishments of covert action than for the long-term development of agents required for clandestine collection. Clandestine activities will remain an element of United States foreign policy, and policymakers will directly affect the level of operations. The prominence of the Clandestine Service within the Agency may moderate as money for and high-level Executive interest in covert actions diminish. However, DDO incentives which emphasize operations over collection and which create an internal demand for projects will continue to foster covert action unless an internal conversion process forces a change.

In the past the orientation of DCIs such as Dulles and Helms also contributed to the Agency's emphasis on clandestine activities. It is no coincidence that of those DCIs who have been Agency careerists, all have come from the Clandestine Service. Except for James Schlesinger's brief appointment, the Agency has never been directed by a trained analyst. The qualities demanded of individuals in the DDO—essentially management of people—serve as the basis for bureaucratic skills in the organization. As a result, the Agency's leadership has been dominated by DDO careerists.

Clandestine collection and covert action have had their successes, i.e. individual activities have attained their stated objectives. What the relative contribution of clandestine activities has been—the extent to which they have contributed to or detracted from the implementation of United States foreign policy and whether the results have been worth the risks—cannot be evaluated without wide access to records on covert operations, access the Committee did not have.

Organizational arrangements within the Agency and the decision-making structure outside the Agency have permitted the extremes in CIA activity. The ethos of secrecy which pervaded the DDO had the effect of setting the Directorate apart within the Agency and allowed the Clandestine Service a measure of autonomy not accorded other Directorates. More importantly, the compartmentation principle allowed units of the DDO freedom in defining operations. In many cases the burden of responsibility fell on individual judgments—a situation in which lapses and deviations are inevitable. Previous excesses of drug testing, assassination planning, and domestic activities were supported by an internal structure that permitted individuals to conduct operations without the consistent necessity or expectation of justifying or revealing their activities.

Ultimately, much of the responsibility for the scale of covert action and for whatever abuses occurred must fall to senior policymakers. The decisionmaking arrangements at the NSC level created an environment of blurred accountability which allowed consideration of actions without the constraints of individual responsibility. Historically the ambiguity and imprecision derived from the initial expectation that covert operations would be limited and therefore could be managed by a small, informal group. Such was the intention in 1948. By 1951 with the impetus of the Korean War, covert action had become a fixed element in the U.S. foreign policy repertoire. The frequency of covert action forced the development of more formalized decisionmaking arrangements. Yet structural changes did not alter ambiguous procedures. In the 1950's the relationship between Secretary of State John Foster Dulles and Allen Dulles allowed informal agreements and personal understandings to prevail over explicit and precise decisions. In addition, as the scale of covert action expanded, policymakers found it useful to maintain the ambiguity of the decisionmaking process to insure secrecy and to allow "plausible deniability" of covert operations.

No one in the Executive—least of all the President—was required to formally sign off on a decision to implement a covert action program. The DCI was responsible for the execution of a project but not for taking the decision to implement it. Within the NSC a group of individuals held joint responsibility for defining policy objectives, but they did not attempt to establish criteria placing moral and constitutional limits on activities undertaken to achieve the objectives. Congress has functioned under similar conditions. Within the Congress a handful of committee members passed on the Agency's budget. Some members were informed of most of the CIA's major activities; others preferred not to be informed. The result was twenty-nine years of acquiescence.

At each level of scrutiny in the National Security Council and in the Congress a small group of individuals controlled the approval processes. The restricted number of individuals involved as well as the assumption that their actions would not be subject to outside scrutiny contributed to the scale of covert action and to the development of questionable practices.

The DDO and the DDI evolved out of separate independent organizations, serving different policy needs. Essentially, the two Directorates have functioned as separate organizations. They maintain totally independent career tracks and once recruited into one, individuals are rarely posted to the other.

In theory the DDO's candestine collection function should have contributed to the DDI's analytic capacity. However, DDO concerns about maintaining the security of its operations and protecting the identity of its agents, and DDI concerns about measuring the reliability of its sources restricted interchange between the two Directorates. Fundamentally, this has deprived the DDI of a major source of information Although DDI–DDO contact has increased during the last five years, it remains limited.

The DDI has traditionally not been informed of sensitive covert operations undertaken by the DDO. This has affected the respective missions of both Directorates. The Clandestine Service has not had the benefit of intelligence support during consideration and implementation of its operations. The Bay of Pigs invasion was an instance in which DDI analysts, even the Deputy Director for Intelligence, were uninformed and represents a situation in which timely analysis of political trends and basic geography might have made a difference— either in the decision to embark on the operation or in the plans for the operation. In the DDI, lack of knowledge about operations has complicated and undermined the analytic effort. Information on a CIA-sponsored political action program would affect judgments about the results of a forthcoming election; information provided by a foreign government official would be invaluable in assessing the motives, policies, and dynamics of that government; information on a CIA-sponsored propaganda campaign might alter analyses of the press or public opinion in that country. Essentially, the potential quality of the finished intelligence product suffers.

The Agency was created in part to rectify the problem of duplication among the departmental intelligence services. Rather than minimizing the problem the Agency has contributed to it by becoming yet another source of intelligence production. Growth in the range of American foreign policy interests and the DDI's response to additional requirements have resulted in an increased scale of collection and analysis. Today, the CIA's intelligence products include: current intelligence in such disparate areas as science, economics, politics, strategic affairs, and technology; quick responses to specific requests from government agencies and officials; basic or long-term research; and national intelligence estimates. With the exception of national intelligence estimates, other intelligence organizations engage in overlapping intelligence analysis.

Rather than fulfilling the limited mission in intelligence analysis and coordination for which it was created, the Agency became a producer of finished intelligence and consistently expanded its areas of responsibility. In political and strategic intelligence the inadequacy of analysis by the State Department and by the military services allowed the Agency to lay claim to the two areas. As the need for specialized research in other subjects developed, the DDI responded—as the only potential source for objective national intelligence. Over time the DDI has addressed itself to a full range of consumers in the broadest number of subject areas. Yet the extent to which the analysis satisfied policymakers' needs and was an integral part of the policy process has been limited.

The size of the DDI and the administrative process involved in the production of finished intelligence—a process which involves numerous stages of drafting and review by large numbers of individuals—precluded close association between policymakers and analysts, between the intelligence product and policy informed by intelligence analysis. Even the National Intelligence Estimates were relegated to briefing papers for second and third level officials rather than the principal intelligence source for senior policymakers that they were intended to be. Recent efforts to improve the interaction include creating the NIO system and assigning two full-time analysts on location at the Treasury Department. Yet these changes cannot compensate for the nature of the intelligence production system itself, which employs hundreds of analysts, most of whom have little sustained contact with their consumers.

At the Presidential level the DCI's position is essential to the utilization of intelligence. The DCI must be constantly informed, must press for access, must vigorously sell his product, and must anticipate future demands. Those DCIs who have been most successful in this dimension have been those whose primary identification was not with the DDO.

Yet the relationship between intelligence analysis and policymaking is a reciprocal one. Senior policymakers must actively utilize the intelligence capabilities at their disposal. Presidents have looked to the Agency more for covert operations than for intelligence analysis. While only the Agency could perform covert operations, decisionmaking methods determined Presidential reliance on the CIA's intelligence capabilities. Preferences for small staffs, individual advisors, the need for specialized information quickly—all of these factors circumscribe a President's channel of information, of which intelligence analysis may be a part. It was John F. Kennedy who largely determined John McCone's relative influence by defining the DCI's role and by including McCone in the policy process; it was Lyndon Johnson and Richard Nixon who limited the roles of Richard Helms and William Colby. Although in the abstract objectivity may be the most desirable quality in intelligence analysis, objective judgments are frequently not what senior officials want to hear about their policies. In most cases, Presidents are inclined to look to the judgments of individuals they know and trust. Whether or not a DCI is included among them is the President's choice.

Over the past thirty years the United States has developed an institution and a corps of individuals who constitute the the U.S. intelligence profession. The question remains as to how both the institution and the individuals will best be utilized.

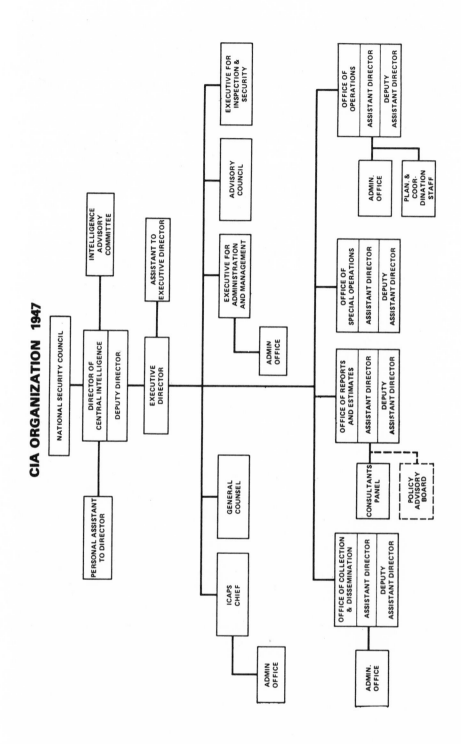

CIA ORGANIZATION 1947

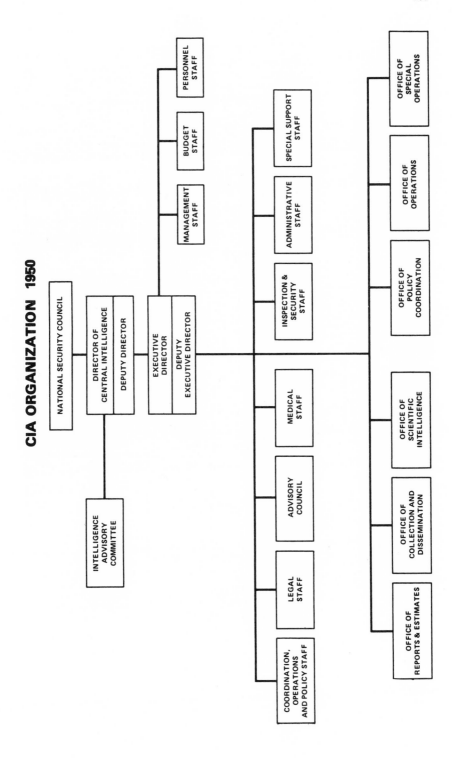

CIA ORGANIZATION 1950

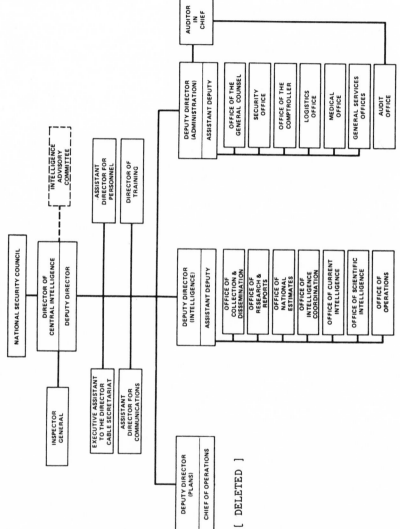

CIA ORGANIZATION 1953

NATIONAL SECURITY COUNCIL

INSPECTOR GENERAL

DIRECTOR OF CENTRAL INTELLIGENCE

DEPUTY DIRECTOR

INTELLIGENCE ADVISORY COMMITTEE

ASSISTANT DIRECTOR FOR PERSONNEL

DIRECTOR OF TRAINING

EXECUTIVE ASSISTANT TO THE DIRECTOR CABLE SECRETARIAT

ASSISTANT DIRECTOR FOR COMMUNICATIONS

DEPUTY DIRECTOR (PLANS)

CHIEF OF OPERATIONS

[DELETED]

DEPUTY DIRECTOR (INTELLIGENCE)

ASSISTANT DEPUTY

OFFICE OF COLLECTION & DISSEMINATION

OFFICE OF RESEARCH & REPORTS

OFFICE OF NATIONAL ESTIMATES

OFFICE OF INTELLIGENCE COORDINATION

OFFICE OF CURRENT INTELLIGENCE

OFFICE OF SCIENTIFIC INTELLIGENCE

OFFICE OF OPERATIONS

DEPUTY DIRECTOR (ADMINISTRATION)

ASSISTANT DEPUTY

OFFICE OF THE GENERAL COUNSEL

SECURITY OFFICE

OFFICE OF THE COMPTROLLER

LOGISTICS OFFICE

MEDICAL OFFICE

GENERAL SERVICES OFFICES

AUDIT OFFICE

AUDITOR IN CHIEF

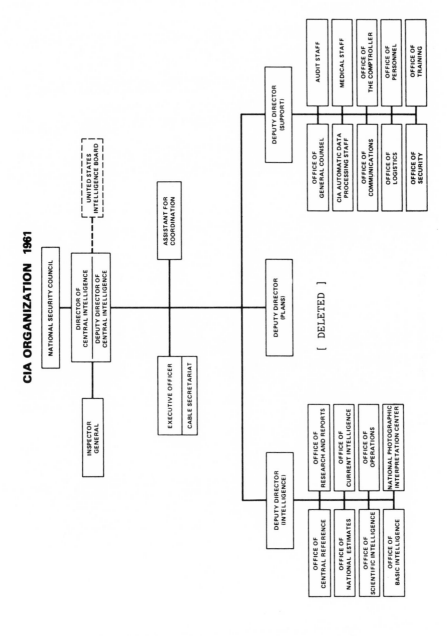

CIA ORGANIZATION 1961

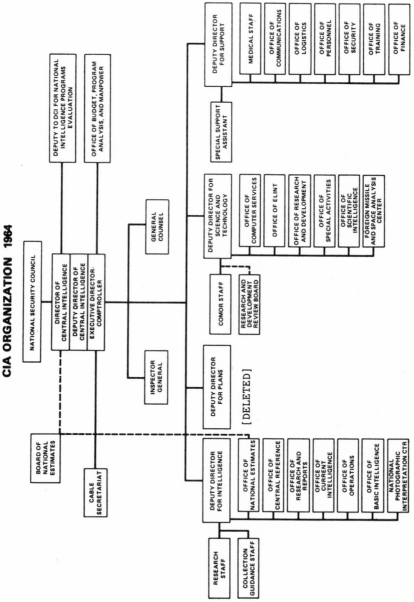

CIA ORGANIZATION 1964

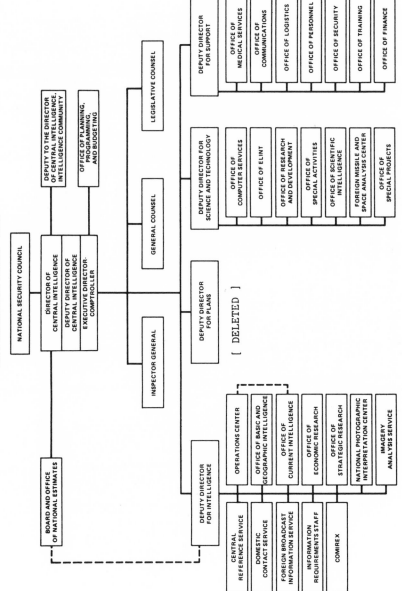

CIA ORGANIZATION 1972

CIA ORGANIZATION 1975

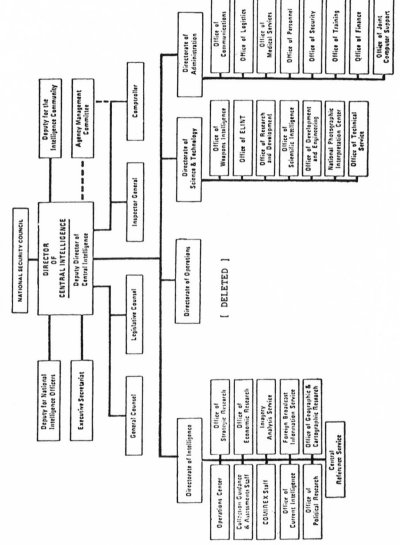

LIST OF ACRONYMS

ADDP: Assistant Deputy Director for Plans, second person in line of command of the DDP.

ADPC: Assistant Director for Policy Coordination, the senior administrative officer in the Office of Policy Coordination.

ADSO: Assistant Director for Special Operations, the senior administrative officer in the Office of Special Operations.

ARC: Ad Hoc Requirements Committee, an interdepartmental group established in 1955 to coordinate intelligence collection requirements among the Departments for the U–2 program. Succeeded by COMOR in 1960.

BID: Basic Intelligence Division, a component of ORR, responsible for production of National Intelligence Surveys. Became Office of Basic Intelligence in 1955.

CA Staff: Covert Action Staff, a component of the DDP, responsible for review of covert action projects for the Directorate as well as management and control of some field operations.

CIG: Central Intelligence Group, 1946–1947, predecessor of the CIA.

CI Staff: Counterintelligence Staff, a component of the DDP, which until recently maintained virtual control over counterintelligence operations.

COMINT: Communications Intelligence, technical and intelligence information derived from foreign communications, not including foreign press, propaganda, or public broadcasts.

COMIREX: Committee on Imagery Requirements and Exploitation, established in 1967 to succeed COMOR as the USIB subcommittee responsible for the management of collection planning.

COMOR: Committee on Overhead Reconnaissance, a USIB subcommittee established in 1960 to coordinate intelligence collection requirements among the Departments for the development and operation of all overhead reconnaissance systems.

CRS: Central Reports Staff, a component of the CIG, responsible for correlation and evaluation of information drawn from other Departments.

DCI: Director of Central Intelligence, chief officer of the CIG and the CIA.

DCID: Director of Central Intelligence Directive, a directive issued by the DCI which outlines general policies and procedures to be followed by the intelligence community. It is generally more specific than an NSCID.

DCS: Domestic Contact Service, a component of CIG, responsible for soliciting domestic sources for foreign intelligence information. Renamed the Domestic Contact Division in 1951; became a component of the DDI in 1952; renamed the Domestic Contact Service in 1965; transferred to DDO in 1973 and renamed the Domestic Collection Division.

DDA: Directorate for Administration, established in 1950, responsible for personnel, budget, security, medical services and logistical support for overseas operations.

DDCI: Deputy Director of Central Intelligence, second person in line of command of CIA.

DDI: Directorate for Intelligence, created in 1952, responsible for production of finished intelligence (excluding scientific and technical intelligence since 1963) and for collection of overt information.

DDP: Directorate for Plans, created in 1952 from the integration of OSO and OPC, also known as the "Clandestine Service." Responsible for clandestine collection, counterintelligence, and covert operations. Renamed the Directorate for Operations in 1973.

DDR: Directorate for Research, created in 1962, immediate predecessor to the Directorate for Science and Technology.

DDS&T: Directorate for Science and Technology, organized in 1963, combining OSI, the Data Processing Staff, the Office of ELINT, the DPD, and a newly created Office of Research and Development. Responsible for research development and operation of technical collection systems and for production of finished scientific and technical intelligence.

DIA: Defense Intelligence Agency, created by Secretary of Defense Robert McNamara in 1961, responsible for production of military intelligence.

DPD: Development Projects Division, a component of the DDP, responsible for overhead reconnaissance. Transferred to DDS&T in 1963.

EIC: Economic Intelligence Committee, a subcommittee of the IAC created in 1951, charged with interdepartmental coordination of economic intelligence activities and the production of publications. Continued under USIB.

ELINT: Electronic Intelligence, technical and intelligence information derived from the collection (or interception) and processing of foreign electromagnetic radiations such as radar.

ERA: Economic Research Area, established in 1950 as a component of ORR, responsible for production of economic intelligence. Eventually developed into OER.

EXCOM: Executive Committee, established in 1965 for the management of overhead reconnaissance, giving the CIA and the Department of Defense decisionmaking authority over the national reconnaissance program.

FBID: Foreign Broadcast Information Division, as element of CIG which monitored overseas broadcasts. Became a component of the DDI in 1952; renamed the Foreign Broadcast Information Service in 1965.

GMAIC: Guided Missiles and Astronautics Intelligence Committee, a USIB subcommittee established in 1958, responsible for interdepartmental coordination of intelligence related to guided missiles.

GMIC: Guided Missiles Intelligence Committee, an IAC subcommittee created in 1956, responsible for interdepartmental coordination of intelligence related to guided missiles. Succeeded by GMAIC in 1958.

GRA: Geographic Research Area, created in 1950 as a component of ORR; in 1965 transferred to OBI, which was renamed Office of Basic and Geographic Intelligence; OBGI became the Office of Geographic and Cartographic Research in 1974.

IAB: Intelligence Advisory Board, an advisory group to the DCI, composed of the heads of the military and civilian intelligence agencies. Existed for the life of CIG.

IAC: Intelligence Advisory Committee, created in 1947 to serve as a coordinating body in establishing intelligence requirements, among the Departments. Merged with USCIB in 1958 to form USIB.

IC Staff: Intelligence Community staff, established in 1972 as a replacement for the NIPE staff. Responsible for assisting the DCI in the management of intelligence community activities.

ICAPS: Interdepartmental Coordinating and Planning Staff, a component of the CIG, which handled the administrative aspects of CIG's contacts with the Departments.

INR: Bureau of Intelligence and Research, the State Department's intelligence analysis component.

IRAC: Intelligence Resources Advisory Committee, an interdepartmental group established in 1971 to advise the DCI in preparing a consolidated intelligence program budget for the President. Members included representatives from the Departments of State, Defense, OMB, and CIA.

JAEIC: Joint Atomic Energy Intelligence Committee, a subcommittee of USIB, responsible for interdepartmental coordination of intelligence relating to atomic energy.

JAG: Joint Analysis Group, an interdepartmental body established in 1962, to provide regular assessments on Soviet and Chinese future military strengths.

KIQs: Key Intelligence Questions, initiated in 1974 and designed to produce intelligence on topics of particular importance to national policymakers, as defined by the DCI.

MBO: Management by Objectives, a system established in 1974 to measure performance against explicitly stated goals.

MONGOOSE: Operation MONGOOSE, a program conducted between 1961 and 1962, aimed at discrediting and ultimately toppling the Castro government.

NIA: National Intelligence Authority, supervisory body of the Central Intelligence Group (CIG), comprised of the Secretaries of State, War, and Navy, and the personal representative of the President.

NIE: National Intelligence Estimate, a predictive judgment on the capabilities, vulnerabilities, and courses of action of foreign nations. It represents the composite view of the intelligence community.

NIOs: National Intelligence Officers, a senior group of analysts, organized in 1973 to replace ONE. Responsible for the management of intelligence collection and production.

NIPE Staff: National Intelligence Programs Evaluation Staff, established in 1963 under the DCI to serve as a coordinating body in the management of interdepartmental intelligence activities. Replaced by IC Staff in 1971.

NIPP: National Intelligence Projections for Planning, interagency assessments on Soviet and Chinese future military strengths, produced by the JAG.

NIRB: National Intelligence Review Board, established in 1968, to advise the DCI in making judgments on foreign intelligence resource needs. Replaced in 1971 by IRAC.

NIS: National Intelligence Survey, a compendium of factual information on foreign countries drawn from throughout the intelligence community. The program was terminated in 1974.

NPIC: National Photographic Interpretation Center, established in 1961 under the direction of the DCI to analyze photography derived from overhead reconnaissance.

NSC: National Security Council, the senior decisionmaking body in the Executive branch. Established in 1947, comprised of the President, the Vice President, the Secretaries of State and Defense with representatives of the JCS, Special Assistant to the President and other officials attending as required.

NSCID: National Security Council Intelligence Directive, a directive issued by the NSC to the intelligence agencies. NSCIDs are often augmented by more specific DCIDs and by internal departmental or agency regulations.

OCB: Operations Coordinating Board, established in 1953 to replace the PSB as a senior review body for covert operations. Its members included deputy-level officials from the Departments of State, Defense, the office of the President, and from the foreign aid program.

OCD: Office of Collection and Dissemination, a component of the DDI charged with the dissemination of intelligence and the storage and retrieval of unevaluated intelligence. Renamed the Office of Central Reference in 1955; renamed the Central Reference Service in 1967.

OCI: Office of Current Intelligence, a component of the DDI, established in 1951. Responsible for the production of current intelligence in numerous areas.

OER: Office of Economic Research, a component of the DDI, established in 1967. Responsible for production of economic intelligence.

ONE: Office of National Estimates, organized in 1950, to produce National Intelligence Estimates. Dissolved in 1973.

OO: Office of Operations, a component of the DDI, charged with the collection of overt information. Dissolved in 1965.

OPC: Office of Policy Coordination, a component attached to the CIA but reporting to the Departments of State and Defense. Established in 1948 with responsibility for the conduct of covert operations. Merged with OSO in 1952 to form the DDP.

OPR: Office of Political Research, established in 1974 as a component of the DDI. Responsible for long-term political research.

ORE: Office of Research and Evaluation, a component of CIG and CIA, established in 1946. Responsible for intelligence production and interagency coordination. Dissolved in 1951.

ORR: Office of Research and Reports, established in 1950, became a component of DDI in 1952. Responsible primarily for economic and strategic research. Dissolved in 1967.

OSI : Office of Scientific Intelligence, created in 1949. Responsible for basic science and technical research. Became a component of the DDI in 1952. Transferred to the DDS&T in 1963.

OSO : Office of Special Operations, a component of CIG and CIA, established in 1946, responsible for espionage and counterespionage. Merged with OPC in 1952 to form the Directorate for Plans.

OSR : Office of Strategic Research, established in 1967 as a component of the DDI, combining military intelligence units in OCI and ORR.

OSS : Office of Strategic Services, U.S. intelligence agency from 1942–1945. Responsibilities included research, analysis, espionage and overseas operations.

PBCFIA : President's Board of Consultants on Foreign Intelligence Activities, an advisory body created in 1956 by President Eisenhower. Renamed President's Foreign Intelligence Advisory Board (PFIAB) in 1961.

PSB : Psychological Strategy Board, a subcommittee of NSC established in 1951, charged with directing psychological warfare programs. Its members included departmental representatives and Board staff members. Replaced by OCB in 1953.

SEC : Scientific Estimates Committee, a subcommittee of the IAC, established in 1952, charged with interagency coordination of scientific intelligence and the production of publications. Renamed the Scientific Intelligence Committee in 1959.

SIGINT : Signals Intelligence, which involves the interception, processing, analysis and dissemination of information derived from foreign electrical communications and other signals.

SNIE : Special National Intelligence Estimate, request by policymakers for a judgment on a particular question.

SPG : Special Procedures Group, a component of OSO, established in 1947. Responsible for the conduct of covert psychological operations.

SSU : Strategic Services Unit, a component of the War Department charged with clandestine collection and counterespionage. Transferred to CIG in 1946.

SWNCC : State, War, Navy Coordinating Committee, established in 1944, the predecessor body to the NSC.

TSD : Technical Services Division, a component of the DDP, engaged in research and development to provide operational support for clandestine activities. Transferred to DDS&T in 1973.

USCIB : United States Communications Intelligence Board, established in 1946 to advise and make recommendations on communications intelligence to the Secretary of Defense.

USIB : United States Intelligence Board, an interdepartmental body established in 1958, through the merger of the IAC and the USCIB. Responsible for coordinating intelligence activities among the Departments.

Documents

Document One

Memorandum for the President
by William J. Donovan, November 18, 1944

November 18, 1944

MEMORANDUM FOR THE PRESIDENT

Pursuant to your note of 31 October 1944 I have given consideration to the organization of an intelligence service for the post-war period.

In the early days of the war, when the demands upon intelligence services were mainly in and for military operations, the OSS was placed under the JCS.

Once our enemies are defeated the demand will be equally pressing for information that will aid us in solving the problems of peace.

This will require two things:

1. That intelligence control be returned to the supervision of the President.

2. The establishment of a central authority reporting directly to you, with responsibility to frame intelligence objectives and to collect and coordinate the intelligence material required by the Executive Branch in planning and carrying out national policy and strategy.

I attach in the form of a draft directive (Tab A) the means by which I think this could be realized without difficulty or loss of time. You will note that coordination and centralization are placed at the policy level but operational intelligence (that pertaining primarily to Department action) remains within the existing agencies concerned. The creation of a central authority thus would not conflict with or limit necessary intelligence functions within the Army, Navy, Department of State and other agencies.

In accordance with your wish, this is set up as a permanent long-range plan. But you may want to consider whether this (or part of it) should be done now, by executive or legislative action. There are common sense reasons why you may desire to lay the keel of the ship at once.

The immediate revision and coordination of our present intelligence system would effect substantial economies and aid in the more efficient and speedy termination of the war.

Information important to the national defense, being gathered now by certain Departments and agencies, is not being used to full advantage in the war. Coordination at the strategy level would prevent waste, and avoid the present confusion that leads to waste and unnecessary duplication.

Though in the midst of war, we are also in a period of transition which, before we are aware, will take us into the tumult of rehabilitation. An adequate and orderly intelligence system will contribute to informed decisions.

We have now in the Government the trained and specialized personnel needed for the task. This talent should not be dispersed.

William J. Donovan
Director

SUBSTANTIVE AUTHORITY NECESSARY IN ESTABLISHMENT OF A CENTRAL INTELLIGENCE SERVICE

In order to coordinate and centralize the policies and actions of the Government relating to intelligence:

1. There is established in the Executive Office of the President a central intelligence service, to be known as the ———, at the head of which shall be a Director appointed by the President. The Director shall discharge and perform his functions and duties under the direction and supervision of the President. Subject to the approval of the President, the Director may exercise his powers, authorities and duties through such officials or agencies and in such manner as he may determine.

2. There is established in the ——— an Advisory Board consisting of the Secretary of State, the Secretary of War, the Secretary of the Navy, and such other members as the President may subsequently appoint. The Board shall advise and assist the Director with respect to the formulation of basic policies and plans of the ———.

3. Subject to the direction and control of the President, and with any necessary advice and assistance from the other Departments and agencies of the Government, the ——— shall perform the following functions and duties:

(a) Coordination of the functions of all intelligence agencies of the Government, and the establishment of such policies and objectives as will assure the integration of national intelligence efforts;

(b) Collection either directly or through existing Government Departments and agencies, of pertinent information, including military, economic, political and scientific, concerning the capabilities, intentions and activities of foreign nations, with particular reference to the effect such matters may have upon the national security, policies and interests of the United States;

(c) Final evaluation, synthesis and dissemination within the Government of the intelligence required to enable the Government to determine policies with respect to national planning and security in peace and war, and the advancement of broad national policy;

(d) Procurement, training and supervision of its intelligence personnel;

(e) Subversive operations abroad;

(f) Determination of policies for and coordination of facilities essential to the collection of information under subparagraph "(b)" hereof; and

(g) Such other functions and duties relating to intelligence as the President from time to time may direct.

4. The ———— shall have no police or law enforcement functions, either at home or abroad.

5. Subject to Paragraph 3 hereof, existing intelligence agencies within the Government shall collect, evaluate, synthesize and disseminate departmental operating intelligence, herein defined as intelligence required by such agencies in the actual performance of their functions and duties.

6. The Director shall be authorized to call upon Departments and agencies of the Government to furnish appropriate specialists for such supervisory and functional positions within the ———— as may be required.

7. All Government Departments and agencies shall make available to the Director such intelligence materials as the Director, with the approval of the President, from time to time may request.

8. The ———— shall operate under an independent budget.

9. In time of war or unlimited national emergency, all programs of the ———— in areas of actual or projected military operations shall be coordinated with military plans and shall be subject to the approval of the Joint Chiefs of Staff. Parts of such programs which are to be executed in a theater of military operations shall be subject to the control of the Theater Commander.

10. Within the limits of such funds as may be made available to the ————, the Director may employ necessary personnel and make provision for necessary supplies, facilities and services. The Director shall be assigned, upon the approval of the President, such military and naval personnel as may be required in the performance of the functions and duties of the ————. The Director may provide for the internal organization and management of the ———— in such manner as he may determine.

Document Two

President Harry S. Truman Establishes the Central Intelligence Group, January 22, 1946

January 22, 1946

To the Secretary of State, the Secretary of War,
and the Secretary of the Navy:

1. It is my desire, and I hereby direct, that all Federal foreign intelligence activities be planned, developed and coordinated so as to assure the most effective accomplishment of the intelligence mission related to the national security. I hereby designate you, together with another person to be named by me as my personal representative, as the National Intelligence Authority to accomplish this purpose.

2. Within the limits of available appropriations, you shall each from time to time assign persons and facilities from your respective Departments, which persons shall collectively form a Central Intelligence Group and shall, under the direction of a Director of Central Intelligence, assist the National Intelligence Authority. The Director of Central Intelligence shall be designated by me, shall be responsible to the National Intelligence Authority, and shall sit as a non-voting member thereof.

3. Subject to existing law, and to the direction and control of the National Intelligence Authority, the Director of Central Intelligence shall:

a. Accomplish the correlation and evaluation of intelligence relating to the national security, and the appropriate dissemination within the Government of the resulting strategic and national policy intelligence. In so doing, full use shall be made of the staff and facilities of the intelligence agencies of your Departments.

b. Plan for the coordination of such of the activities of the intelligence agencies of your Departments as relate to the national security and recommend to the National Intelligence Authority the establishment of such over-all policies and objectives as will assure the most effective accomplishment of the national intelligence mission.

    c. Perform, for the benefit of said intelligence agencies, such services of common concern as the National Intelligence Authority determines can be more efficiently accomplished centrally.

    d. Perform such other functions and duties related to intelligence affecting the national security as the President and the National Intelligence Authority may from time to time direct.

    4. No police, law enforcement or internal security functions shall be exercised under this directive.

    5. Such intelligence received by the intelligence agencies of your Department as may be designated by the National Intelligence Authority shall be freely available to the Director of Central Intelligence for correlation, evaluation or dissemination. To the extent approved by the National Intelligence Authority, the operations of said intelligence agencies shall be open to inspection by the Director of Central Intelligence in connection with planning functions.

    6. The existing intelligence agencies of your Departments shall continue to collect, evaluate, correlate and disseminate departmental intelligence.

    7. The Director of Central Intelligence shall be advised by an Intelligence Advisory Board consisting of the heads (or their representatives) of the principal military and civilian intelligence agencies of the Government having functions related to national security, as determined by the National Intelligence Authority.

    8. Within the scope of existing law and Presidential directives, other departments and agencies of the executive branch of the Federal Government shall furnish such intelligence information relating to the national security as is in their possession, and as the Director of Central Intelligence may from time to time request pursuant to regulations of the National Intelligence Authority.

    9. Nothing herein shall be construed to authorize the making of investigations inside the continental limits of the United States and its possessions, except as provided by law and Presidential directives.

    10. In the conduct of their activities the National Intelligence Authority and the Director of Central Intelligence shall be responsible for fully protecting intelligence sources and methods.

Sincerely Yours,
Harry S. Truman

Document Three

The National Security Act of 1947
[excerpts]

THE NATIONAL SECURITY ACT OF 1947
Public Law 253, July 26, 1947

*   *   *   *

SEC. 102. (a) There is hereby established under the National Security Council a Central Intelligence Agency with a Director of Central Intelligence, who shall be the head thereof. The Director shall be appointed by the President, by and with the advice and consent of the Senate, from among the commissioned officers of the armed services or from among individuals in civilian life. The Director shall receive compensation at the rate of $14,000 a year.

(b) (1) If a commissioned officer of the armed services is appointed as Director then—

(A) in the performance of his duties as Director, he shall be subject to no supervision, control, restriction, or prohibition (military or otherwise) other than would be operative with respect to him if he were a civilian in no way connected with the Department of the Army, the Department of the Navy, the Department of the Air Force, or the armed services of any component thereof; and

(B) he shall not possess or exercise any supervision, control, powers, or functions (other than such as he possesses, or is authorized or directed to exercise, as Director) with respect to the armed services or any component thereof, the Department of the Army, the Department of the Navy, or the Department of the Air Force, or any branch, bureau, unit or division thereof, or with respect to any of the foregoing.

(2) Except as provided in paragraph (1), the appointment to the office of Director of a commissioned officer of the armed services, and his acceptance

of any service in such office, shall in no way affect any status, office, rank, or grade he may occupy or hold in the armed services, or any emolument, perquisite, right, privilege, or benefit incident to or arising out of any such status, office, rank, or grade. Any such commissioned officer shall, while serving in the office of Director, receive the military pay and allowances (active or retired, as the case may be) payable to a commissioned officer of his grade and length of service and shall be paid, from any funds available to defray the expenses of the Agency, annual compensation at a rate equal to the amount by which $14,000 exceeds the amount of his annual military pay and allowances.

(c) Notwithstanding the provisions of section 6 of the Act of August 24, 1912 (37 Stat. 555), or the provisions of any other law, the Director of Central Intelligence may, in his discretion, terminate the employment of any officer or employee of the Agency whenever he shall deem such termination necessary or advisable in the interests of the United States, but such termination shall not affect the right of such officer or employee to seek or accept employment in any other department or agency of the Government if declared eligible for such employment by the United States Civil Service Commission.

(d) For the purpose of coordinating the intelligence activities of the several Government departments and agencies in the interest of national security, it shall be the duty of the Agency, under the direction of the National Security Council—

(1) to advise the National Security Council in matters concerning such intelligence activities of the Government departments and agencies as relate to national security;

(2) to make recommendations to the President through the National Security Council for the coordination of such intelligence activities of the departments and agencies of the Government as relate to the national security;

(3) to correlate and evaluate intelligence relating to the national security, and provide for the dissemination of such intelligence within the Government using where appropriate existing agencies and facilities: *Provided,* That the Agency shall have no police, subpoena, law-enforcement powers, or internal-security functions: *Provided further,* That the departments and other agencies of the Government shall continue to collect, evaluate, correlate, and disseminate departmental intelligence: *And provided further,* That the Director of Central Intelligence shall be responsible for protecting intelligence sources and methods from unauthorized disclosure;

(4) to perform, for the benefit of the existing intelligence agencies, such additional services of common concern as the National Security Council determines can be more efficiently accomplished centrally;

(5) to perform such other functions and duties related to intelligence

affecting the national security as the National Security Council may from time to time direct.

(e) To the extent recommended by the National Security Council and approved by the President, such intelligence of the departments and agencies of the Government, except as hereinafter provided, relating to the national security shall be open to the inspection of the Director of Central Intelligence, and such intelligence as relates to the national security and is possessed by such departments and other agencies of the Government, except as hereinafter provided, shall be made available to the Director of Central Intelligence for correlation, evaluation, and dissemination: *Provided however,* That upon the written request of the Director of Central Intelligence, the Director of the Federal Bureau of Investigation shall make available to the Director of Central Intelligence such information for correlation, evaluation, and dissemination as may be essential to the national security.

(f) Effective when the Director first appointed under subsection (a) has taken office—

(1) the National Intelligence Authority (11 Fed. Reg. 1337, 1339, February 5, 1946) shall cease to exist; and

(2) the personnel, property, and records of the Central Intelligence Group are transferred to the Central Intelligence Agency, and such Group shall cease to exist. Any unexpended balances of appropriations, allocations, or other funds available or authorized to be made available for such Group shall be available and shall be authorized to be made available in like manner for expenditure by the Agency.

*   *   *   *

Document Four

National Security Council Directive 10/2, June 18, 1948, Establishing the Office of Special Projects

NSC 10/2 June 18, 1948

NATIONAL SECURITY COUNCIL DIRECTIVE
on
OFFICE OF SPECIAL PROJECTS

1. The National Security Council, taking cognizance of the vicious covert activities of the USSR, its satellite countries and Communist groups to discredit and defeat the aims and activities of the United States and other Western powers, has determined that, in the interests of world peace and US national security, the overt foreign activities of the US Government must be supplemented by covert operations.

2. The Central Intelligence Agency is charged by the National Security Council with conducting espionage and counter-espionage operations abroad. It therefore seems desirable, for operational reasons, not to create a new agency for covert operations, but in time of peace to place the responsibility for them within the structure of the Central Intelligence Agency and correlate them with espionage and counter-espionage operations under the over-all control of the Director of Central Intelligence.

3. Therefore, under the authority of Section 102(d)(5) of the National Security Act of 1947, the National Security Council hereby directs that in time of peace:

a. A new office of Special Projects shall be created within the Central Intelligence Agency to plan and conduct covert operations; and in coordination with the Joint Chiefs of Staff to plan and prepare for the conduct of such operations in wartime.

b. A highly qualified person, nominated by the Secretary of State, acceptable to the Director of Central Intelligence and approved by the National Security Council, shall be appointed as Chief of the Office of Special Projects.

c. The Chief of the Office of Special Projects shall report directly to the Director of Central Intelligence. For purposes of security and of flexibility of operations, and to the maximum degree consistent with efficiency, the Office of Special Projects shall operate independently of other components of Central Intelligence Agency.

d. The Director of Central Intelligence shall be responsible for:

(1) Ensuring, through designated representatives of the Secretary of State and of the Secretary of Defense, that covert operations are planned and conducted in a manner consistent with US foreign and military policies and with overt activities. In disagreements arising between the Director of Central Intelligence and the representative of the Secretary of State or the Secretary of Defense over such plans, the matter shall be referred to the National Security Council for decision.

(2) Ensuring that plans for wartime covert operations are also drawn up with the assistance of a representative of the Joint Chiefs of Staff and are accepted by the latter as being consistent with and complementary to approved plans for wartime military operations.

(3) Informing, through appropriate channels, agencies of the US Government, both at home and abroad (including diplomatic and military representatives in each area), of such operations as will affect them.

e. Covert operations pertaining to economic warfare will be conducted by the Office of Special Projects under the guidance of the departments and agencies responsible for the planning of economic warfare.

f. Supplemental funds for the conduct of the proposed operations for fiscal year 1949 shall be immediately requested. Thereafter operational funds for these purposes shall be included in normal Central Intelligence Agency Budget requests.

4. In time of war, or when the President directs, all plans for covert operations shall be coordinated with the Joint Chiefs of Staff. In active theaters of war where American forces are engaged, covert operations will be conducted under the direct command of the American Theater Commander and orders therefore will be transmitted through the Joint Chiefs of Staff unless otherwise directed by the President.

5. As used in this directive, "covert operations" are understood to be all activities (except as noted herein) which are conducted or sponsored by this Government against hostile foreign states or groups or in support of friendly foreign states or groups but which are so planned and executed that any US Government responsibility for them is not evident to unauthorized persons and that if uncovered the US Government can plausibly disclaim any responsibility for them. Specifically, such operations shall include any covert ac-

tivities related to: propaganda, economic warfare; preventive direct action, including sabotage, anti-sabotage, demolition and evacuation measures; subversion against hostile states, including assistance to underground resistance movements, guerrillas and refugee liberations groups, and support of indigenous anti-communist elements in threatened countries of the free world. Such operations shall not include armed conflict by recognized military forces, espionage, counter-espionage, and cover and deception for military operations.

6. This Directive supersedes the directive contained in NSC 4-A, which is hereby cancelled.

Document Five

The Dulles-Jackson-Correa Report to
the National Security Council on
the Central Intelligence Agency and
National Organization for Intelligence,
January 1, 1949 [summary]

January 1, 1949

THE CENTRAL INTELLIGENCE AGENCY AND NATIONAL
ORGANIZATION FOR INTELLIGENCE
A REPORT TO THE NATIONAL SECURITY COUNCIL
By

Allen W. Dulles, Chairman
William H. Jackson
Mathias F. Correa

SUMMARY

The primary object of this survey has been the Central Intelligence Agency, its organization and activities, and the relationship of these activities to the intelligence work of other Government agencies. Examination has been made of these other intelligence agencies only to the extent that their activities bear upon the carrying out by the Central Intelligence Agency of its assigned functions.

Section 102 (d) of the National Security Act of 1947 creates the Central Intelligence Agency as an independent agency under the direction of the National Security Council. It gives to the Council broad powers in the assignment of functions to the Central Intelligence Agency and creates a framework upon which a sound intelligence system can be built. The Central Intelligence Agency has been properly placed under the National Security

Council for the effective carrying out of its assigned function. It should, however, be empowered and encouraged to establish, through its Director, closer liaison with the two members of the National Security Council on whom it chiefly depends and who should be the main recipients of its product—the Secretary of State and the Secretary of Defense.

The National Security Act, as implemented by directives of the National Security Council, imposes upon the Central Intelligence Agency responsibility for carrying out three essential functions:

(1) The coordination of intelligence activities;

(2) The correlation and evaluation of intelligence relating to the national security, which has been interpreted by directive as meaning the production of national intelligence;

(3) The performance centrally of certain intelligence services of common concern. These include services of a static nature, such as research in fields of common usefulness, and operational services such as the collection through the central agency of secret intelligence.

These three functions constitute the basis of an integrated system of intelligence and they have been used as the frame of reference for the examination of the Central Intelligence Agency and the related activities of other intelligence agencies of the Government represented on the National Security Council, particularly the Department of State and the Departments in the National Military Establishment.

No amendment to the provision of the Act relating to intelligence is required at this time. What is needed is action to give effect to its true intent.

THE RESPONSIBILITY OF THE CENTRAL INTELLIGENCE AGENCY FOR COORDINATING INTELLIGENCE ACTIVITIES

Under the statute, the Central Intelligence Agency has broad responsibility to coordinate intelligence activities relating to the national security. In the discharge of this responsibility, the Central Intelligence Agency should review the intelligence field and ascertain where there are gaps or overlaps. The agency best equipped to do a particular job should fill any gaps. Where two or more agencies are doing similar work, the one best equipped ought to carry on the job and the others drop out or their efforts be coordinated.

This vitally important responsibility for coordination is to be exercised by recommending directives for approval by the National Security Council. The Central Intelligence Agency has the duty of planning for coordination and, in consultation with the other intelligence agencies, of taking the initiative in seeking directives to effect it. Today this coordinating function of the Central Intelligence Agency is not being adequately exercised.

To assist it in carrying out this task the Central Intelligence Agency has available the Intelligence Advisory Committee. This group includes the Director of Central Intelligence as chairman, the heads of the intelligence staffs of the Departments of State, Army, Navy and Air Force, the Atomic Energy Commission and the Joint Intelligence Group of the Joint Staff.

A number of formal directives for the coordination of intelligence activities have been issued by the National Security Council upon the recommendation of the Central Intelligence Agency and the Intelligence Advisory Committee. These directives, except those specifically assigning to the Central Intelligence Agency the carrying out of certain common services described below, have not gone far enough in defining the scope and limits of departmental intelligence activities. These activities continue to present many of the same jurisdictional conflicts and duplication which the National Security Act was intended to eliminate. Consequently, the absence of coordinated intelligence planning, as between the Central Intelligence Agency, the Service agencies and the State Department, remains serious. What is needed is continuing and effective coordinating action under existing directives and also directives establishing more precisely the responsibility of the various intelligence agencies.

The field of scientific and technological intelligence is an example of lack of coordination. Responsibilities are scattered, collection efforts are uncoordinated, atomic energy intelligence is divorced from scientific intelligence generally, and there is no recognized procedure for arriving at authoritative intelligence estimates in the scientific field, with the possible exception of atomic energy matters.

Another important example of lack of coordination is in the field of domestic intelligence and counter-intelligence relating to the national security. Jurisdiction over counter-intelligence and counter-espionage activities is assigned to the Federal Bureau of Investigation in the United States and the Central Intelligence Agency abroad. However, fifth column activities and espionage do not begin or end at our geographical frontiers, and our intelligence to counter them cannot be sharply divided on any such geographical basis. In order to meet the specific problem presented by the need for coordination of activities in the field of domestic intelligence and counter-intelligence relating to the national security, it is recommended that the Director of the Federal Bureau of Investigation be made a permanent member of the Intelligence Advisory Committee.

The Intelligence Advisory Committee so far has had little impact on the solution of the problem of coordination, except in formally approving proposed directives. It should be re-activated and called upon to play an important role.

To assist the Director of Central Intelligence in carrying out his duties to plan for the coordination of intelligence, the staff in the Central Intelligence Agency known as the Interdepartmental Coordinating and Planning Staff should be reconstituted and strengthened. It should be composed of personnel definitely assigned to, and responsible to, the Director of Central Intelligence and charged, on a full-time basis, with carrying on continuous planning for coordination of specific intelligence activities. This staff, which might be called the "Coordination Division," should support the Director in fulfilling one of his most important and difficult duties under the National Security Act.

In concluding the consideration of this most vital problem of coordination of intelligence activities, it should be emphasized that coordination can most effectively be achieved by mutual agreement among the various agencies. With the right measure of leadership on the part of the Central Intelligence Agency, a major degree of coordination can be accomplished in that manner.

THE RESPONSIBILITY OF THE CENTRAL INTELLIGENCE AGENCY FOR THE PRODUCTION OF INTELLIGENCE RELATING TO THE NATIONAL SECURITY

A long-felt need for the coordination, on the highest level, of intelligence opinion relating to broad aspects of national policy and national security was probably the principal moving factor in bringing about the creation of the Central Intelligence Agency. The lack of any provision for the prompt production of coordinated national intelligence of this kind was one of the most significant causes of the Pearl Harbor intelligence failure.

This type of national intelligence, expressed in the form of coordinated national estimates, transcends in scope and breadth the interest and competence of any single intelligence agency. Hence, such estimates should be fully participated in by all of the principal intelligence agencies. All jointly should share in the responsibility for them.

With one or two significant exceptions, whose occurrence was largely fortuitous, the Central Intelligence Agency has not as yet effectively carried out this most important function.

The Office of Reports and Estimates in the Central Intelligence Agency was given responsibility for production of national intelligence. It has, however, been concerned with a wide variety of activities and with the production of miscellaneous reports and summaries which by no stretch of the imagination could be considered national estimates.

Where the Office of Reports and Estimates produces estimates, it usually does so on the basis of its own research and analysis and offers its product as competitive with the similar product of other agencies, rather than as the coordinated result of the best intelligence product which each of the interested agencies is able to contribute.

The failure of this type of intelligence product to meet the requirements of a coordinated national estimate is not substantially mitigated by the existing procedure whereby the Office of Reports and Estimates circulates its estimates to the intelligence agencies of State, Army, Navy and Air Force and obtains a formal notation of dissent or concurrence. Under this procedure, none of the agencies regards itself as a full participant contributing to a truly national estimate and accepting a share in the responsibility for it.

It is believed that this situation can be remedied if the Central Intelligence Agency recognizes the responsibility which it has under the statute and assumes the leadership in organizing its own work and in drawing upon that of the other intelligence agencies of Government for the production of coordinated intelligence. Thus, within its own organization, the Central Intelligence Agency should have, in lieu of the present Office of Reports and Estimates, a small group of specialists, which might appropriately be called "Estimates Division." It would be the task of this group to review the intelligence products of other intelligence agencies and of the Central Intelligence Agency, and to prepare drafts of national intelligence estimates for consideration by the Intelligence Advisory Committee.

The final process of coordination should take place in the Intelligence Advisory Committee which would review and discuss the proposed estimates. The finished estimate should be clearly established as the product of all of the contributing agencies in which all share and for which all take responsibility. It should be recognized as the most authoritative estimate available to the policy-makers.

Where particular scientific or technical intelligence matters are involved, the Intelligence Advisory Committee should secure the views of the best qualified technical experts available to them, including experts from the Research and Development Board and the Atomic Energy Commission.

There should also be provision for the prompt handling of major emergency situations so that, as a matter of course, when quick estimates are required, there is immediate consultation and collective appraisal by the Intelligence Advisory Committee on the basis of all available information.

The inclusion of the Federal Bureau of Investigation as a permanent member should assure that intelligence estimates will be made in the light of domestic as well as foreign intelligence. Provision should be made for the representation on the Intelligence Advisory Committee of other agencies of the Government when matters within their competence are under discussion.

PERFORMANCE CENTRALLY OF SERVICES OF COMMON CONCERN

Under the National Security Act, the Central Intelligence Agency should perform, for the benefit of the existing intelligence agencies, such services of common concern as may be assigned to it by the National Security Council.

These services, as now being performed by the Central Intelligence

Agency, can be broken down into (1) static services, consisting of intelligence research and production on certain assigned subjects which do not fall exclusively within the function of any one existing intelligence agency, and (2) operating services, consisting of certain types of intelligence collection and related secret operations.

STATIC SERVICES OF COMMON CONCERN

At the present time the static services of intelligence research and reporting are carried out in the Office of Reports and Estimates. If the duties of this Office in relation to the production of national intelligence are assigned to a newly constituted Estimates Division, the miscellaneous reporting functions presently carried out by the Office of Reports and Estimates and a part at least of the personnel engaged in them could be reconstituted as the nucleus of a separate division of the Central Intelligence Agency to be known as the "Research and Reports Divison." This Division would also include the Foreign Documents Branch of the Office of Operations and the various reference and library functions now carried on in the Office of Collection and Dissemination.

The economic, scientific and technological fields are ones in which all of our intelligence agencies have varying degrees of interest. At the present time there is serious duplication in these fields of common concern. Central production and coordination by the proposed Research and Reports Division, would result in great economy of effort and improvement of the product. For example, the organization within this division of a scientific branch, staffed by highly qualified personnel and empowered to draw upon the scientific personnel of such organizations of Government as the Research and Development Board and the Atomic Energy Commission for the purpose of dealing with specialized scientific problems, is a project which should have the highest priority.

This division of the Central Intelligence Agency should be staffed in part by representatives of the departmental intelligence services so that the reports produced would represent authoritative and coordinated opinion and be accepted as such by the various consumer agencies.

The Director's planning staff for coordination of activities, the proposed Coordination Division, should review the question as to what subjects might appropriately be assigned to the new Research and Reports Division for central research and report and what services now centrally performed in the Central Intelligence Agency might be eliminated. The Intelligence Advisory Committee would be the agency to determine the allocation of work, and in case of any failure to agree the matter would be referred to the National Security Council.

OPERATING SERVICES OF COMMON CONCERN

The operating services of common concern presently performed by the Central Intelligence Agency consist of the collection, through the Office of Operations, of certain types of intelligence in the United States—i.e., intelligence from private individuals, firms, educational and scientific institutions, etc.; the collection of secret intelligence abroad through the Office of Special Operations; and the conduct of secret operations abroad through the Office of Policy Coordination.

All of these services are appropriately allocated to the Central Intelligence Agency. These operating functions are so inter-related and inter-dependent that they should have common direction at some point below the Director of Central Intelligence.

[DELETED]

In its secret intelligence work, the Office of Special Operations requires a closer liaison with the other intelligence agencies, especially those of the military services and of the State Department which are its chief consumers and which should be able to guide its collection efforts more effectively than they do at present. The counter-intelligence function of the Office of Special Operations requires more emphasis and there is need for better coordination of all its activities with the military, particularly in the occupied areas.

THE ORGANIZATION AND DIRECTION OF THE CENTRAL INTELLIGENCE AGENCY

The principal defect of the Central Intelligence Agency is that its direction, administrative organization and performance do not show sufficient appreciation of the Agency's assigned functions, particularly in the fields of intelligence coordination and the production of intelligence estimates. The result has been that the Central Intelligence Agency has tended to become just one more intelligence agency producing intelligence in competition with older established agencies of the Government departments.

Since it is the task of the Director to see that the Agency carries out its assigned functions, the failure to do so is necessarily a reflection of inadequacies of direction.

There is one over-all point to be made with respect to the administration of the Central Intelligence Agency. The organization is over-administered in the sense that administrative considerations have been allowed to guide and, on occasion, even control intelligence policy to the detriment of the latter. Under the arrangements proposed in this report, the heads of the newly constituted Coordination, Estimates, Research and Reports, and Operations Divisions would be included in the immediate staff of the Director. In this way the Director, who at present relies chiefly on his administrative staff, would be brought into intimate contact with the day-to-day operations of his agency and be able to give policy guidance to them.

In commenting on administration, the question of security should also be stressed. The Director is charged under the law with protecting intelligence sources and methods from unauthorized disclosure. One of the best methods of achieving this is to correct the present situation where the Agency is viewed and generally publicized as the collector of secret intelligence and to bury its secret functions within a Central Intelligence Agency whose chief recognized activities are the coordination of intelligence and the production of intelligence estimates.

In reviewing the work of the directorate, consideration has been given to the question whether or not the Director should be a civilian. The work of the Agency, from its very nature, requires continuity in that office which is not likely to be achieved if a military man holds the post on a "tour of duty" basis. For this reason, as well as because freedom from Service ties is desirable, the Director should be a civilian. This recommendation does not exclude the possibility that the post might be held by a military man who has severed his connection with the Service by retirement.

THE SERVICE INTELLIGENCE AGENCIES AND THE INTELLIGENCE FUNCTIONS OF THE STATE DEPARTMENT

The Service intelligence agencies and the intelligence organization of the State Department have been reviewed from the point of view of the over-all coordination of intelligence and of the contribution which these agencies should make to the assembly and production of national intelligence.

As regards the Service intelligence agencies, the active exercise by the Central Intelligence Agency of its coordinating functions should result in a more efficient allocation of effort than is presently the case. The Service agencies should concern themselves principally with military intelligence questions, leaving the Central Intelligence Agency to perform agreed central services of common interest. In addition, continuing responsibility of the Central Intelligence Agency for coordination should be exercised with respect to certain Service activities, for example, espionage and counter-espionage in occupied areas. The Joint Intelligence Committee would continue to operate with its membership unchanged and would concern itself exclusively with military and strategic questions as directed by the Joint Chiefs of Staff. The Services would participate in the formulation of national intelligence estimates through their membership in the Intelligence Advisory Committee and would share in the collective responsibility for these estimates.

In the case of the Research and Intelligence staff of the State Department, the conclusion has been reached that this staff, as at present constituted, is not sufficiently close to operation and policy matters in the Department to furnish the necessary liaison or the political intelligence estimates required by the Central Intelligence Agency for the preparation of national estimates. Accordingly, it is desirable that a high official of the State Department be designated as its Intelligence Officer to coordinate these activities, to act as the Department's representative on the Intelligence Advisory Committee and, in general, to act as liaison with the Central Intelligence Agency with respect to the intelligence and related activities of the two agencies and to develop close working relations between them.

CONCLUSION

While organization charts can never replace individual initiative and ability, the Central Intelligence Agency, reorganized along the functional lines indicated in this report, should be able more effectively to carry out the duties assigned it by law and thus bring our over-all intelligence system closer to that point of efficiency which the national security demands.

Document Six

Report of the Special Study Group
[Doolittle Committee] on the Covert Activities
of the Central Intelligence Agency,
September 30, 1954 [excerpts]

September 30, 1954

REPORT ON THE COVERT ACTIVITIES OF THE
CENTRAL INTELLIGENCE AGENCY

I. INTRODUCTION

The acquisition and proper evaluation of adequate and reliable intelligence on the capabilities and intentions of Soviet Russia is today's most important military and political requirement. Several agencies of Government and many thousands of capable and dedicated people are engaged in the accomplishment of this task. Because the United States is relatively new at the game, and because we are opposed by a police state enemy whose social discipline and whose security measures have been built up and maintained at a high level for many years, the usable information we are obtaining is still far short of our needs.

As long as it remains national policy, another important requirement is an aggressive covert psychological, political and paramilitary organization more effective, more unique and, if necessary, more ruthless than that employed by the enemy. No one should be permitted to stand in the way of the prompt, efficient and secure accomplishment of this mission.

In the carrying out of this policy and in order to reach minimal standards for national safety under present world conditions, two things must be done. First, the agencies charged by law with the collection, evaluation and distribution of intelligence must be strengthened and coordinated to the greatest practical degree. This is a primary concern of the National Security Council and must be accomplished at the national policy level. Those elements of the problem that fall within the scope of our directive are dealt with in the report which follows. The second consideration is less tangible but equally important. It is now clear that we are facing an implacable enemy whose avowed objective is world domination by whatever means and at whatever cost. There are no rules in such a game. Hitherto acceptable norms of human conduct do not apply. If the United States is to survive, long-standing American concepts of "fair play" must be reconsidered. We must develop effective espionage and counterespionage services and must learn to subvert, sabotage and destroy our enemies by more clever, more sophisticated and more effective methods than those used against us. It may become necessary that the American people be made acquainted with, understand and support this fundamentally repugnant philosophy.

Because of the tight security controls that have been established by the U.S.S.R. and its satellites, the problem of infiltration by human agents is extremely difficult. Most borders are made physically secure by elaborate systems of fencing, lights, mines, etc., backed by constant surveillance. Once across borders—by parachute, or by other means—escape from detection is extremely difficult because of constant checks on personnel activities and personal documentation. The information we have obtained by this method of acquisition has been negligible and the cost in effort, dollars and human lives prohibitive.

This leads to the conviction that much more effort should be expended in exploring every possible scientific and technical avenue of approach to the intelligence problem. The study group has been extensively briefed by C.I.A. personnel and by the Armed Services in the methods and equipment that are presently in use and under development in this area. We have also had the benefit of advice from certain civilian consultants who are working on such special projects. We are impressed by what has been done, but feel that there is an immense potential yet to be explored. We believe that every known technique should be intensively applied and new ones should be developed to increase our intelligence acquisition by [DELETED]

II. CONCLUSIONS AND RECOMMENDATIONS

With respect to the Central Intelligence Agency in general we conclude: (a) that its placement in the overall organization of the Government is proper; (b) that the laws under which it operates are adequate; (c) that the established provisions for its financial support are sufficiently flexible to meet its current operational needs; (d) that in spite of the limitations imposed by its relatively short life and rapid expansion it is doing a creditable job; (e) that it is gradually improving its capabilities; and (f) that it is exercising care to insure the loyalty of its personnel. . . .

J. H. Doolittle, chairman
William B. Franke
Morris Hadley
William D. Pawley

Document Seven

National Security Council Directive 5412/2, December 28, 1955, on Covert Operations

NSC 5412/2   December 28, 1955

NATIONAL SECURITY COUNCIL DIRECTIVE
on
COVERT OPERATIONS

1. The National Security Council, taking cognizance of the vicious activities of the USSR and Communist China and the governments, parties and groups dominated by them (hereinafter collectively referred to as "International Communism") to discredit and defeat the aims and activities of the United States and other powers of the free world, determined, as set forth in NSC directives 10/2 and 10/5, that, in the interests of world peace and U.S. national security, the overt foreign activities of the U.S. Government should be supplemented by covert operations.

2. The Central Intelligence Agency had already been charged by the National Security Council with conducting espionage and counter-espionage operations abroad. It therefore seemed desirable, for operational reasons, not to create a new agency for covert operations, but, subject to directives from the NSC, to place the responsibility for them on the Central Intelligence Agency and correlate them with espionage and counter-espionage operations under the over-all control of the Director of Central Intelligence.

3. The NSC has determined that such covert operations shall to the greatest extent practicable, in the light of U.S. and Soviet capabilities and taking into account the risk of war, be designed to:

a. Create and exploit troublesome problems for International Communism, impair relations between the USSR and Communist China and between them and their satellites, complicate control within the USSR,

Communist China and their satellites, and retard the growth of the military and economic potential of the Soviet bloc.

b. Discredit the prestige and ideology of International Communism, and reduce the strength of its parties and other elements.

c. Counter any threat of a party or individuals directly or indirectly responsive to Communist control to achieve dominant power in a free world country.

d. Reduce International Communist control over any areas of the world.

e. Strengthen the orientation toward the United States of the peoples and nations of the free world, accentuate, wherever possible, the identity of interest between such peoples and nations and the United States as well as favoring, where appropriate, those groups genuinely advocating or believing in the advancement of such mutual interests, and increase the capacity and will of such peoples and nations to resist International Communism.

f. In accordance with established policies and to the extent practicable in areas dominated or threatened by International Communism, develop underground resistance and facilitate covert and guerrilla operations and ensure availability of those forces in the event of war, including wherever practicable provisions of a base upon which the military may expand these forces in time of war within active theaters of operations as well as provision for stay-behind assets and escape and evasion facilities.

4. Under the authority of Section 102(d)(5) of the National Security Act of 1947, the National Security Council hereby directs that the Director of Central Intelligence shall be responsible for:

a. Ensuring, through designated representatives of the Secretary of State and of the Secretary of Defense, that covert operations are planned and conducted in a manner consistent with United States foreign and military policies and with overt activities, and consulting with and obtaining advice from the Operations Coordinating Board and other departments or agencies as appropriate.

b. Informing, through appropriate channels and on a need-to-know basis, agencies of the U.S. Government, both at home and abroad (including diplomatic and military representatives), of such operations as will affect them.

5. In addition to the provisions of paragraph 4, the following provisions shall apply to wartime covert operations:

a. Plans for covert operations to be conducted in active theaters of war and any other areas in which U.S. forces are engaged in combat operations will be drawn up with the assistance of the Department of Defense and will be in consonance with and complementary to approved war plans of the Joint Chiefs of Staff.

b. Covert operations in active theaters of war and any other areas in which U.S. forces are engaged in combat operations will be conducted under such command and control relationships as have been or may in the future be approved by the Department of Defense.

6. As used in this directive, "covert operations" shall be understood to be all activities conducted pursuant to this directive which are so planned and executed that any U.S. Government responsibility for them is not evident to unauthorized persons and that if uncovered the U.S. Government can plausibly disclaim any responsibility for them. Specifically, such operations shall include any covert activities related to: propaganda, political action; economic warfare; preventive direct action, including sabotage, anti-sabotage, demolition; escape and evasion and evacuation measures; subversion against hostile states or groups including assistance to underground resistance movements, guerrillas and refugee liberation groups; support of indigenous and anti-communist elements in threatened countries of the free world; deception plans and operations; and all activities compatible with this directive necessary to accomplish the foregoing. Such operations shall not include: armed conflict by recognized military forces, espionage and counter-espionage, nor cover and deception for military operations.

7. Except as the President otherwise directs, designated representatives of the Secretary of State and of the Secretary of Defense of the rank of Assistant Secretary or above, and a representative of the President designated for this purpose, shall hereafter be advised in advance of major covert programs initiated by CIA under this policy or as otherwise directed, and shall be the normal channel for giving policy approval for such programs as well as for securing coordination of support therefore among the Department of State and Defense and the CIA.

8. This directive supersedes and rescinds NSC 10/2, NSC 10/5, NSC 5412, NSC 5412/1, and subparagraphs "a" and "b" under the heading "Additional Functions of the Operations Coordinating Board" on page 1 of the President's memorandum for the Executive Secretary, National Security Council, supplementing Executive Order 10483.

ANNEX TO NSC 5412/2

Standard Procedures for Insuring Implementation
of Paragraph 7 of NSC 5412/2

(1) With respect to a covert program to be recommended by CIA for policy approval, the NSC 5412/2 Group may decide at any meeting whether to proceed at such meeting to consider and act upon an oral presentation of such covert program or to base such consideration on a detailed paper to be circulated to the Group members in advance of a subsequent meeting. Any paper so circulated will be handled on a "read-and-return" basis in order to

avoid duplicate files, thereby enhancing the security of the information contained in such paper.

(2) At a meeting held to discuss a detailed paper circulated pursuant to (1) above, the Group members will decide in each instance on the procedures to be followed to provide coordinated consideration prior to the Group's giving final policy approval and to provide coordinated support after such approval.

(3) CIA will keep the State and Defense Department advised on a need-to-know and secure basis of developments pertaining to the implementation of programs to which policy approval has been given by the Group.

(4) In accordance with the exception provided for in paragraph 7 of NSC 5412/2, the standard procedure set forth above shall not apply to the case of a particularly sensitive project which relates exclusively to U.S. foreign policy and which does not involve military implications. In such case, approval of such project by the Secretary of State shall constitute both sufficient authorization for initiation of the project by the Director of Central Intelligence and policy approval therefore. The Director of Central Intelligence shall report any such exception (without identification) to the NSC 5412/2 Group.*

---

* In approving the above recommendations, the President directed that whenever the Secretary of State takes action under this paragraph, he shall inform the President.

Document Eight

Final Report of the Senate's Select
Committee on Intelligence,
April 26, 1976 [General Findings]

*　　*　　*　　*　　*

B. GENERAL FINDINGS

The Committee finds that United States foreign and military intelligence agencies have made important contributions to the nation's security, and generally have performed their missions with dedication and distinction. The Committee further finds that individual men and women serving America in difficult and dangerous intelligence assignments deserve the respect and gratitude of the nation.

The Committee finds that there is a continuing need for an effective system of foreign and military intelligence. United States interests and responsibilities in the world will be challenged, for the foreseeable future, by strong and potentially hostile powers. This requires the maintenance of an effective American intelligence system. The Committee has found that the Soviet KGB and other hostile intelligence services maintain extensive foreign intelligence operations, for both intelligence collection and covert operational purposes. These activities pose a threat to the intelligence activities and interests of the United States and its allies.

The Committee finds that Congress has failed to provide the necessary statutory guidelines to ensure that intelligence agencies carry out their missions in accord with constitutional processes. Mechanisms for, and the practice of, congressional oversight have not been adequate. Further, Congress has not devised appropriate means to effectively use the valuable information developed by the intelligence agencies. Intelligence information and analysis that exist within the executive branch clearly would contribute to sound judgments and more effective legislation in the areas of foreign policy and national security.

The Committee finds that covert action operations have not been an exceptional instrument used only in rare instances when the vital interests of the United States have been at stake. On the contrary, presidents and administrations have made excessive, and at times self-defeating, use of covert action. In addition, covert action has become a routine program with a bureaucratic momentum of its own. The long-term impact, at home and abroad, of repeated disclosure of U.S. covert action never appears to have been assessed. The cumulative effect of covert actions has been increasingly costly to America's interests and reputation. The Committee believes that covert action must be employed only in the most extraordinary circumstances.

Although there is a question concerning the extent to which the Constitution requires publication of intelligence expenditures information, the Committee finds that the Constitution at least requires public disclosure and public authorization of an annual aggregate figure for United States national intelligence activities. Congress' failure as a whole to monitor the intelligence agencies' expenditures has been a major element in the ineffective legislative oversight of the intelligence community. The permanent intelligence oversight committee(s) of Congress should give further consideration to the question of the extent to which further public disclosure of intelligence budget information is prudent and constitutionally necessary.

At the same time, the Committee finds that the operation of an extensive and necessarily secret intelligence system places severe strains on the nation's constitutional government. The Committee is convinced, however, that the competing demands of secrecy and the requirements of the democratic process—our Constitution and our laws—can be reconciled. The need to protect secrets must be balanced with the assurance that secrecy is not used as a means to hide the abuse of power or the failures and mistakes of policy. Means must and can be provided for lawful disclosure of unneeded or unlawful secrets.

The Committee finds that intelligence activities should not be regarded as ends in themselves. Rather, the nation's intelligence functions should be organized and directed to assure that they serve the needs of those in the executive and legislative branches who have responsibility for formulating or carrying out foreign and national security policy.

The Committee finds that Congress has failed to provide the necessary statutory guidelines to ensure that intelligence agencies carry out their necessary missions in accord with constitutional processes.

In order to provide firm direction for the intelligence agencies, the Committee finds that new statutory charters for these agencies must be written that take account of the experience of the past three and a half decades. Further, the Committee finds that the relationship among the various intelligence agencies and between them and the Director of Central Intelligence should be restructured in order to achieve better accountability, coordination, and more efficient use of resources.

These tasks are urgent. They should be undertaken by the Congress in consultation with the executive branch in the coming year. The recent proposals and executive actions by the President are most welcome. However, further action by Congress is necessary.

*   *   *   *   *

Document Nine

Executive Order No. 12063, January 24, 1978,
Governing Intelligence Activities [excerpts]

United States Foreign
Intelligence Activities

Executive Order 12036.   *January 24, 1978*

United States Intelligence
Activities

By virtue of the authority vested in me by the Constitution and statutes of
the United States of America including the National Security Act of 1947, as
amended, and as President of the United States of America, in order to
provide for the organization and control of United States foreign intelligence
activities, it is hereby ordered as follows:

Section 1
Direction, Duties and Responsibilities
with Respect to the National Intelligence Effort

1-1. *National Security Council.*

1-101. *Purpose.* The National Security Council (NSC) was established by
the National Security Act of 1947 to advise the President with respect to the
integration of domestic, foreign, and military policies relating to the national
security. The NSC shall act as the highest Executive Branch entity that
provides review of, guidance for, and direction to the conduct of all national
foreign intelligence and counterintelligence activities.

1-102. *Committees.* The NSC Policy Review Committee and Special Coordination Committee, in accordance with procedures established by the
Assistant to the President for National Security Affairs, shall assist in carrying
out the NSC's responsibilities in the foreign intelligence field.

1-2. *NSC Policy Review Committee.*

1-201. *Membership.* The NSC Policy Review Committee (PRC), when carrying out responsibilities assigned in this Order, shall be chaired by the Director of Central Intelligence and composed of the Vice President, the Secretary of State, the Secretary of the Treasury, the Secretary of Defense, the Assistant to the President for National Security Affairs, and the Chairman of the Joint Chiefs of Staff, or their designees, and other senior officials, as appropriate.

1-202. *Duties.* The PRC shall:

(a) Establish requirements and priorities for national foreign intelligence;

(b) Review the National Foreign Intelligence Program and budget proposals and report to the President as to whether the resource allocations for intelligence capabilities are responsive to the intelligence requirements of the members of the NSC.

(c) Conduct periodic reviews of national foreign intelligence products, evaluate the quality of the intelligence product, develop policy guidance to ensure quality intelligence and to meet changing intelligence requirements; and

(d) Submit an annual report on its activities to the NSC.

1-203. *Appeals.* Recommendations of the PRC on intelligence matters may be appealed to the President or the NSC by any member of the PRC.

1-3. *NSC Special Coordination Committee.*

1-301. *Membership.* The NSC Special Coordination Committee (SCC) is chaired by the Assistant to the President for National Security Affairs and its membership includes the statutory members of the NSC and other senior officials, as appropriate.

1-302. *Special Activities.* The SCC shall consider and submit to the President a policy recommendation, including all dissents, on each special activity. When meeting for this purpose, the members of the SCC shall include the Secretary of State, the Secretary of Defense, the Attorney General, the Director of the Office of Management and Budget, the Assistant to the President for National Security Affairs, the Chairman of the Joint Chiefs of Staff, and the Director of Central Intelligence.

1-303. *Sensitive Foreign Intelligence Collection Operations.* Under standards established by the President, proposals for sensitive foreign intelligence collection operations shall be reported to the Chairman by the Director of Central Intelligence for appropriate review and approval. When meeting for the purpose of reviewing proposals for sensitive foreign intelligence collection operations, the members of the SCC shall include the Secretary of State, the Secretary of Defense, the Attorney General, the Assistant to the President for National Security Affairs, the Director of Central Intelligence, and such other members designated by the Chairman to ensure proper consideration of these operations.

1-304. *Counterintelligence.* The SCC shall develop policy with respect to the conduct of counterintelligence activities. When meeting for this purpose the members of the SCC shall include the Secretary of State, the Secretary of Defense, the Attorney General, the Director of the Office of Management and Budget, the Assistant to the President for National Security Affairs, the Chairman of the Joint Chiefs of Staff, the Director of Central Intelligence, and the Director of the FBI. The SCC's counterintelligence functions shall include:

(a) Developing standards and doctrine for the counterintelligence activities of the United States;

(b) Resolving interagency differences concerning implementation of counterintelligence policy;

(c) Developing and monitoring guidelines consistent with this Order for the maintenance of central records of counterintelligence information;

(d) Submitting to the President an overall annual assessment of the relative threat to United States interests from intelligence and security services of foreign powers and from international terrorist activities, including an assessment of the effectiveness of the United States counterintelligence activities; and

(e) Approving counterintelligence activities which, under such standards as may be established by the President, require SCC approval.

1-305. *Required Membership.* The SCC shall discharge the responsibilities assigned by sections 1-302 through 1-304 only after consideration in a meeting at which all designated members are present or, in unusual circumstances when any such member is unavailable, when a designated representative of the member attends.

1-306. *Additional Duties.* The SCC shall also:

(a) Conduct an annual review of ongoing special activities and sensitive national foreign intelligence collection operations and report thereon to the NSC; and

(b) Carry out such other coordination and review activities as the President may direct.

1-307. *Appeals.* Any member of the SCC may appeal any decision to the President or the NSC.

1-4. *National Foreign Intelligence Board.*

1-401. *Establishment and Duties.* There is established a National Foreign Intelligence Board (NFIB) to advise the Director of Central Intelligence concerning:

(a) Production, review, and coordination of a national foreign intelligence;

(b) The National Foreign Intelligence Program budget;

(c) Interagency exchanges of foreign intelligence information;

(d) Arrangements with foreign governments on intelligence matters;

(e) The protection of intelligence sources and methods;

(f) Activities of common concern; and

(g) Other matters referred to it by the Director of Central Intelligence.

1-402. *Membership.* The NFIB shall be chaired by the Director of Central

Intelligence and shall include other appropriate officers of the CIA, the Office of the Director of Central Intelligence, the Department of State, the Department of Defense, the Department of Justice, the Department of the Treasury, the Department of Energy, the Defense Intelligence Agency, the offices within the Department of Defense for reconnaissance programs, the National Security Agency and the FBI. A representative of the Assistant to the President for National Security Affairs may attend meetings of the NFIB as an observer.

1-403. *Restricted Membership and Observers.* When the NFIB meets for the purpose of section 1-401(a), it shall be composed solely of the senior intelligence officers of the designated agencies. The senior intelligence officers of the Army, Navy and Air Force may attend all meetings of the NFIB as observers.

1-5. *National Intelligence Tasking Center.*

1-501. *Establishment.* There is established a National Intelligence Tasking Center (NITC) under the direction, control and management of the Director of Central Intelligence for coordinating and tasking national foreign intelligence collection activities. The NITC shall be staffed jointly by civilian and military personnel including designated representatives of the chiefs of each of the Department of Defense intelligence organizations engaged in national foreign intelligence activities. Other agencies within the Intelligence Community may also designate representatives.

1-502. *Responsibilities.* The NITC shall be the central mechanism by which the Director of Central Intelligence:

(a) Translates national foreign intelligence requirements and priorities developed by the PRC into specific collection objectives and targets for the Intelligence Community;

(b) Assigns targets and objectives to national foreign intelligence collection organizations and systems;

(c) Ensures the timely dissemination and exploitation of data for national foreign intelligence purposes gathered by national foreign intelligence collection means, and ensures the resulting intelligence flow is routed immediately to relevant components and commands;

(d) Provides advisory tasking concerning collection of national foreign intelligence to departments and agencies having information collection capabilities or intelligence assets that are not a part of the National Foreign Intelligence Program. Particular emphasis shall be placed on increasing the contribution of departments or agencies to the collection of information through overt means.

1-503. *Resolution of Conflicts.* The NITC shall have the authority to resolve conflicts of priority. Any PRC member may appeal such a resolution to the PRC; pending PRC's decision, the tasking remains in effect.

1-504. *Transfer of Authority.* All responsibilities and authorities of the Director of Central Intelligence concerning the NITC shall be transferred to the Secretary of Defense upon the express direction of the President. To maintain readiness for such transfer, the Secretary of Defense shall, with advance agreement of the Director of Central Intelligence, assume temporarily during regular practice exercises all responsibilities and authorities of the Director of Central Intelligence concerning the NITC.

1-6. *The Director of Central Intelligence.*

1-601. *Duties.* The Director of Central Intelligence shall be responsible directly to the NSC and, in addition to the duties specified elsewhere in this Order, shall:

(a) Act as the primary adviser to the President and the NSC on national foreign intelligence and provide the President and other officials in the Executive Branch with national foreign intelligence;

(b) Be the head of the CIA and of such staff elements as may be required for discharge of the Director's Intelligence Community responsibilities;

(c) Act, in appropriate consultation with the departments and agencies, as the Intelligence Community's principal spokesperson to the Congress, the news media and the public, and facilitate the use of national foreign intelligence products by the Congress in a secure manner;

(d) Develop, consistent with the requirements and priorities established by the PRC, such objectives and guidance for the Intelligence Community as will enhance capabilities for responding to expected future needs for national foreign intelligence;

(e) Promote the development and maintenance of services of common concern by designated foreign intelligence organizations on behalf of the Intelligence Community;

(f) Ensure implementation of special activities;

(g) Formulate policies concerning intelligence arrangements with foreign governments, and coordinate intelligence relationships between agencies of the Intelligence Community and the intelligence or internal security services of foreign governments;

(h) Conduct a program to protect against overclassification of foreign intelligence information;

(i) Ensure the establishment by the Intelligence Community of common security and access standards for managing and handling foreign intelligence systems, information and products;

(j) Participate in the development of procedures required to be approved by the Attorney General governing the conduct of intelligence activities;

(k) Establish uniform criteria for the determination of relative priorities for the transmission of critical national foreign intelligence, and advise the Secretary of Defense concerning the communications requirements of the Intelligence Community for the transmission of such intelligence;

(l) Provide appropriate intelligence to departments and agencies not within the Intelligence Community; and

(m) Establish appropriate committees or other advisory groups to assist in the execution of the foregoing responsibilities.

1-602. *National Foreign Intelligence Program Budget.* The Director of Central Intelligence shall, to the extent consistent with applicable law, have full and exclusive authority for approval of the National Foreign Intelligence Program budget submitted to the President. Pursuant to this authority:

(a) The Director of Central Intelligence shall provide guidance for program and budget development to program managers and heads of component activities and to department and agency heads;

(b) The heads of departments and agencies involved in the National Foreign Intelligence Program shall ensure timely development and submission to the Director of Central Intelligence of proposed national programs and budgets in the format designated by the Director of Central Intelligence, by the program managers and heads of component activities, and shall also ensure that the Director of Central Intelligence is provided, in a timely and responsive manner, all information necessary to perform the Director's program and budget responsibilities;

(c) The Director of Central Intelligence shall review and evaluate the national program and budget submissions and, with the advice of the NFIB and the departments and agencies concerned, develop the consolidated National Foreign Intelligence Program budget and present it to the President through the Office of Management and Budget;

(d) The Director of Central Intelligence shall present and justify the National Foreign Intelligence Program budget to the Congress;

(e) The heads of the departments and agencies shall, in consultation with the Director of Central Intelligence, establish rates of obligation for appropriated funds;

(f) The Director of Central Intelligence shall have full and exclusive authority for reprogramming National Foreign Intelligence Program funds, in accord with guidelines established by the Office of Management and Budget, but shall do so only after consultation with the head of the department affected and appropriate consultation with the Congress;

(g) The departments and agencies may appeal to the President decisions by the Director of Central Intelligence on budget or reprogramming matters of the National Foreign Intelligence Program.

(h) The Director of Central Intelligence shall monitor National Foreign Intelligence Program implementation and may conduct program and performance audits and evaluations.

1-603. *Responsibility For National Foreign Intelligence.* The Director of Central Intelligence shall have full responsibility for production and dissemination of national foreign intelligence and have authority to levy analytic tasks on departmental intelligence production organizations, in consultation with those organizations. In doing so, the Director of Central Intelligence shall ensure that diverse points of view are considered fully and that differences of judgment within the Intelligence Community are brought to the attention of national policymakers.

1-604. *Protection of Sources, Methods and Procedures.* The Director of Central Intelligence shall ensure that programs are developed which protect intelligence sources, methods and analytical procedures, provided that this responsibility shall be limited within the United States to:

(a) Using lawful means to protect against disclosure by present or former employees of the CIA or the Office of the Director of Central Intelligence, or by persons or organizations presently or formerly under contract with such entities; and

(b) Providing policy, guidance and technical assistance to departments and agencies regarding protection of intelligence information, including information that may reveal intelligence sources and methods.

1-605. *Responsibility of Executive Branch Agencies.* The heads of all Executive Branch departments and agencies shall, in accordance with law and relevant Attorney General procedures, give the Director of Central Intelligence access to all information relevant to the national intelligence needs of the United States and shall give due consideration to requests from the Director of Central Intelligence for appropriate support for CIA activities.

1-606. *Access to CIA Intelligence.* The Director of Central Intelligence, shall, in accordance with law and relevant Attorney General procedures, give the heads of the departments and agencies access to all intelligence, developed by the CIA or the staff elements of the office of the Director of Central Intelligence, relevant to the national intelligence needs of the departments and agencies.

1-7. *Senior Officials of the Intelligence Community.* The senior officials of each of the agencies within the Intelligence Community shall:

1-701. Ensure that all activities of their agencies are carried out in accordance with applicable law;

1-702. Make use of the capabilities of other agencies within the Intelligence Community in order to achieve efficiency and mutual assistance;

1-703. Contribute in their areas of responsibility to the national foreign intelligence products;

1-704. Establish internal policies and guidelines governing employee conduct and ensure that such are made known to each employee;

1-705. Provide for strong, independent, internal means to identify, inspect, and report on unlawful or improper activity;

1-706. Report to the Attorney General evidence of possible violations of federal criminal law by an employee of their department or agency, and report to the Attorney General evidence of possible violations by any other person of those federal criminal laws specified in guidelines adopted by the Attorney General;

1-707. In any case involving serious or continuing breaches of security, recommend to the Attorney General that the case be referred to the FBI for further investigation;

1-708. Furnish the Director of Central Intelligence, the PRC and the SCC, in accordance with applicable law and Attorney General procedures, the information required for the performance of their respective duties;

1-709. Report to the Intelligence Oversight Board, and keep the Director of Central Intelligence appropriately informed, concerning any intelligence activities of their organizations which raise questions of legality or propriety;

1-710. Protect intelligence and intelligence sources and methods consistent with guidance from the Director of Central Intelligence and the NSC;

1-711. Disseminate intelligence to cooperating foreign governments under arrangements established or agreed to by the Director of Central Intelligence;

1-712. Execute programs to protect against overclassification of foreign intelligence;

1-713. Instruct their employees to cooperate fully with the Intelligence Oversight Board; and

1-714. Ensure that the Inspectors General and General Counsel of their agencies have access to any information necessary to perform their duties assigned by this Order.

1-8. *The Central Intelligence Agency.* All duties and responsibilities of the CIA shall be related to the intelligence functions set out below. As authorized by the National Security Act of 1947, as amended, the CIA Act of 1949, as amended, and other laws, regulations and directives, the CIA, under the direction of the NSC, shall:

1-801. Collect foreign intelligence, including information not otherwise obtainable, and develop, conduct, or provide support for technical and other programs which collect national foreign intelligence. The collection of information within the United States shall be coordinated with the FBI as required by procedures agreed upon by the Director of Central Intelligence and the Attorney General;

1-802. Produce and disseminate foreign intelligence relating to the national security, including foreign political, economic, scientific, technical, military, geographic and sociological intelligence to meet the needs of the President, the NSC, and other elements of the United States Government;

1-803. Collect, produce and disseminate intelligence on foreign aspects of narcotics production and trafficking;

1-804. Conduct counterintelligence activities outside the United States and coordinate counterintelligence activities conducted outside the United States by other agencies within the Intelligence Community;

1-805. Without assuming or performing any internal security functions, conduct counterintelligence activities within the United States, but only in coordination with the FBI and subject to the approval of the Attorney General;

1-806. Produce and disseminate counterintelligence studies and reports;

1-807. Coordinate the collection outside the United States of intelligence information not otherwise obtainable;

1-808. Conduct special activities approved by the President and carry out such activities consistent with applicable law;

1-809. Conduct services of common concern for the Intelligence Community as directed by the NSC;

1-810. Carry out or contract for research, development and procurement of technical systems and devices relating to authorized functions;

1-811. Protect the security of its installations, activities, information and personnel by appropriate means, including such investigations of applicants, employees, contractors, and other persons with similar associations with the CIA as are necessary;

1-812. Conduct such administrative and technical support activities within and outside the United States as are necessary to perform the functions described in sections 1-801 through 1-811 above, including procurement and essential cover and proprietary arrangements;

1-813. Provide legal and legislative services and other administrative support to the Office of the Director of Central Intelligence. . . .

Section 2
Restrictions on Intelligence
Activities

2-1. *Adherence to Law.*

2-101. *Purpose.* Information about the capabilities, intentions and activities of foreign powers, organizations, or persons and their agents is essential to informed decision-making in the areas of national defense and foreign relations. The measures employed to acquire such information should be responsive to legitimate governmental needs and must be conducted in a manner that preserves and respects established concepts of privacy and civil liberties.

2-102. *Principles of Interpretation.* Sections 2-201 through 2-309 set forth limitations which, in addition to other applicable laws, are intended to achieve the proper balance between protection of individual rights and acquisition of essential information. Those sections do not authorize any activity not authorized by sections 1-101 through 1-1503 and do not provide any exemption from any other law.

2-2. *Restrictions on Certain Collection Techniques.*

2-201. *General Provisions.*

(a) The activities described in Sections 2-202 through 2-208 shall be undertaken only as permitted by this Order and by procedures established by the head of the agency concerned and approved by the Attorney General. Those procedures shall protect constitutional rights and privacy, ensure that information is gathered by the least intrusive means possible, and limit use of such information to lawful governmental purposes.

(b) Activities described in sections 2-202 through 2-205 for which a warrant would be required if undertaken for law enforcement rather than intelligence purposes shall not be undertaken against a United States person without a judicial warrant, unless the President has authorized the type of activity involved and the Attorney General has both approved the particular activity and determined that there is probable cause to believe that the United States person is an agent of a foreign power.

2-202. *Electronic Surveillance.* The CIA may not engage in any electronic surveillance within the United States. No agency within the Intelligence Community shall engage in any electronic surveillance directed against a United States person abroad or designed to intercept a communication sent from, or intended for receipt within, the United States except as permitted by the procedures established pursuant to section 2-201. Training of personnel by agencies in the Intelligence Community in the use of electronic communications equipment, testing by such agencies of such equipment, and the use of measures to determine the existence and capability of electronic surveillance equipment being used unlawfully shall not be prohibited and shall also be governed by such procedures. Such activities shall be limited in scope and duration to those necessary to carry out the training, testing or countermeasures purpose. No information derived from communications intercepted in the course of such training, testing or use of countermeasures may be retained or used for any other purpose.

2-203. *Television Cameras and Other Monitoring.* No agency within the Intelligence Community shall use any electronic or mechanical device surreptitiously and continuously to monitor any person within the United States, or any United States person abroad, except as permitted by the procedures established pursuant to Section 2-201.

2-204. *Physical Searches.* No agency within the Intelligence Community except the FBI may conduct any unconsented physical searches within the United States. All such searches conducted by the FBI, as well as all such searches conducted by any agency within the Intelligence Community outside the United States and directed against United States persons, shall be undertaken only as permitted by procedures established pursuant to Section 2-201.

2-205. *Mail Surveillance.* No agency within the Intelligence Community shall open mail or examine envelopes in United States postal channels, except in accordance with applicable statutes and regulations. No agency within the Intelligence Community shall open mail of a United States person abroad except as permitted by procedures established pursuant to Section 2-201.

2-206. *Physical Surveillance.* The FBI may conduct physical surveillance directed against United States persons or others only in the course of a lawful investigation. Other agencies within the Intelligence Community may not undertake any physical surveillance directed against a United States person unless:

(a) The surveillance is conducted outside the United States and the person being surveilled is reasonably believed to be acting on behalf of a foreign power, engaging in international terrorist activities, or engaging in narcotics production or trafficking;

(b) The surveillance is conducted solely for the purpose of identifying a person who is in contact with someone who is the subject of a foreign intelligence or counterintelligence investigation; or

(c) That person is being surveilled for the purpose of protecting foreign intelligence and counterintelligence sources and methods from unauthorized disclosure or is the subject of a lawful counterintelligence, personnel, physical or communications security investigation.

(d) No surveillance under paragraph (c) of this section may be conducted within the United States unless the person being surveilled is a present employee, intelligence agency contractor or employee of such a contractor, or is a military person employed by a non-intelligence element of a military service. Outside the United States such surveillance may also be conducted against a former employee, intelligence agency contractor or employee of a contractor or a civilian person employed by a non-intelligence element of an agency within the Intelligence Community. A person who is in contact with such a present or former employee or contractor may also be surveilled, but only to the extent necessary to identify that person.

2-207. *Undisclosed Participation in Domestic Organizations.* No employees may join, or otherwise participate in, any organization within the United States on behalf of any agency within the Intelligence Community without disclosing their intelligence affiliation to appropriate officials of the organization, except as permitted by procedures established pursuant to Section 2-201. Such procedures shall provide for disclosure of such affiliation in all cases unless the agency head or a designee approved by the Attorney General finds that non-disclosure is essential to achieving lawful purposes, and that finding is subject to review by the Attorney General. Those procedures shall further limit undisclosed participation to cases where:

(a) The participation is undertaken on behalf of the FBI in the course of a lawful investigation;

(b) The organization concerned is composed primarily of individuals who are not United States persons and is reasonably believed to be acting on behalf of a foreign power; or

(c) The participation is strictly limited in its nature, scope and duration to that necessary for other lawful purposes relating to foreign intelligence and is a type of participation approved by the Attorney General and set forth in a public document. No such participation may be undertaken for the purpose of influencing the activity of the organization or its members.

2-208. *Collection of Nonpublicly Available Information.* No agency within the Intelligence Community may collect, disseminate or store information concerning the activities of United States persons that is not available publicly, unless it does so with their consent or as permitted by procedures established pursuant to Section 2-201. Those procedures shall limit collection, storage or dissemination to the following types of information:

(a) Information concerning corporations or other commercial organizations or activities that constitutes foreign intelligence or counterintelligence;

(b) Information arising out of a lawful counterintelligence or personnel, physical or communications security investigation;

(c) Information concerning present or former employees, present or former intelligence agency contractors or their present or former employees, or applicants for any such employment or contracting, which is needed to protect foreign intelligence or counterintelligence sources or methods from unauthorized disclosure;

(d) Information needed solely to identify individuals in contact with those persons described in paragraph (c) of this section or with someone who is the subject of a lawful foreign intelligence or counterintelligence investigation;

(e) Information concerning persons who are reasonably believed to be potential sources or contacts, but only for the purpose of determining the suitability or credibility of such persons;

(f) Information constituting foreign intelligence or counterintelligence gathered abroad or from electronic surveillance conducted in compliance with Section 2-202 or from cooperating sources in the United States;

(g) Information about a person who is reasonably believed to be acting on behalf of a foreign power, engaging in international terrorist activities or narcotics production or trafficking, or endangering the safety of a person protected by the United States Secret Service or the Department of State;

(h) Information acquired by overhead reconnaissance not directed at specific United States persons;

(i) Information concerning United States persons abroad that is obtained in response to requests from the Department of State for support of its consular responsibilities relating to the welfare of those persons;

(j) Information collected, received, disseminated or stored by the FBI and necessary to fulfill its lawful investigative responsibilities; or

(k) Information concerning persons or activities that pose a clear threat to any facility or personnel of an agency within the Intelligence Community.

Such information may be retained only by the agency threatened and, if appropriate, by the United States Secret Service and the FBI.

2-3. *Additional Restrictions and Limitations.*

2-301. *Tax Information.* No agency within the Intelligence Community shall examine tax returns or tax information except as permitted by applicable law.

2-302. *Restrictions on Experimentation.* No agency within the Intelligence Community shall sponsor, contract for, or conduct research on human subjects except in accordance with guidelines issued by the Department of Health, Education and Welfare. The subject's informed consent shall be documented as required by those guidelines.

2-303. *Restrictions on Contracting.* No agency within the Intelligence Community shall enter into a contract or arrangement for the provision of goods or services with private companies or institutions in the United States unless the agency sponsorship is known to the appropriate officials of the company or institution. In the case of any company or institution other than an academic institution, intelligence agency sponsorship may be concealed where it is determined, pursuant to procedures approved by the Attorney General, that such concealment is necessary to maintain essential cover or proprietary arrangements for authorized intelligence purposes.

2-304. *Restrictions on Personnel Assigned to Other Agencies.* An employee detailed to another agency within the federal government shall be responsible to the host agency and shall not report to the parent agency on the affairs of the host agency unless so directed by the host agency. The head of the host agency, and any successor, shall be informed of the employee's relationship with the parent agency.

2-305. *Prohibition on Assassination.* No person employed by or acting on behalf of the United States Government shall engage in, or conspire to engage in, assassination.

2-306. *Restrictions on Special Activities.* No component of the United States Government except an agency within the Intelligence Community may conduct any special activity. No such agency except the CIA (or the military services in wartime) may conduct any special activity unless the President determines, with the SCC's advice, that another agency is more likely to achieve a particular objective.

2-307. *Restrictions on Indirect Participation in Prohibited Activities.* No agency of the Intelligence Community shall request or otherwise encourage, directly or indirectly, any person, organization, or government agency to undertake activities forbidden by this Order or by applicable law.

2-308. *Restrictions on Assistance to Law Enforcement Authorities.* Agencies within the Intelligence Community other than the FBI shall not, except as expressly authorized by law:

(a) Provide services, equipment, personnel or facilities to the Law Enforcement Assistance Administration (or its successor agencies) or to state or local police organizations of the United States; or

(b) Participate in or fund any law enforcement activity within the United States.

2-309. *Permissible Assistance to Law Enforcement Authorities.* The restrictions in Section 2-308 shall not preclude:

(a) Cooperation with appropriate law enforcement agencies for the purpose of protecting the personnel and facilities of any agency within the Intelligence Community;

(b) Participation in law enforcement activities, in accordance with law and this Order, to investigate or prevent clandestine intelligence activities by foreign powers, international narcotics production and trafficking, or international terrorist activities; or

(c) Provision of specialized equipment, technical knowledge, or assistance of expert personnel for use by any department or agency or, when lives are endangered, to support local law enforcement agencies. Provision of assistance by expert personnel shall be governed by procedures approved by the Attorney General.

2-310. *Permissible Dissemination and Storage of Information.* Nothing in Sections 2-201 through 2-309 of this Order shall prohibit:

(a) Dissemination to appropriate law enforcement agencies of information which indicates involvement in activities that may violate federal, state, local or foreign laws;

(b) Storage of information required by law to be retained;

(c) Dissemination of information covered by Section 2-208 (a)-(j) to agencies within the Intelligence Community or entities of cooperating foreign governments; or

(d) Lawful storage or dissemination of information solely for administrative purposes not related to intelligence or security.

Section 3
Oversight of Intelligence
Organizations

3-1. *Intelligence Oversight Board.*

3-101. *Membership.* The President's Intelligence Oversight Board (IOB) shall function within the White House. The IOB shall have three members who shall be appointed by the President and who shall be from outside the government and be qualified on the basis of ability, knowledge, diversity of background and experience. No member shall have any personal interest in any contractual relationship with any agency within the Intelligence Community. One member shall be designated by the President as chairman.

3-102. *Duties.* The IOB shall:

(a) Review periodically the practices and procedures of the Inspectors General and General Counsel with responsibilities for agencies within the Intelligence Community for discovering and reporting to the IOB intelligence activities that raise questions of legality or propriety, and consider written and oral reports referred under Section 3-201;

(b) Review periodically for adequacy the internal guidelines of each agency within the Intelligence Community concerning the legality or propriety of intelligence activities;

(c) Report periodically, at least quarterly, to the President on its findings; and report in a timely manner to the President any intelligence activities that raise serious questions of legality or propriety;

(d) Forward to the Attorney General, in a timely manner, reports received concerning intelligence activities in which a question of legality has been raised or which the IOB believes to involve questions of legality; and

(e) Conduct such investigations of the intelligence activities of agencies within the Intelligence Community as the Board deems necessary to carry out its functions under this Order.

3-103. *Restriction on Staff.* No person who serves on the staff of the IOB shall have any contractual or employment relationship with any agency within the Intelligence Community.

3-2. *Inspectors General and General Counsel.* Inspectors General and General Counsel with responsibility for agencies within the Intelligence Community shall:

3-201. Transmit timely reports to the IOB concerning any intelligence activities that come to their attention and that raise questions of legality or propriety;

3-202. Promptly report to the IOB actions taken concerning the Board's findings on intelligence activities that raise questions of legality or propriety;

3-203. Provide to the IOB information requested concerning the legality or propriety of intelligence activities within their respective agencies;

3-204. Formulate practices and procedures for discovering and reporting to the IOB intelligence activities that raise questions of legality or propriety; and

3-205. Report to the IOB any occasion on which the Inspectors General or General Counsel were directed not to report any intelligence activity to the IOB which they believed raised questions of legality or propriety.

3-3. *Attorney General.* The Attorney General shall:

3-301. Receive and consider reports from agencies within the Intelligence Community forwarded by the IOB;

3-302. Report to the President in a timely fashion any intelligence activities which raise questions of legality;

3-303. Report to the IOB and to the President in a timely fashion decisions made or actions taken in response to reports from agencies within the Intelligence Community forwarded to the Attorney General by the IOB;

3-304. Inform the IOB of legal opinions affecting the operations of the Intelligence Community; and

3-305. Establish or approve procedures, as required by this Order, for the conduct of intelligence activities. Such procedures shall ensure compliance with law, protect constitutional rights and privacy, and ensure that any intelligence activity within the United States or directed against any United States person is conducted by the least intrusive means possible. The procedures shall also ensure that any use, dissemination and storage of information about United States persons acquired through intelligence activities is limited to that necessary to achieve lawful governmental purposes.

3-4. *Congressional Intelligence Committees.* Under such procedures as the President may establish and consistent with applicable authorities and duties, including those conferred by the Constitution upon the Executive and Legislative Branches and by law to protect sources and methods, the Director of Central Intelligence and heads of departments and agencies of the United States involved in intelligence activities shall:

3-401. Keep the Permanent Select Committee on Intelligence of the House of Representatives and the Select Committee on Intelligence of the Senate fully and currently informed concerning intelligence activities, including any significant anticipated activities which are the responsibility of, or engaged in, by such department or agency. This requirement does not constitute a condition precedent to the implementation of such intelligence activities;

3-402. Provide any information or document in the possession, custody, or control of the department or agency or person paid by such department or agency, within the jurisdiction of the Permanent Select Committee on Intelligence of the House of Representatives or the Select Committee on Intelligence of the Senate, upon the request of such committee; and

3-403. Report in a timely fashion to the Permanent Select Committee on Intelligence of the House of Representatives and the Select Committee on Intelligence of the Senate information relating to intelligence activities that are illegal or improper and corrective actions that are taken or planned. . . .

The White House   Jimmy Carter
January 24, 1978

Document Ten

Executive Order No. 12333, December 4, 1981, Governing Intelligence Activities [excerpts]

Executive Order 12333 of December 4, 1981
United States Intelligence Activities

Timely and accurate information about the activities, capabilities, plans, and intentions of foreign powers, organizations, and persons and their agents, is essential to the national security of the United States. All reasonable and lawful means must be used to ensure that the United States will receive the best intelligence available. For that purpose, by virtue of the authority vested in me by the Constitution and statutes of the United States of America, including the National Security Act of 1947, as amended, and as President of the United States of America, in order to provide for the effective conduct of United States intelligence activities and the protection of constitutional rights, it is hereby ordered as follows:

Part 1
Goals, Direction, Duties and Responsibilities With Respect to the National Intelligence Effort

1.1 *Goals.* The United States intelligence effort shall provide the President and the National Security Council with the necessary information on which to base decisions concerning the conduct and development of foreign, defense and economic policy, and the protection of United States national interests from foreign security threats. All departments and agencies shall cooperate fully to fulfill this goal.

(a) Maximum emphasis should be given to fostering analytical competition among appropriate elements of the Intelligence Community.

(b) All means, consistent with applicable United States law and this Order, and with full consideration of the rights of United States persons, shall be used to develop intelligence information for the President and the National

Security Council. A balanced approach between technical collection efforts and other means should be maintained and encouraged.

(c) Special emphasis should be given to detecting and countering espionage and other threats and activities directed by foreign intelligence services against the United States Government, or United States corporations, establishments, or persons.

(d) To the greatest extent possible consistent with applicable United States law and this Order, and with full consideration of the rights of United States persons, all agencies and departments should seek to ensure full and free exchange of information in order to derive maximum benefit from the United States intelligence effort.

1.2 *The National Security Council.*

(a) *Purpose.* The National Security Council (NSC) was established by the National Security Act of 1947 to advise the President with respect to the integration of domestic, foreign and military policies relating to the national security. The NSC shall act as the highest Executive Branch entity that provides review of, guidance for and direction to the conduct of all national foreign intelligence, counterintelligence, and special activities, and attendant policies and programs.

(b) *Committees.* The NSC shall establish such committees as may be necessary to carry out its functions and responsibilities under this Order. The NSC, or a committee established by it, shall consider and submit to the President a policy recommendation, including all dissents, on each special activity and shall review proposals for other sensitive intelligence operations.

1.3 *National Foreign Intelligence Advisory Groups.*

(a) *Establishment and Duties.* The Director of Central Intelligence shall establish such boards, councils, or groups as required for the purpose of obtaining advice from within the Intelligence Community concerning:

(1) Production, review and coordination of national foreign intelligence;

(2) Priorities for the National Foreign Intelligence Program budget;

(3) Interagency exchanges of foreign intelligence information;

(4) Arrangements with foreign governments on intelligence matters;

(5) Protection of intelligence sources and methods;

(6) Activities of common concern; and

(7) Such other matters as may be referred by the Director of Central Intelligence.

(b) *Membership.* Advisory groups established pursuant to this section shall be chaired by the Director of Central Intelligence or his designated representative and shall consist of senior representatives from organizations within the Intelligence Community and from departments or agencies containing such organizations, as designated by the Director of Central Intelligence. Groups for consideration of substantive intelligence matters will include representatives of organizations involved in the collection, processing and analysis of intelligence. A senior representative of the Secretary of Commerce, the Attorney General, the Assistant to the President for National Security Affairs, and the Office of the Secretary of Defense shall be invited to participate in any group which deals with other than substantive intelligence matters.

1.4 *The Intelligence Community.* The agencies within the Intelligence Community shall, in accordance with applicable United States law and with the other provisions of this Order, conduct intelligence activities necessary for the conduct of foreign relations and the protection of the national security of the United States, including:

(a) Collection of information needed by the President, the National Security Council, the Secretaries of State and Defense, and other Executive Branch officials for the performance of their duties and responsibilities;

(b) Production and dissemination of intelligence;

(c) Collection of information concerning, and the conduct of activities to protect against, intelligence activities directed against the United States, international terrorist and international narcotics activities, and other hostile activities directed against the United States by foreign powers, organizations, persons, and their agents;

(d) Special activities;

(e) Administrative and support activities within the United States and abroad necessary for the performance of authorized activities; and

(f) Such other intelligence activities as the President may direct from time to time.

1.5 *Director of Central Intelligence.* In order to discharge the duties and responsibilities prescribed by law, the Director of Central Intelligence shall be responsible directly to the President and the NSC and shall:

(a) Act as the primary adviser to the President and the NSC on national foreign intelligence and provide the President and other officials in the Executive Branch with national foreign intelligence;

(b) Develop such objectives and guidance for the Intelligence Community as will enhance capabilities for responding to expected future needs for national foreign intelligence;

(c) Promote the development and maintenance of services of common concern by designated intelligence organizations on behalf of the Intelligence Community;

(d) Ensure implementation of special activities;

(e) Formulate policies concerning foreign intelligence and counterintelligence arrangements with foreign governments, coordinate foreign intelligence and counterintelligence relationships between agencies of the Intelligence Community and the intelligence or internal security services of foreign governments, and establish procedures governing the conduct of liaison by any department or agency with such services on narcotics activities;

(f) Participate in the development of procedures approved by the Attorney General governing criminal narcotics intelligence activities abroad to ensure that these activities are consistent with foreign intelligence programs;

(g) Ensure the establishment by the Intelligence Community of common security and access standards for managing and handling foreign intelligence systems, information, and products;

(h) Ensure that programs are developed which protect intelligence sources, methods, and analytical procedures;

(i) Establish uniform criteria for the determination of relative priorities for the transmission of critical national foreign intelligence, and advise the Secretary of Defense concerning the communications requirements of the Intelligence Community for the transmission of such intelligence;

(j) Establish appropriate staffs, committees, or other advisory groups to assist in the execution of the Director's responsibilities;

(k) Have full responsibility for production and dissemination of national foreign intelligence, and authority to levy analytic tasks on departmental intelligence production organizations, in consultation with those organizations, ensuring that appropriate mechanisms for competitive analysis are developed so that diverse points of view are considered fully and differences of judgment within the Intelligence Community are brought to the attention of national policymakers;

(l) Ensure the timely exploitation and dissemination of data gathered by national foreign intelligence collection means, and ensure that the resulting intelligence is disseminated immediately to appropriate government entities and military commands;

(m) Establish mechanisms which translate national foreign intelligence objectives and priorities approved by the NSC into specific guidance for the Intelligence Community, resolve conflicts in tasking priority, provide to departments and agencies having information collection capabilities that are not part of the National Foreign Intelligence Program advisory tasking concerning collection of national foreign intelligence, and provide for the development of plans and arrangements for transfer of required collection tasking authority to the Secretary of Defense when directed by the President;

(n) Develop, with the advice of the program managers and departments and agencies concerned, the consolidated National Foreign Intelligence Program budget, and present it to the President and the Congress;

(o) Review and approve all requests for reprogramming National Foreign Intelligence Program funds, in accordance with guidelines established by the Office of Management and Budget;

(p) Monitor National Foreign Intelligence Program implementation, and, as necessary, conduct program and performance audits and evaluations;

(q) Together with the Secretary of Defense, ensure that there is no unnecessary overlap between national foreign intelligence programs and Department of Defense intelligence programs consistent with the requirement to develop competitive analysis, and provide to and obtain from the Secretary of Defense all information necessary for this purpose;

(r) In accordance with law and relevant procedures approved by the Attorney General under this Order, give the heads of the departments and agencies access to all intelligence, developed by the CIA or the staff elements of the Director of Central Intelligence, relevant to the national intelligence needs of the departments and agencies; and

(s) Facilitate the use of national foreign intelligence products by Congress in a secure manner.

1.6 *Duties and Responsibilities of the Heads of Executive Branch Departments and Agencies.*

(a) The heads of all Executive Branch departments and agencies shall, in accordance with law and relevant procedures approved by the Attorney General under this Order, give the Director of Central Intelligence access to all information relevant to the national intelligence needs of the United States, and shall give due consideration to the requests from the Director of Central Intelligence for appropriate support for Intelligence Community activities.

(b) The heads of departments and agencies involved in the National Foreign Intelligence Program shall ensure timely development and submission to the Director of Central Intelligence by the program managers and heads of component activities of proposed national programs and budgets in the format designated by the Director of Central Intelligence, and shall also ensure that the Director of Central Intelligence, and shall also ensure that the Director of Central Intelligence is provided, in a timely and responsive manner, all information necessary to perform the Director's program and budget responsibilities.

(c) The heads of departments and agencies involved in the National Foreign Intelligence Program may appeal to the President decisions by the Director of Central Intelligence on budget or reprogramming matters of the National Foreign Intelligence Program.

1.7 *Senior Officials of the Intelligence Community.* The heads of departments and agencies with organizations in the Intelligence Community or the heads of such organizations, as appropriate, shall:

(a) Report to the Attorney General possible violations of federal criminal laws by employees and of specified federal criminal laws by any other person as provided in procedures agreed upon by the Attorney General and the head of the department or agency concerned, in a manner consistent with the protection of intelligence sources and methods, as specified in those procedures;

(b) In any case involving serious or continuing breaches of security, recommend to the Attorney General that the case be referred to the FBI for further investigation;

(c) Furnish the Director of Central Intelligence and the NSC, in accordance with applicable law and procedures approved by the Attorney General under this Order, the information required for the performance of their respective duties;

(d) Report to the Intelligence Oversight Board, and keep the Director of Central Intelligence appropriately informed, concerning any intelligence activities of their organizations that they have reason to believe may be unlawful or contrary to Executive order or Presidential directive;

(e) Protect intelligence and intelligence sources and methods from unauthorized disclosure consistent with guidance from the Director of Central Intelligence;

(f) Disseminate intelligence to cooperating foreign governments under arrangements established or agreed to by the Director of Central Intelligence;

(g) Participate in the development of procedures approved by the Attorney General governing production and dissemination of intelligence resulting from criminal narcotics intelligence activities abroad if their departments, agencies, or organizations have intelligence responsibilities for foreign or domestic narcotics production and trafficking;

(h) Instruct their employees to cooperate fully with the Intelligence Oversight Board; and

(i) Ensure that the Inspectors General and General Counsels for their organizations have access to any information necessary to perform their duties assigned by this Order.

1.8 *The Central Intelligence Agency.* All duties and responsibilities of the CIA shall be related to the intelligence functions set out below. As authorized by this Order; the National Security Act of 1947, as amended; the CIA Act of 1949, as amended; appropriate directives or other applicable law, the CIA shall:

(a) Collect, produce and disseminate foreign intelligence and counterintelligence, including information not otherwise obtainable. The collection of foreign intelligence or counterintelligence within the United States shall be coordinated with the FBI as required by procedures agreed upon by the Director of Central Intelligence and the Attorney General;

(b) Collect, produce and disseminate intelligence on foreign aspects of narcotics production and trafficking;

(c) Conduct counterintelligence activities outside the United States and, without assuming or performing any internal security functions, conduct counterintelligence activities within the United States in coordination with the FBI as required by procedures agreed upon by the Director of Central Intelligence and the Attorney General;

(d) Coordinate counterintelligence activities and the collection of information not otherwise obtainable when conducted outside the United States by other departments and agencies;

(e) Conduct special activities approved by the President. No agency except the CIA (or the Armed Forces of the United States in time of war declared by Congress or during any period covered by a report from the President to the Congress under the War Powers Resolution (87 Stat. 855)) may conduct any special activity unless the President determines that another agency is more likely to achieve a particular objective;

(f) Conduct services of common concern for the Intelligence Community as directed by the NSC;

(g) Carry out or contract for research, development and procurement of technical systems and devices relating to authorized functions;

(h) Protect the security of its installations, activities, information, property, and employees by appropriate means, including such investigations of applicants, employees, contractors, and other persons with similar associations with the CIA as are necessary; and

(i) Conduct such administrative and technical support activities within and outside the United States as are necessary to perform the functions described in sections (a) through (h) above, including procurement and essential cover and proprietary arrangements. . . .

Part 2
Conduct of Intelligence Activities

2.1 *Need.* Accurate and timely information about the capabilities, intentions and activities of foreign powers, organizations, or persons and their agents is essential to informed decisionmaking in the areas of national defense and foreign relations. Collection of such information is a priority objective and will be pursued in a vigorous, innovative and responsible manner that is consistent with the Constitution and applicable law and respectful of the principles upon which the United States was founded.

2.2 *Purpose.* This Order is intended to enhance human and technical collection techniques, especially those undertaken abroad, and the acquisition of significant foreign intelligence, as well as the detection and countering of international terrorist activities and espionage conducted by foreign powers. Set forth below are certain general principles that, in addition to and consistent with applicable laws, are intended to achieve the proper balance between the acquisition of essential information and protection of individual interests. Nothing in this Order shall be construed to apply to or interfere with any authorized civil or criminal law enforcement responsibility of any department or agency.

2.3 *Collection of Information.* Agencies within the Intelligence Community are authorized to collect, retain or disseminate information concerning United States persons only in accordance with procedures established by the head of the agency concerned and approved by the Attorney General, consistent with the authorities provided by Part 1 of this Order. Those procedures shall permit collection, retention and dissemination of the following types of information:

(a) Information that is publicly available or collected with the consent of the person concerned;

(b) Information constituting foreign intelligence or counterintelligence, including such information concerning corporations or other commercial organizations. Collection within the United States of foreign intelligence not otherwise obtainable shall be undertaken by the FBI or, when significant foreign intelligence is sought, by other authorized agencies of the Intelligence Community, provided that no foreign intelligence collection by such agencies may be undertaken for the purpose of acquiring information concerning the domestic activities of United States persons;

(c) Information obtained in the course of a lawful foreign intelligence, counterintelligence, international narcotics or international terrorism investigation;

(d) Information needed to protect the safety of any persons or organizations, including those who are targets, victims or hostages of international terrorist organizations;

(e) Information needed to protect foreign intelligence or counterintelligence sources or methods from unauthorized disclosure. Collection within the United States shall be undertaken by the FBI except that other agencies of the Intelligence Community may also collect such information concerning present or former employees, present or former intelligence agency contractors or their present or former employees, or applicants for any such employment or contracting;

(f) Information concerning persons who are reasonably believed to be potential sources or contacts for the purpose of determining their suitability or credibility;

(g) Information arising out of a lawful personnel, physical or communications security investigation;

(h) Information acquired by overhead reconnaissance not directed at specific United States persons;

(i) Incidentally obtained information that may indicate involvement in activities that may violate federal, state, local or foreign laws; and

(j) Information necessary for administrative purposes.

In addition, agencies within the Intelligence Community may disseminate information, other than information derived from signals intelligence, to each appropriate agency within the Intelligence Community for purposes of allowing the recipient agency to determine whether the information is relevant to its responsibilities and can be retained by it.

2.4 *Collection Techniques.* Agencies within the Intelligence Community shall use the least intrusive collection techniques feasible within the United States or directed against United States persons abroad. Agencies are not authorized to use such techniques as electronic surveillance, unconsented physical search, mail surveillance, physical surveillance, or monitoring devices unless they are in accordance with procedures established by the head of the agency concerned and approved by the Attorney General. Such procedures shall protect constitutional and other legal rights and limit use of such information to lawful governmental purposes. These procedures shall not authorize:

(a) The CIA to engage in electronic surveillance within the United States except for the purpose of training, testing, or conducting countermeasures to hostile electronic surveillance;

(b) Unconsented physical searches in the United States by agencies other than the FBI, except for:

(1) Searches by counterintelligence elements of the military services directed against military personnel within the United States or abroad for intelligence purposes, when authorized by a military commander empowered to approve physical searches for law enforcement purposes, based upon a finding of probable cause to believe that such persons are acting as agents of foreign powers; and

(2) Searches by CIA of personal property of non-United States persons lawfully in its possession.

(c) Physical surveillance of a United States person in the United States by agencies other than the FBI, except for:

(1) Physical surveillance of present or former employees, present or former intelligence agency contractors or their present or former employees, or applicants for any such employment or contracting; and

(2) Physical surveillance of a military person employed by a nonintelligence element of a military service.

(d) Physical surveillance of a United States person abroad to collect foreign intelligence, except to obtain significant information that cannot reasonably be acquired by other means.

2.5 *Attorney General Approval.* The Attorney General hereby is delegated the power to approve the use for intelligence purposes, within the United States or against a United States person abroad, of any technique for which a warrant would be required if undertaken for law enforcement purposes, provided that such techniques shall not be undertaken unless the Attorney General has determined in each case that there is probable cause to believe that the technique is directed against a foreign power or an agent of a foreign power. Electronic surveillance, as defined in the Foreign Intelligence Surveillance Act of 1978, shall be conducted in accordance with that Act, as well as this Order.

2.6 *Assistance to Law Enforcement Authorities.* Agencies within the Intelligence Community are authorized to:

(a) Cooperate with appropriate law enforcement agencies for the purpose of protecting the employees, information, property and facilities of any agency within the Intelligence Community;

(b) Unless otherwise precluded by law or this Order, participate in law enforcement activities to investigate or prevent clandestine intelligence activities by foreign powers, or international terrorist or narcotics activities;

(c) Provide specialized equipment, technical knowledge, or assistance of expert personnel for use by any department or agency, or, when lives are endangered, to support local law enforcement agencies. Provision of assistance by expert personnel shall be approved in each case by the General Counsel of the providing agency; and

(d) Render any other assistance and cooperation to law enforcement authorities not precluded by applicable law.

2.7 *Contracting.* Agencies within the Intelligence Community are authorized to enter into contracts or arrangements for the provision of goods or services with private companies or institutions in the United States and need not reveal the sponsorship of such contracts or arrangements for authorized intelligence purposes. Contracts or arrangements with academic institutions may be undertaken only with the consent of appropriate officials of the institution.

2.8 *Consistency With Other Laws.* Nothing in this Order shall be construed to authorize any activity in violation of the Constitution or statutes of the United States.

2.9 *Undisclosed Participation in Organizations Within the United States.* No one acting on behalf of agencies within the Intelligence Community may join or otherwise participate in any organization in the United States on behalf of any agency within the Intelligence Community without disclosing his intelligence affiliation to appropriate officials of the organization, except in accordance with procedures established by the head of the agency concerned and approved by the Attorney General. Such participation shall be authorized only if it is essential to achieving lawful purposes as determined by the agency head or designee. No such participation may be undertaken for the purpose of influencing the activity of the organization or its members except in cases where:

(a) The participation is undertaken on behalf of the FBI in the course of a lawful investigation; or

(b) The organization concerned is composed primarily of individuals who are not United States persons and is reasonably believed to be acting on behalf of a foreign power.

2.10 *Human Experimentation.* No agency within the Intelligence Community shall sponsor, contract for or conduct research on human subjects except in accordance with guidelines issued by the Department of Health and Human Services. The subject's informed consent shall be documented as required by those guidelines.

2.11 *Prohibition on Assassination.* No person employed by or acting on behalf of the United States Government shall engage in, or conspire to engage in, assassination.

2.12 *Indirect Participation.* No agency of the Intelligence Community shall participate in or request any person to undertake activities forbidden by this Order. . . .

The White House   Ronald Reagan
December 4, 1981

Bibliographical Essay

The roots of permanent intelligence organizations in the United States are traced best in Jeffery M. Dorwart, *The Office of Naval Intelligence: The Birth of America's First Intelligence Agency, 1865–1918* (Annapolis, 1979), and *Conflict of Duty: The U.S. Navy's Intelligence Dilemma, 1919–1945* (Annapolis, 1983), and in Rhodri Jeffrey-Jones, *American Espionage: From Secret Service to CIA* (New York, 1977). R. Harris Smith, *OSS: The Secret History of America's First Central Intelligence Agency* (Berkeley, 1972), and Bradley F. Smith, *The Shadow Warriors: O.S.S. and the Origins of the C.I.A.* (New York, 1983), are essential for the CIA's immediate predecessor. For the OSS's dynamic leader, see Anthony Cave Brown, *The Last Hero: Wild Bill Donovan* (New York, 1982), and Richard Dunlop, *Donovan: America's Master Spy* (Chicago, 1982). Thomas F. Troy, *Donovan and the CIA: A History of the Establishment of the Central Intelligence Agency* (Frederick, Md., 1981), a declassified "in-house" study, details the transition from OSS to CIA, but see also Tom Braden, "The Birth of the CIA," *American Heritage, 28* (1977), 4–13. Important comments by a perceptive contemporary observer can be found in a series of articles by Hanson W. Baldwin in the *New York Times*, July 20, 22, 23, 24, and 25, 1948.

As pointed out by David H. Hunter, "The Evolution of Literature on United States Intelligence," *Armed Forces and Society, 5* (1978), 31–52, accounts of the CIA published before the mid-1960s tend to be laudatory. Typical if more informative than most is the three-part article by Richard and Gladys Harkness, "The Mysterious Doings of CIA," *Saturday Evening Post*, October 30, November 6 and 13, 1954. Written in response to Senator Joseph McCarthy's attacks on the agency, the authors examine the record (with evident CIA cooperation), highlight intelligence triumphs, and conclude that the CIA is "Communist-proof."

The Bay of Pigs fiasco and subsequent criticism of the CIA sparked a spirited defense of the organization by former director Allen W. Dulles. Part history, part memoir, and part polemic, *The Craft of Intelligence* (New York, 1963), is a classic. His audience no doubt was reassured to learn that the CIA never could pose a threat to American freedoms because it was prohibited by law from a domestic role and because it could not act without the authority and approval of "the highest policymaking organizations of the government" (p. 257).

Other noteworthy books appearing during the 1960s include Lyman B. Kirkpatrick, Jr., *The Real CIA* (New York, 1968), a summary by a former CIA inspector general of what the agency permitted to be said about itself at the time, and Andrew Tully, *CIA: The Inside Story* (New York, 1962), a journalist's informative, largely favorable but not uncritical account of CIA operations. Sharply critical are David Wise and Thomas B. Ross, *The Invisible Government* (New York, 1964), and Fred Cook, "The CIA," *Nation*, 192 (June 24, 1961), 529–72. Also, not to be missed are Paul W. Blackstock, *The Strategy of Subversion: Manipulating the Politics of Other Nations* (New York, 1964), an early scholarly critique of covert operations, and Stewart Alsop, *The Center: People and Power in Political Washington* (New York, 1968), which contains an interesting chapter on the CIA.

Victor Marchetti and John D. Marks, *The CIA and the Cult of Intelligence* (New York, 1974), marked an important turning point in literature about the CIA. Marchetti, an intelligence analyst with the agency who once served as executive assistant to the deputy director, and Marks, a former employee of the State Department, combined their talents to produce an exposé of the CIA that called for greater Congressional supervision of the agency and dismantling the Clandestine Service. Obtaining a copy of the manuscript, the CIA ordered Marchetti (who had signed a secrecy oath) to delete 339 passages due to violations of security. The matter ended up in court, where a federal judge excised eighteen passages of varying length. As finally published, the book revealed far more about the CIA's internal organization and covert activities than any previous study.

The revelations of Marchetti and Marks were only the beginning. In 1975–76, Congressional investigations—to the dismay of many at the CIA—placed in the public record an unprecedented corpus of information about the nation's secret intelligence service. Essential data on the CIA can be found in U.S. Congress, Senate, Select Committee to Study Governmental Operations with respect to Intelligence, *Hearings*, 7 vols., 94th Cong., 1st sess. (1975), and *Final Report* [No. 94–755], 5 books, 94th Cong., 2d sess (1976), and U.S. Congress, House, Select Committee on Intelligence, *Hearings: The Performance of the Intelligence Community*, 6 parts, 94th Cong., 1st and 2d sess. (1975). Also valuable are U.S. Commission on CIA Activities Within the United States [Rockefeller Commission], *Report to the President* (Washington, D.C., 1975), and U.S. Commission on the Organization of the Government for the Conduct of Foreign Policy [Murphy Commission], *Report* (Washington, D.C., 1975).

The mid-1970s marked the appearance of a spate of memoirs by former intelligence officers. Some were chatty: E. Howard Hunt, *Undercover: Memoirs of an American Secret Agent* (New York, 1974), records the author's career in the CIA and subsequent Watergate adventures, while Joseph B. Smith, *Portrait of a Cold Warrior* (New York, 1976), is a treasure trove of information about CIA activities in Asia during the 1950s by a longtime covert action specialist. Other accounts were hostile, especially Philip Agee, *Inside* the Company: CIA Diary (London, 1975), which provides an insight into the daily activities of a field agent in Latin America, along with the names of every CIA employee who had the misfortune to cross the author's path. Critical accounts by disaffected but by no means disloyal employees include Frank Snepp, Decent Interval (New York, 1977) an angry and moving narrative of the last, painful days in Vietnam; John Stockwell, In Search of Enemies (New York, 1978), about CIA operations in Angola; and Ralph W. McGehee, Deadly Secrets: My 25 Years in the CIA (New York, 1983), the memoirs of a former case officer with extensive experience in Asia that includes an informative appendix on the CIA's recent attempts to enforce secrecy agreements—and sanitize unfriendly books to the point of innocuousness.

Retired intelligence officers quickly rose to the CIA's defense, often revealing more about agency activities than the critics. David Atlee Phillips, The Night Watch (New York, 1977), is a well-written memoir by a former chief of Latin American operations who resigned in 1975 to defend the agency, while Peer de Silva, Sub Rosa: The CIA and the Uses of Intelligence (New York, 1978), is by a station chief in Europe and Asia who wanted to correct what he saw as a distorted picture of the CIA. Other favorable accounts include Ray S. Cline, Secrets, Spies, and Scholars (Washington, D.C., 1976), a discussion of the CIA from the perspective of an intelligence analyst, station chief (Taiwan, 1958–62), and deputy director; Harry Rositzki, The CIA's Secret Operations (New York, 1977), by a Soviet specialist who promises more than he delivers; and Cord Meyer, Facing Reality: From World Federalism to the CIA (New York, 1980), an uneven retelling of the author's twenty-six years with the agency.

The view from the top is given by William Colby and Peter Forbath, Honorable Men: My Life in the CIA (New York, 1978), the forthright memoir of an embattled CIA director and honorable man. The bitterness of his predecessor can be glimpsed in Thomas Powers, The Man Who Kept the Secrets: Richard Helms and the CIA (New York, 1979). There is no reliable biography of CIA director Allen Dulles, but R. Harris Smith's forthcoming study is eagerly awaited.

CIA covert operations around the world have attracted the attention of insiders, journalists, and scholars. Broad in scope are L. Fletcher Prouty, The Secret Team (Englewood Cliffs, N.J., 1973), written by a former air force liaison officer for contacts between the CIA and Department of Defense on matters pertaining to covert action; William R. Corson, The Armies of Ignorance (New York, 1977), a critical examination of CIA operations by a former marine corps officer with intelligence connections; and Stephen Ambrose, Ike's Spies: Eisenhower and the Espionage Establishment (Garden City, N.Y., 1981), a scholar's treatment of the topic which is better for the wartime than presidential period.

Christopher Felix (pseud.), A Short Course in the Secret War (New York,

1963), contains an intriguing personal account of early covert operations in Eastern Europe, while Philip Agee and Louis Wolf, *Dirty Work: The CIA in Western Europe* (Secaucus, N.J., 1979), is an informative exposé that should be used with care. Trevor Barnes, "The Secret Cold War: The C.I.A. and American Foreign Policy in Europe, 1946–1956," *The Historical Journal*, 2 parts, *24* (1981), 399–415, and *25* (1982), 649–70, is by far the best treatment of the topic.

Books abound on CIA machinations in Asia. Joseph C. Goulden, *Korea: The Untold Story of the War* (New York, 1982), includes an interesting chapter on covert activities, while William M. Leary, *Perilous Missions: Civil Air Transport and CIA Covert Operations in Asia* (University, Ala., 1984), focuses on operational and administrative aspects of the agency's first air proprietary. The CIA's early involvement in Southeast Asia is sketched by Roger Hilsman, *To Move a Nation* (New York, 1967), and Edward G. Lansdale, *In the Midst of Wars: An American's Mission to Southeast Asia* (New York, 1972), a circumspect account by a senior intelligence officer. Considerable information can be culled from *The Pentagon Papers*, Gravel edition, 5 vols. (Boston, 1971).

The CIA's role in Central America during the mid-1950s has been examined by Richard H. Immerman, *The CIA in Guatemala* (Austin, Tex., 1982), and Stephen Schlesinger and Stephen Kinzer, *Bitter Fruit: The Untold Story of the American Coup in Guatemala* (Garden City, N.Y., 1982). Among the many accounts of the CIA's major misadventure in Latin America, Peter Wyden, *Bay of Pigs: The Untold Story* (New York, 1979), contains the most operational details, while Arthur M. Schlesinger, Jr., *A Thousand Days* (Boston, 1965), paints the broad picture. Also valuable are Lyman B. Kirkpatrick, Jr., "Paramilitary Case Study: The Bay of Pigs," *Naval War College Review, 25* (1972), 32–42, and the recently declassified (in part) *Operation Zapata: The 'Ultrasensitive' Report and Testimony of the Board of Inquiry of the Bay of Pigs* (Frederick, Md., 1981). For glimpses of later CIA operations, see Bradley Earl Ayers, *The War That Never Was: An Insider's Account of CIA Covert Operations Against Cuba* (New York, 1976), and Tad Szulc, *The Illusion of Peace: Foreign Policy in the Nixon Years* (New York, 1978).

Information on covert activities elsewhere around the world can be found in Miles Copeland, *The Game of Nations* (London, 1969), dealing with early ventures in the Middle East; Wilbert Crane Eveland, *Ropes of Sand: America's Failure in the Middle East* (New York, 1980); Kermit Roosevelt, *Countercoup: The Struggle for Control of Iran* (New York, 1979); Chris Mullin, "The CIA: Tibetan Conspiracy," *Far Eastern Economic Review,* September 1975, pp. 30–34; Stephen R. Weissman, "CIA Covert Action in Zaire and Angola," *Political Science Quarterly, 45* (1979), 263–86, and his essay "CIA Operations" in René Lemarchand (ed.), *American Foreign Policy in Southern Africa* (Washington, D.C., 1978), pp. 383–432.

The CIA's involvement with communications intelligence is outlined in David Kahn, *The Code Breakers* (New York, 1967), and James Bamford, *The Puzzle Palace* (Boston, 1982). Sherman Kent, *Strategic Intelligence for American World Policy* (Princeton, 1949), is the classic treatment of intelligence analysis by a man who went on to serve as chairman of the CIA's Board of Estimates (1950–67), but it should be read with John Prados, *The Soviet Estimate: U.S. Intelligence Analysis and Russian Military Strength* (New York, 1982), and Chester L. Cooper, "The CIA and Decision-Making," *Foreign Affairs, 50* (January 1972), 223–36. David Wise and Thomas B. Ross, *The U-2 Affair* (New York, 1962), sheds light on the CIA's highly successful program of aerial reconnaissance during the 1950s, while Roy Varner and Wayne Collier, *A Matter of Risk* (New York, 1978), recounts later efforts to recover intelligence materials from a sunken Soviet submarine. A less successful venture is exposed by John D. Marks, *The Search for the Manchurian Candidate: The CIA and Mind Control* (New York, 1979), and U.S. Congress, Senate, Select Committee on Intelligence and the Subcommittee on Health and Scientific Research of the Committee on Human Resources, *Project MKULTRA, The CIA's Program of Research in Behavioral Modification,* Hearings, 95th Cong., 1st sess. (1977). Attempts to penetrate the murky world of counterespionage include David C. Martin, *Wilderness of Mirrors* (New York, 1980), and William Hood, *Mole* (New York, 1982), a former intelligence officer's fascinating account of a classic operation against the Soviet Union during the 1950s.

Harry Howe Ransom, *The Intelligence Establishment* (Cambridge, Mass., 1970), is the starting point for serious inquiries about the CIA's proper role in government, while Tyrus G. Fain (comp.), *The Intelligence Community: History, Organization, and Issues* (New York, 1977), provides an ample selection of essential material. For a sampling of recent questions (and hostile answers) about the propriety, utility, and legality of certain CIA practices, see Morton H. Halperin, et al., *The Lawless State: The Crimes of the U.S. Intelligence Agencies* (New York, 1976); Howard Frazier (ed.), *Uncloaking the CIA* (New York, 1978); Frank Church, "Covert Action: Swampland of American Foreign Policy," *Bulletin of Atomic Scientists, 32* (1976), 7–11; Richard A. Falk, "CIA Covert Action and International Law," *Society, 12* (1975), 39–44; and Henry S. Commager, "Intelligence: The Constitution Betrayed," *New York Review of Books,* September 29, 1976, pp. 32–37. Taking an opposite view are Theodore Shackley, *The Third Option: An American View of Counterinsurgency Operations* (New York, 1981), a defense of the CIA's paramilitary role by a legendary field officer, and Roy Godson and Ernest W. Lefever, *The CIA and the American Ethic: An Un-*

finished Debate (Washington, D.C., 1979), a sympathetic treatment of an important if less violent issue.

Stansfield Turner and George Thibault, "Intelligence: The Right Rules," *Foreign Policy, 48* (1982), 122–38, is a thoughtful statement on the question of oversight by a former CIA director and his assistant, but see also Loch K. Johnson, "The CIA: Controlling the Quiet Option," *Foreign Policy, 39* (1980), 143–53, and "The U.S. Congress and the CIA: Monitoring the Dark Side of Government," *Legislative Studies Quarterly, 5* (1980), 477–99.

Useful on a variety of issues are the papers being produced by the Consortium for the Study of Intelligence. There are five volumes to date, edited by Roy Godson, in a series entitled "Intelligence Requirements for the 1980's": *Elements of Intelligence* (1979), *Analysis and Estimates* (1980), *Counterintelligence* (1980), *Covert Action* (1981), and *Clandestine Collection* (1982).

Myron J. Smith, Jr., *The Secret Wars: A Guide to Sources in English*, 3 vols. (Santa Barbara, Calif., 1980), is by far the best bibliographical aid for browsing or research. Also helpful are Marjorie W. Cline, Carla E. Christiansen, and Judith M. Fontaine (eds.), *Scholar's Guide to Intelligence Literature: Bibliography of the Russell J. Bowen Collection* (Frederick, Md., 1983), and Paul W. Blackstock and Frank L. Schaf, Jr., *Intelligence, Espionage, Counterespionage, and Covert Operations: A Guide to Information Sources* (Detroit, 1978).

Index